Summers Away

Kara DeMaio

This is a work of fiction. All of the characters, organizations, and events portrayed in this novel are either a production of the author's imagination or are used fictitiously.

ISBN: 978-1-7358455-2-4 (pbk.)

For more information, visit LifeTranscribed.com

For my parents,

Neil & Roberta

For teaching me acceptance, unconditional love
and the value of a true friend.

You helped me find my voice and
recognize the importance of
standing up for others.

Because I don't say it enough,

Thank you.

Prologue

It's back; the overwhelming, suffocating sadness that seems to spring when I least expect it. I can feel it as it begins its journey over my body, choking every bit of happiness in its wake. I try to shove the feelings back down where they usually rest, hidden beneath the surface, but the tears typically come before I can.

Sometimes it happens when I'm alone in my car. A song will play on the radio that will bring back a memory of one of our adventures and the blanket of sadness begins. Sometimes I smell the scent of his soap when walking by someone and turn around expecting him to be there. When he's not, it's like a punch to the gut. Sometimes I'll be dancing in a group of people at a party and I have to leave immediately. I am surrounded by people and still feel the weight of loneliness without him with me.

On the worst days, I forget that he is gone and pick up the phone to share a story with him or some good news before realizing that no one will pick up on his end. The reality that he won't ever answer my call again hits me in the chest with striking force. All air escapes my lungs and I momentarily forget how to breathe.

Summer used to be my favorite season, but now something is missing. There's a hole in my heart that matches the emptiness I feel when I think about him, which is often.

I haven't always been this way. I haven't always been dark and twisted inside. They did this to me. They did this to him. They did this to all of us. There is a definitive line that marks the change for us; a night I will never forget — the night my best friend died in my arms.

One

I am fifteen years old when I meet Ryan Gematti for the first time. Ryan is seventeen at the time, a full head taller than me, and his smile is hypnotizing. Seriously, you forget every thought in your head when he smiles at you. I know right away he comes from money. He and his father speak with a casual arrogance that I find common among anyone above the working class. Plus, the huge boat that pulls up to the dock kind of gives it away.

I am working at the local marina for the summer, manning the gas pump and helping boaters fill their tanks and collecting payments. It's a boring job, but an easy one, and I always have a freckled tan by the end of the summer from being in the sun all day.

The day I meet Ryan, his father pulls up in a forty-five-foot Hunter Center Cockpit Cruiser and asks me to fill it up with diesel. He barely glances at me, but I smile and nod as he makes his way toward the marina store.

My mind travels elsewhere as it typically does while I set the diesel nozzle and begin filling his tank. I'm in the middle of a fantastical daydream involving me stealing the boat and sailing it around the world when I hear a voice behind me. It startles me out of my thoughts as I stumble backward off the edge of the dock directly into the Hudson River.

The water is shockingly cold, even with the air temperature as high as it is. I resurface with a splash, choking and gasping for air and that's when I see him for the first time. Ryan is standing at the edge of the dock with the sun at his back, which makes him look like something forged by the heavens, down to the sparkling smile he's trying to hold back as he stares at me. I shake my head and close my mouth, which I hope hasn't been dangling open in awe for too long.

Well, this is typical.

I have always been very good at making a fool of myself.

Apparently, Ryan had been aboard the boat the whole time, but my daydreams had kept me from hearing him approach. He looks genuinely worried, even while trying not to laugh at me, and reaches a hand down to help me back to the dock.

"I'm sorry about that. I didn't mean to scare you," Ryan says, finally releasing his full smile.

The words I begin to respond with stick in my throat as I lose them to his smile. Momentarily stupefied, I stand in front of him and try to smile back, dripping onto the dock and his very expensive-looking shoes. He looks down at the droplets, now forming a puddle underneath me, as I manage to remember how to form words again.

"It was mostly my fault. I was in my own little world and you caught me off guard."

I smile back at Ryan to assure him I'm not mad, but shiver as goosebumps spread over my arms and legs.

"Geez, you're soaked now. I feel like a jerk."

Ryan reaches out a hand and squeezes my braid, which bleeds water beneath his touch. I let out a loud, nervous laugh and Ryan locks eyes with me. My breath catches in my throat before I respond.

"Really, it's okay. I'm embarrassed to admit this isn't the first time I've fallen in."

I laugh again. Sadly, this is the truth. I have a tendency to be a bit clumsy. Thankfully, Ryan laughs, too.

"I'm Ryan Gematti," he says as he lets go of my hair.

I reach out a soggy hand to give Ryan a wet handshake.

"I'm Ayla DeLuca," I say, my eyes never leaving his face.

At that moment, Ryan's father walks out from the marina store and over to where we are standing. He smacks Ryan in the back of the head playfully as he tries to hand me a hundred-dollar bill.

"Please take this. I saw the whole thing through the window. I'll admit the guys inside all had a good laugh about it, but you're soaking wet. I should have warned you that Ryan might pop out of the cabin. By the way, I'm Ryan's father, Scott."

I shake my head in refusal as he tries to push the hundred dollars into my wet hand.

"Oh, no, sir. Thank you, but I can't accept that. I'll dry quickly anyway. Besides, my shift ends in another hour."

I shield my eyes and look up into the sunglass covered eyes of Mr. Gematti. I laugh to myself because my entire outfit, shoes and all, cost me less than fifty dollars, something I am damn proud of.

"What if I wanted to give you a nice tip? Would you refuse a tip from me?"

Mr. Gematti smiles at me and I can see that Ryan inherited his charm.

I shake my head once more.

"Not that big of a tip!"

Mr. Gematti laughs, but continues to hold the money out to me, not giving up. I glance at my feet, which are making a squishing sound as I shift my weight back and forth. My clothes cling to me and I self-consciously pull at them, but I refuse to take the money. I've always been pretty stubborn — stubborn and clumsy.

Mr. Gematti pushes his sunglasses to the top of his head and squints at me in the sun.

"If you won't take the tip, then you have to join us for dinner on the boat tonight. I won't take no for an answer."

I start to protest again, but both Ryan and Scott insist. I reluctantly agree to dinner later tonight and watch them as they pull away from the dock, a wave of nervous panic making my knees weak.

I finish my shift, trying to ignore the incessant teasing from the guys I work with. My clothes are almost dry by the time my mother picks me up. When she asks what happened, I hurriedly tell her the story.

"What are you going to wear?" is the first question my mother asks me.

I shrug, looking out the window, my stomach tying in knots. I hadn't thought of that. I've been more worried about my inherent clumsiness and what I could possibly talk about with Ryan and Scott because I stumble over small talk when I'm nervous. I mentally cross off all of the outfits I have in my closet, unsure of what to even wear to dinner on a boat.

A few hours later, I am back at the waterfront in a black dress and sandals, thanks to a last-minute shopping trip with Mom. Ryan meets me at the edge of the dock and extends his arm to me.

"So you can't fall in again," Ryan says when I look at him in question.

I laugh out loud.

"Fair enough."

I link my arm through his as we walk toward the boat.

I don't eat much at dinner, mostly because I don't care for seafood, but I talk with Ryan and his father easily, feeling more comfortable than I expect to.

Over the next week while Ryan and his father are in town, I see him every day. They stop at the marina when I am working to have lunch and chat with me. Ryan meets me at the end of the dock after my shifts and we spend most of our time talking and laughing. He lives in Virginia and is spending some time with his father traveling on the boat.

"Bonding Time," Ryan tells me his father calls it.

Throughout the week, I take Ryan to some of my favorite places in town. I tell him about the best places to eat and visit while they are here. One night, I show Ryan where I go to high school and the football field where I spend Friday nights during school, cheering for my friends who play.

I live in a small town with nothing much in it but apple orchards and the Hudson River. I worry that he will find it boring, but Ryan seems to be interested in everything I show him. He promises to show me where he grew up, too. I smile, not really thinking too much about it.

On the very last night Ryan and Mr. Gematti are in town, Ryan asks me to dinner. I take him to my favorite place, and after the meal, we find ourselves down at the river. I point out a secret local spot which leads to a flat cliff above the Hudson. When we walk through the trail and into the clearing on the cliff, Ryan stops in his tracks. The sky is full of stars and the view is pretty amazing from this high up.

"Thank you for taking me here," Ryan says to me, keeping his gaze on the sky.

I smile shyly, the realization of how romantic it all is making me blush.

"You're welcome. I have to admit, I've never been here before myself. I've heard about it, and you can see it from the bridge over there," I say as I turn around to point, "but I've never actually made it up here. It really is beautiful."

We spend a few hours on the cliff, talking in the darkness with the stars as our only light.

Later, we make our way back to his father's boat. Ryan takes a seat at the back of the boat. He pats the cushioned seat next to him and I sit down, butterflies fluttering in my stomach. I close my eyes as Ryan leans in to kiss me. It is only my second kiss ever, but it is a good one: soft and sweet. When he pulls away, he takes my hand. We sit like this on his father's boat for another hour, Ryan's hand never leaving mine. It's not until after I'm home later the same night that I realize it was my kiss goodbye.

When I get a call from Ryan three days later inviting me to stay with his family in Virginia for the month of August, I don't know what to say. I'm filled with excitement, but I worry about being so far from home and am not sure my parents will allow it. I can already hear my father telling me that I barely know this boy and his family. I explain to Ryan that I have a job and need to make money for the summer, but Ryan insists that I can work for his father like he does. I'm not even sure what Ryan's father does, but I know from our conversations that he owns his own company.

After Ryan convinces me, it's my turn to convince my parents, which is no easy task. I don't know what stars aligned to get them to say yes, and I'm sure that the chat with Mr. Gematti was a large part of it, but they finally agree to let me go. Thankfully they both got to meet Ryan and his dad when they were in town, and Dad got a "good feeling" about the two of them. I think my mother is more excited than I am because Ryan is handsome, and she is forever trying to match me up with a nice, good-looking guy. She keeps a picture of me on her desk at work and makes sure to show it to any guy around my age.

True story.

Dad tells me later that while he'll worry about me the entire time that I am there, he knows that I'm responsible and will make smart decisions. He gives me the look when he says this, a crooked smile on his face. I grin at him and put an arm over his shoulder, knowing exactly what the look means and promise him that I'll make him proud.

When I call Ryan to tell him that my parents said yes, he laughs into the receiver and the sweet sound echoes in my ears.

"Pack your bags, Ayla. I can't wait for you to get here!"

I hang up the phone with Ryan and dance excitedly around my room.

It's settled. I leave for Virginia in a week.

Two

I make the long trip from New York to Virginia in a company car that is sent by Ryan's father. By the time I get to Onancock, my nerves have officially worked themselves in a knot. As we pass the small downtown area of shops, galleries and restaurants, I am mesmerized by the serenity of it all. Slowly the nervousness leads way to excitement and by the time we make our way through the abundance of large Victorian era homes, I can't wait to jump out of the car and start the rest of the summer. Then we turn into Ryan's driveway and the butterflies quickly return.

My legs are shaking when I get out of the car in front of the large brick mansion that is home to the Gematti family. It is two stories tall and surrounded by large white columns with perfectly manicured landscape beds framing the front of the house. The company car pulls up in front of the attached three-car garage and I let out a long whistle. The driver, John, who has been kindly trying to calm me down as I talk his ear off for the entire ride, laughs and helps me with my bags.

I turn around to look at the half-mile long dock that protrudes out into the purple-black water in front of the house. It is breathtaking and as I take a few steps toward the dock, I recognize Ryan making his way to me. He has a fishing pole in hand and looks like something out of a J. Crew catalog. On his arm is a blonde in a red bikini. She is giggling and twirling her hair. Right then and there I decide that I hate her.

As Ryan approaches, he lets go of the girl's arm, drops his fishing pole and jogs the rest of the way to give me a hug.

"I'm so glad you're finally here," Ryan says excitedly.

I nod into Ryan's shoulder, making sure to take note of the flash of jealousy in red bikini's eyes before she gives me a huge, perfect grin.

"Ayla, this is a family friend, Ashleigh Weathers. Ash, this is Ayla, and she'll be staying with us for the next month."

As Ryan finishes introductions, I shake Ashleigh's hand, making sure to have a stronger handshake than she does. Ryan explains that his father and Ashleigh's father are best friends and business partners, and that Ryan and Ashleigh grew up together. When Ryan says, "grew up together," she makes sure to put her arms around him and squeeze, as if letting me know he and I will never be as close as they are now.

Ryan walks ahead of us to bring my bags inside, just out of earshot. Ashleigh takes the opportunity to threaten me through clenched teeth.

"Our families have been trying to hook the two of us up since grade school. I don't know what exactly you think you're doing here, but newsflash: Ryan invited you to occupy his younger brother, Tate. You're clearly trash, and you don't belong here."

Ryan is already inside the front door waiting for us to catch up. I stop in my tracks, turn and give Ashleigh the biggest smile I can fake while Ryan watches.

"Since grade school, huh? And to think I only met him two weeks ago and I've already been invited to stay with his family for the summer. Isn't that something?"

And with an even bigger smile, I walk right up the steps and into the front door of my new home for the next month without so much as a glance back in Ashleigh's direction.

Ashleigh walks around back with a scowl, to where Mr. Gematti and her father are having a drink. Ryan puts his hand on my lower back, guiding me through the house so I can get familiar with where I'll be staying.

The inside of the house is as breathtaking as the outside is. The staircase that welcomes us inside the front door is made of black walnut wood and the cathedral ceilings seem endless. I refrain myself from yelling to see if it will echo, not wanting to come off as the "trash" that Ashleigh described me as. From there, Ryan takes me into the kitchen, where their chef Cora greets me and hands me a glass of homemade lemonade from the center island. Cora is warm and friendly, and I like her right away.

The kitchen and dining area are a large, open room, separated only by an island bar, which seats four. There is a huge bay window behind the dining table that looks out on the water and Cora informs me that this is the best seat in the house to watch the sunset. The family room hosts a number of very comfortable-looking loveseats, chair and a halfs, and recliners, all in coordinating patterns. All are facing each other around a large stone fireplace. I can't help but notice that there isn't a television anywhere in the room.

Ryan's father sleeps in a master bedroom suite on the first floor of the house, and Ryan and his brother, Tate, each have their own room and bathrooms on the second floor. That floor also is home to an elaborate game room, office library and balcony that is the full length of the house. At the end of the hall on the second floor is a small set of stairs that leads to the attic where I will be staying. Ryan's father doesn't feel comfortable with me staying on the same floor as the boys, so he rearranged the guest suite in the attic.

My family's attic at home is hot and humid, full of mice and an occasional bat, and not high enough to stand up straight. Whenever anyone needs something from the attic, we usually draw straws because none of us ever want to volunteer to go up there. This attic is nothing like the one at home. First of all, there is a staircase that leads up to the attic and at home we have something similar to a folding ladder that drops down from the ceiling. At the top of the staircase is a large open room complete with a queen size bed — at home I sleep on a twin — with a beautiful wooden headboard and matching double dresser, armoire, and vanity to the left, and a white armchair and loveseat with coffee table and television to my right. There are small circular windows that look out on the water and even a small balcony with wicker chairs. As I walk toward the bed to feel the flowered embroidery of the duvet cover, I realize the room opens up to a walk-in closet with full-length mirror and a small bathroom with a claw-foot tub. And when I say small bathroom, I mean in comparison to the rest of the house. This small bathroom is close to the size of my bedroom at home.

Worried my face will give away my every thought, I turn to Ryan and smile as he lugs my two bags up the stairs and tells me to make myself at home.

"Dad thought this would be the best room for you. Susan comes once a week to clean the house and will take care of your laundry for you if you leave it in that basket," as he points to a white wicker and linen basket that sits underneath the countertop in the bathroom. "I'll let you get settled a little bit and come get you when dinner is ready."

And with one of his winning smiles, Ryan turns and makes his way back down the staircase. At the first step, he turns around.

"Ayla, I'm really happy you came. We are going to have a great summer together."

Before I can say anything in reply, Ryan is gone.

I start to unpack and hang clothes in my walk-in closet. As a true type A personality, I hang everything by color and length. I spread out my clothes on the hangers so it looks like I have more than I do. I am stuffing my empty bags underneath the bed when I hear someone come bounding up the stairs and flop themselves on the mattress above me.

I hop up thinking it is Ryan only to find a boy around my age sprawled across the bed. He locks eyes with me and smiles an identical grin to Ryan's. They even have the same dimple in their chin.

"You must be Tate," I say to him and stick out my hand in an attempt to be friendly.

Tate jumps off the bed and picks me up in a hug that lifts me off the ground.

"Tate I am!" he says into my ear and returns my feet to the floor.

I laugh and push him back onto the bed. I like Tate already. I feel comfortable with him immediately, which is a nice change to the nervous ache in my stomach that returns every time I am around Ryan.

Tate is fifteen and just finished his freshman year of high school, too. He is shy of six feet tall, has the same bright green eyes that Ryan does, but has longer, blonde hair where Ryan's is short and dark. Tate is more muscular than Ryan, but he also seems more awkward, like he is still getting used to his long arms and legs.

"Nice to meet you, Tate-I-Am," I say as I sit on the bed next to him.

He looks at me for what feels like a long time, staring into my eyes. Just at the point where I am starting to get uncomfortable with the gaze, his face breaks out into a slow grin as he grabs my hand to pull me off the bed toward the stairs.

"C'mon, dinner's ready, Ayla. You're in the hot seat tonight!"

Hot seat?! Well, that doesn't sound fun.

And great, the butterflies have returned.

Three

I sit at the dining room table silently praying that no one will ask me anything directly and attempting to hide my shaking legs underneath me. Tate, who is sitting next to me, slides his hand to my knee and gives it a reassuring squeeze.

I guess I wasn't hiding them that well.

I glance toward Tate and gave him a quick smile in appreciation.

Across from me at the table sits Ashleigh in a white gauze dress that, as my father would say, doesn't leave much to the imagination. Next to her and across from Tate sits Ryan. I notice that Ashleigh keeps trying to reach for Ryan's hand while we eat, but he patiently avoids it each time. I celebrate silently just as Ashleigh's dad clears his throat.

"So, Ayla, how do you feel about working for me and Scott this summer?" he asks as he gestures toward Mr. Gematti.

Even though he has asked me twice now, I still can't get used to calling Scott by his first name.

I shrug, hoping this isn't some sort of test that I'm failing.

"Well, I don't know much about what we will be doing, but I'm looking forward to learning as much as I can."

Ashleigh's dad nods at me with kind eyes and then looks at Mr. Gematti. He seems like such a nice man that it is hard to imagine he raised Ashleigh. I was introduced to him as we were sitting down to dinner. He is a pleasant man who seems to smile with his eyes. He has a round belly and balding head but manages to look handsome anyway.

"I guess that's my cue from Paul to tell you a little more about what you will be helping us with this summer, Ayla."

Mr. Gematti sets down his fork and knife and folds his hands together in front of him. He is slightly taller than Paul, but with broad shoulders and a serious look in his eyes. I already know that Mr. Gematti is kind, but he has the ability to look sternly at you and make you want to cry. My own father has that same ability.

"Paul and I own and run a company, a few companies actually, right here in Virginia. One of the divisions of the company handles all of our philanthropic efforts and works with the community to host events to raise funds for various charities that we support. Each summer, the company hosts a large charitable event that happens at the end of August. This year, we are planning a large party to raise funds for the Chincoteague National Wildlife Refuge over on Chincoteague Island. You, Ashleigh, Ryan and Tate will all assist my event director, Jessica, with anything she needs to get ready for the event."

"Wow, that sounds wonderful!"

I try to contain my excitement. Even at fifteen, I already know that I want to become a producer. My dream is to produce large award shows, concerts and events. I am so excited that I don't let the fact that I will be working with Ashleigh all summer ruin it for me. I am extremely happy to be working alongside Ryan and Tate. I have a feeling it will be fun for all of us to work together.

Cora walks in with the most beautiful strawberry shortcake I have ever seen. She puts it at the center of the table and for a moment it just sits there. I think everyone is in agreement that it is too perfect to eat. Tate eventually hands his plate to Cora and I do the same. It is the best strawberry shortcake that I have ever tasted. The strawberries are juicy, sweet and a little tart, but the best part is the homemade biscuit that the strawberries sit on. It melts in your mouth like butter. I eat it slowly and enjoy every last bite. I begin to ask Cora for another piece when Ashleigh snorts and interrupts me.

"I guess someone isn't concerned about her figure," she sneers as she pushes herself back from the table and walks out on the back patio where Ryan, Paul and Scott are all now enjoying a cigar.

Tate scowls in Ashleigh's direction, grabs my plate and scoops another helping of Cora's shortcake onto it. He does the same to his own plate and scoops a third helping onto a third plate and hands it to Cora. She smiles shyly and sits down where Ashleigh was just sitting to eat with us.

"Cora, this is amazing! You have to teach me how to make it."

I smile at her and catch Tate grinning at me out of the corner of my eye.

"Do you cook, Miss Ayla?" Cora asks me in between bites.

"I try to. I'm not that great at it. My grandmother says it's because I'm impatient, but I really do enjoy it."

"Then I'll just have to show you a few things," Cora says as she gathers up the rest of the shortcake and clears away our empty plates. "We have a big meal here every Sunday. You can help me prepare some of it if you'd like?"

As I nod in agreement, she walks back toward the refrigerator and places another helping into a Tupperware container. She covers the rest of the shortcake with a glass top, places that in the fridge and hands the Tupperware container to Tate. I look at him in question, but at that moment Paul comes back through the dining room to say goodnight. He tells the both of us that he'll see us on Monday morning and then he leaves. Cora packs up for the night and says she'll see us in the morning for breakfast.

I look at Tate and put my head in my hands. I yawn once as I realize I completely missed the sunset.

"You better not be tired yet, Sunshine. We still have a whole night ahead of us! Ryan invited all of the guys over to meet you. They'll be here in the next hour or two."

I glance quickly at the clock on the wall above us. It is almost ten.

Ryan's dad lets them have people over at midnight?

As if reading my mind, Tate pulls me out of my thoughts.

"Dad is happy as long as we are home having fun and not out causing trouble somewhere. C'mon, let's go find Ryan and The Beast."

I laugh out loud at Tate's nickname for Ashleigh as he grabs me by the hand and leads me out onto the back patio. We round the corner of the house and head toward the dock. The moon shimmers off the water and it sparkles like someone dumped glitter on top. Each wave that laps the shore makes a soft noise as it hits the sand and the rhythm of it makes me pause for a moment.

"You coming, Sunshine?" Tate calls back to me.

I start walking to him and that's when I see them. Ashleigh and Ryan are sitting on the edge of the long dock. She has her arms around shoulders and her hands are grabbing his hair. His hands are resting on her waist and they are kissing. They look like Barbie and Ken.

They are kissing in the moonlight on the water for goodness sake!

I suddenly feel completely out of place and I miss home.

Tate, who seems to read me so well already even though he barely knows me, walks up beside me, puts his arm around my shoulder and yells out to them.

"Aren't you afraid you'll catch something from that thing?"

I love Tate at this moment.

Ryan's head snaps up and he hops to his feet, half jogging toward us. I see Ashleigh's pouting face in the background as Ryan half waves as he approaches.

"Jackson and Zac are on their way for a beer run. Jackson's older brother hooked us up tonight. You ready for some fun, Ayla?"

And out comes the dimple, which makes me forget that he was just locking lips with the devil.

Damn that dimple.

Four

"So, lemme guess, you have a thing for Ryan like every other girl I've ever met?"

Tate is sitting on my bed while I pace back and forth in front of him.

"What? No, it's not that. Well, maybe it is. I don't know how I feel about Ryan, but I can't believe he'd show any interest in her at all!"

I flop onto the bed next to Tate. He rolls onto his back and with his arms bent at the elbows, puts his hands under his head. He smiles a wicked grin.

"The only time he shows an interest in her is when he wants some."

"Wants some?" I question Tate with raised eyebrows.

"Oh, come on, Sunshine, you know what I mean!"

And with that, Tate pounces on me, tickling my stomach as I giggle. As my laughing gets louder, Tate looks up at the ceiling and groans, faking noises that make me blush.

I shove him off the bed and punch him in the arm.

"There is something wrong with you, you know that?!"

"You ain't seen nothing yet, kid!" Tate says as he starts toward the stairs.

I get up to follow him, but he puts his hand up to stop me.

"I have to run out real quick to get some stuff for the party, but I'll be back before anyone gets here, so don't worry."

"I can go with you"

I start to grab my sweatshirt off the bed, but Tate shakes his head at me.

"No, that's okay. I think you need to shower and change anyway, if you want to compete with The Beast, that is. You may want to stuff your bra while you're at it, too!"

As Tate runs down the stairs laughing, one of my sneakers just misses hitting him in the shoulder.

I smile to myself.

I really like Tate.

Even if things with Ryan are as confusing as ever and even if I am forced to spend the last month of my summer with a Barbie double, it doesn't seem so bad with Tate around. I've only known him for a few hours and I already feel like we're friends.

I turn toward my closet and my meager choice of clothing. I should be able to make something in here work. I choose a pair of worn jeans and a bright yellow top and sandals in honor of my new nickname, Sunshine. I make my way to the bathroom and drop my dirty clothes in the wicker hamper for Susan. Living here is definitely going to take some getting used to for me, although my Gram always does my laundry at home, so this part won't be much of an adjustment.

I hop into a hot shower and as the steam fills the stall around me, I start to get excited about tonight. I had just started going to real parties back home, except our crazy parties involved apple orchards, four wheelers and tents, and any random mismatch of beer that the party goers could scrounge up from their parents' basement fridge. I envision tonight being slightly different.

I turn off the hot water and step back into the bathroom. I walk up to the full-length mirror and wipe away the fog so it only shows my face in the reflection. My large dark eyes stare back at me and my dark hair hangs limp and wet down my back.

This might take some work.

I stare into my own eyes.

After forty-five minutes of trying to do my hair, I finally give up. The southern humidity is doing some dreadful curling thing that has my hair growing in size by the minute. I finally toss in some mousse and hope that wavy hair is in down here. I throw on my jeans, yellow top and sandals and decide to put a yellow flower in my hair to keep it off my face.

Makeup is another story. I have some with me, but don't really know what I am doing when it comes to applying it. At home, I'm not allowed to wear it unless it's a special occasion. I scrounge under my bed for the magazines I read during the long drive here that I had hastily thrown in my empty suitcase. I flip through a few pages until I find something that I can attempt to do myself and get to work on trying to apply eyeliner without blinding myself.

As I finish, someone walks up the stairs to my room. Assuming it is Tate, I turn around with my lips puckered and my best attempt at The Beast's "come get me" face. Out of the corner of my eye, I catch Ryan at the top step just as I spin around. His smiling face and raised eyebrows are enough to make my heart jump.

My sandal catches in the rug and I land flat on my face, my hands not reacting fast enough to brace my fall. I hear Ryan trying to stifle a laugh.

"You know, we really have to stop meeting like this," Ryan says with a smile as he reaches out a hand to help me back up.

I can feel the crimson creeping up my shoulders and across my face.

"You really have to stop sneaking up on me!"

I laugh, trying to hide my absolute humiliation.

I can't imagine The Beast does much tripping and falling on her face, although I wouldn't mind watching it happen.

Ryan sits down on the love seat in my room and motions for me to sit next to him. Being this close to him makes my pulse speed up.

Thump-thump, thump-thump.

The butterflies return immediately and now are dancing furiously in my stomach.

"Listen, Ayla, I feel like I haven't been the most gracious host since you got here. What you saw on the dock before... I just feel like I need to explain to you what that was—"

Ryan's voice trails off, looking to me for a reaction. I shrug nonchalantly, pretending not to care.

"Ryan, you don't owe me an explanation. I never asked if you had a girlfriend. I came here to see your hometown. I have this great new room," I spread my arms to accentuate my point, "and an awesome job that sure beats pumping gas on a marina dock. I'm excited to be spending the next month with you and your family. You don't need to feel bad and I don't need a babysitter. Plus, Tate's been wonderful, and I like spending time with him, too."

At the mention of Tate's name, Ryan's eyes spark a bit and a faint smile shadows his lips before it explodes into one of his awe-inspiring grins.

"Yeah, Tate seems to like you a lot. And Ashleigh is not my girlfriend. It's... complicated. I invited you here because I want you here and now you are."

Ryan smiles at me and my pulse is hammering so loudly that I swear he can hear it, too.

Thump-thump, thump-thump.

He places an arm around my shoulder while I try to figure out what he meant when he said, "complicated." Ryan is talking again, so I try to focus on what he is saying instead.

"All of the guys are on their way over and I've been running my mouth about how beautiful and fun you are," Ryan says with a grin.

I blush for what seems like the millionth time tonight and shrug off the compliment.

Ryan thinks I'm beautiful.

"Let's head down to the game room if you're ready and we can have a drink together before everyone gets here."

He takes my hand lightly and leads me down the stairs. Still confused if Ryan is single or not, I let the thought go as the tingles from him holding my hand leap up into my wrist and arm.

As Ryan reaches the last step, he stops as Tate comes down the hall toward us. I stop also and Ryan abruptly releases his hand from mine. I flinch inwardly.

Tate's whistle shakes the negative thoughts away.

"Wow, Sunshine, you outdid yourself! My new nickname for you suits you in all that yellow."

And with an exaggerated bow, Tate offers me his arm, which I graciously take and make sure to lightly check Ryan with my hip as I walk by him.

"Okay, Tate-I-Am, let's get this party started!"

I try to mimic his big smile but fail miserably. I end up walking into the game room, my arm hooked through Tate's and biting my lip nervously instead.

The Beast is there in yet another outfit, this time all Kelly green from head to toe. It is a strapless dress that I know I've seen in Victoria's Secret catalogs and skintight, making it clear she has no underwear on of any kind underneath the dress.

"Wow, glad to see you got so dressed up for all of us," she snorts as I walk in, rolling her eyes and smirking at me.

I realize at that moment that I'm the only one in jeans. Ryan and Tate both have on linen pants and loafers. The two guys who I haven't been introduced to yet aren't wearing jeans either. One has on a pair of khaki shorts and the other is wearing navy blue linen pants. I suddenly feel self-conscious and sit abruptly on one of the round basket chairs in the game room. I fling a pillow on my lap and tuck my feet underneath me in an attempt to hide as much of my jeans as possible. I consider briefly running back upstairs to change but refuse to give The Beast the satisfaction. I can't believe how much I dislike her already and I haven't even known her a full day.

The two guys on the couch opposite me are Zac and Jackson. Ryan quickly introduces me to them and they both insist on standing up and giving me a hug.

Everyone is so friendly here. I haven't received this many hugs in one day, well, ever.

Jackson is wearing the navy-blue linen pants with a grey collared shirt. He has olive skin, short, cropped dark hair and very blue eyes. He's the same age and height as Ryan, but he looks younger, closer to my age. Zac is much taller than both Ryan and Jackson, even though he's the same age, and has shoulder-length brown hair underneath a baseball cap. He is wearing the khaki shorts with a striped rugby shirt that does nothing to hide his muscles underneath.

Geez, where did these guys come from? One is better looking than the next.

It's at this moment that I notice Tate is gone. I have been chatting with Zac and Jackson and didn't even notice. I take a few sips of a beer, which Jackson's brother has so kindly purchased for us, and crinkle my nose as the foam tickles it.

"Up for a game of beer pong, Ayla?" Zac asks as he leans against the ping-pong table that I am standing next to.

He has a killer smile and I think then that I'd probably play anything he wants me to if he asks with that smile. I don't even know what beer pong is, but I act as though I am ecstatic to play.

"Weathers over here won't drink beer," and he nods his head toward Ashleigh, "so we need someone to play on Ryan's team to make it even."

I turn toward Ryan who is in a conversation with Ashleigh, although she rolls her eyes at Zac, so I know they've both heard him.

"Sure!" I say a little too enthusiastically and Zac high-fives me.

He gives me a quick explanation of the game while he sets up the cups. He stacks red Solo cups in a triangle at the end of each side of the ping-pong table. After Jackson fills each cup halfway with beer, he tosses me a ping-pong ball to practice. The object of the game is to sink your ball in the opposing teams' cups causing them to drink the beer in that cup. The first team to eliminate the opposing team's cups wins and the losing team is forced to drink the remaining cups on the winner's side.

I close one eye and sink my first shot in front of Jackson.

"Beginner's luck!" he yells, but winks at me as he tosses the ball back.

I sink the second and the third shot.

"I think we're getting hustled, Jacks," Zac says and slaps me on the back.

"I've never played before, I swear!"

I laugh and am silently thanking my dad for all the hours of softball training, although I'm not quite sure using the skills for beer pong is what he had in mind.

I hear a plastic cup hit the floor, a splash, and Ryan yell.

"Shit, Ash—you dumped your drink all over me!"

I can tell by her smile that she did it on purpose.

"Sorry, babe, guess you're going to have to change."

She says this to Ryan but looks me dead in the eye. I fight back the immediate urge to punch her and uncurl my hand that unconsciously curled into a fist.

"I'll be right back guys and then we can play."

Ryan leaves the room and Ashleigh makes an obvious effort to avoid the spilled drink that managed to make it past Ryan's pants and onto the floor. She walks over to the table across the room to make herself another drink. Not only is the puddle now spreading underneath the couch, but her red cup is slowly rolling that way, too. Realizing she has no intention of cleaning it up, I grab a handful of paper towels from the table and start mopping up the mess.

From this position on the floor, I absent-mindedly throw the empty cup into the garbage a few feet away. Jackson makes a big deal about me making the shot without looking, but to be honest I probably couldn't have done it again if I tried.

Ashleigh looks up from making her drink when Jackson says this.

"That's right, Ayla. On the floor cleaning up my mess—just where you belong."

Before I can let angry words surface, Tate's voice interrupts me.

"She isn't just beautiful, she cleans, too?!"

He is standing in the doorway leaning against the frame. Tate has on worn jeans, the same color as mine.

He changed into jeans so I'd feel more comfortable. I love this kid.

He walks over and helps clean up the rest of the sopping paper towels.

"Perfect timing. I'm in need of a teammate."

I grab Tate's arm and pull him over to the table. We start to play, and I learn quickly that Zac has an ace shot and Jackson isn't too bad either. I start to worry that we are the ones being hustled as I swallow my third cup of beer for the night. Being the super-competitive person that I am, I put my game face on and sink the next shot. As Jackson chugs that cup, Tate sinks his shot in another cup from behind me. The game goes back and forth a few times. There are two cups left on either team's side and it's anyone's game now. The rest of the guys have now all arrived, and even though I haven't been officially introduced to any of them yet, they all seem to be cheering for Tate and me. I can guess that Zac doesn't lose much at anything sports-related and the guys love every second of the tied-game excitement.

Ryan has pretty much abandoned Ashleigh, and she sits pouting in the corner of the room. He is cheering me on and slapping Tate on the back after every shot. Zac sinks another shot, but Jackson misses the last, lonely cup. Tate and I decide to throw our balls at the same time and somehow, they both land in their own cup simultaneously. The room explodes in cheering as everyone realizes that Tate and I just won. Tate picks me up in one of his bear-hug embraces and spins me in a circle. Zac throws his empty cup across the room in frustration but manages a smile as he walks toward me.

"I still think we got hustled, but I'll give you this one, cutie."

He hugs me for a few seconds before he lets me go. Jackson's hug quickly follows, and he hands me a bottle of water. Ryan interrupts the celebration to introduce everyone to me.

"Guys, this is Ayla, even though you've all kind of met her already. She's working with us on the refugee project, too."

I raise my eyebrows at Ryan. Does that mean we all will be working on this event for Ryan's dad together?

There are ten of them altogether, including Ryan and Tate. Their families vacation together and have parties with each other. They jokingly refer to each other as family, and even though they don't look much alike, they are all handsome in their own way.

The oldest of the group is Mikey. He's stockier than the rest, with almost no neck and very broad, muscular shoulders. He looks like a body builder. His family moved to Onancock when he was fifteen, so he's the only one who didn't grow up in Virginia. He has a Staten Island accent, which reminds me of home because some of my family is from Staten Island. I find out that Mikey just graduated high school and is heading to Marist College in Poughkeepsie in the fall. I excitedly explain to him how close that is to my house and we start chatting about Marist.

Alex is a little taller than me and has a sarcastic sense of humor, so I know we'll get along well. He has dark, short hair and grey eyes. He can come across as a bit of a jerk at times, but he has a softer side and makes me laugh throughout the night.

Jesse and Ace are brothers. Ace is 17, Ryan's age, and Jesse is a year older than Tate and me, who are the youngest of the group. Jesse and Ace look so much alike that sometimes it's hard for me to tell them apart. Ace has a tattoo on his upper right arm and Jesse has one ear pierced, so that helps me separate them. They both have wavy, auburn hair that Jesse wears long over his ears while Ace has his cut shorter. They both have stunning blue-green eyes.

Austin has short, blonde hair and is my idea of a stereotypical southerner. He's polite, not really shy, but stays quiet among the larger group. He has a hearty laugh that shakes his shoulders, which by the look of their build, have seen a lot of physical work. I find out that his family owns a dairy farm in Virginia and he travels an hour each way to work the farm with his father during the week.

Finally, there's Jase. Jase reminds me a lot of my father. Not so much in how he looks, but in his calm demeanor, his smile, and the way he talks. Jase has sandy light-brown hair under a baseball cap that nearly covers his dark blue eyes. Jase's eyes are so dark that they almost look navy. Jase is only 17, but he already owns his own business making furniture. From what the rest of the guys say, Jase is really talented. When I ask him about it, he promises to show me some of it one day.

Austin, Jase, and Alex all work their own summer jobs, but the rest of us are assigned to work with Ryan's dad's event director, Jessica. While Austin works on his family's farm and Jase sells his furniture and helps his dad with the family construction business, Alex works down at the docks. He claims it's a very boring job and mostly involves directing pallets of shipments coming in from the boat yards. I get the sense that these three are closer to my family's income range than the rest, who all look like they've never worked a manual labor job in their life.

The game room now looks like a scene from an Abercrombie photo shoot. There are polo shirts, shoes, ping-pong balls, and red Solo cups strewn all over the room. It's nearly 3am and the guys are starting to disperse in various directions, either heading home or out to another party that apparently is raging on the beach a block or two down.

Tate's curfew is midnight, so he is angry because he can't go and no one else wants to stay at the house. I offer to stay with him, suggesting we watch a movie and all of the guys make disgusting kissing noises. One night and I already feel like I am part of this little family, complete with a bunch of annoying brothers.

I roll my eyes at them and start to clean up the cups around the room. I know my parents would never let me out after midnight either, but I am not about to offer that information to anyone else, except to Tate who smiles at my omission. And when I explain to him that I'm not even allowed out on school nights at all during the year, he seems to return to his normal, happy self again.

Once the room is fairly clean, I head upstairs to change and Tate heads to his room. I'm pulling on sweatpants when Tate's head pops up at the top of the stairs.

"You decent?"

Without waiting for a reply, he continues up the stairs and flops on the loveseat. We nix the movie idea and end up talking until 5am instead. Tate tells me a little more about each of the guys. He explains that Ryan and Jase became close friends when they played little league with each other and they're the two who brought both groups together.

Ryan and Tate had grown up with Jesse and Ace, whose parents were friends before they were born. Zac and Jackson were added to the group when their families moved here back in grade school.

Jase grew up with Austin because their dads are friendly. They met Alex when they were young and the three of them were inseparable for a while. When Ryan and Jase became friends, the two groups came together, and they now do pretty much everything together. Mikey moved to town a few years back and became friends with Alex right away. Eventually he started hanging out with the rest of the group, too.

Tate and I talk about our fathers and I tell Tate how lucky I am to be so close with both of my parents. I tell him that I can tell my father pretty much anything and he always supports everything I want to do, even when everyone else tells me I'm crazy or that it's impossible. Tate gets a sad look in his eyes when I talk about my dad.

"I wish I had that kind of relationship with my dad. I used to, but now we're not as close as I'd like. Him and Ryan are more alike, and I don't know how to talk to him anymore. I get the feeling that he doesn't like me. I didn't even get invited on the boat trip. It sucks sometimes, but whatever."

Tate shrugs it off. It's weird to see Tate sad because he's usually smiling from ear to ear. I can sense that he doesn't want to talk about it anymore, so I try to change the subject.

"What is the deal with Ryan and, um, The Beast?"

Tate groans at the sound of our nickname for her and rolls his eyes skyward.

"She really is a beast and I can't stand her, but she is fake in front of dad and Ryan, so they don't see it. She's never liked me much, though, and pretty much has avoided me for the past year. Honestly, I try to avoid her at all costs."

I nod my head in agreement, resolving that might be my best plan for the rest of my trip as well. My stomach flips at the thought of avoiding Ryan, since she seems to be attached to him.

Tate and I are lying on our backs on my still-made bed. The sunlight is just starting to peek through the small windows. Tate stands up and reaches for my hand.

"Hurry! We're gonna miss it!"

He pulls me on his lap on one of the wicker chairs on the balcony and we watch the most beautiful sunrise I've ever seen in my life. I haven't been this physically close to a guy before without feeling nervous. I don't have much experience with boyfriends, unless you count the one I had back at home for a full three days before we broke up. I tend to be a better "buddy" than "girlfriend" to the guys I hang out with. But, for the first time in my life I'm sitting on a guy's lap, curled up against his chest with my head on his shoulder and I feel completely comfortable.

Something about being next to Tate makes me feel happy and safe, like I belong there.

Five

"Soooo, how is it there? Are you enjoying yourself? What's Ryan's family like? What's their house like? Are you having fun?"

The barrage of questions from my mother comes pouring through the earpiece on the phone that sits next to my bed. I smile at my mother's excitement. She's always like this, and even if she fakes it to act interested in things I'm interested in, I love her for it. In this particular case, I think she is truly excited, and her excitement only makes me happier to hear her voice. Pushing away the slight feeling of homesickness that her voice triggers, I breathlessly tell her about the past twenty-four hours. I omit waking up on Tate's chest this morning, still in the wicker chair we watched the sunrise in, but give her details about the house, my bedroom, the guys (she makes me describe each in detail) and even Ashleigh. I tell her about the nickname that Tate came up with and mom proceeds to refer to her as 'The Beast' from that point forward. I love that she hates Ashleigh as much as I do and has never even met her. My mom always has my back on that kind of thing.

After talking briefly to dad to fill him in on the job I will start on Monday, I tell them both I love them and hang up.

I take one more glance in the mirror before heading back down to the dock where all the guys and Ashleigh are hanging out and fishing. I omitted telling mom about the outfit I have on because I'm not sure she would approve, and I know for sure that my father wouldn't. I have on a yellow bikini that Tate gave me with a card that said, "For my Sunshine." I don't normally wear bikinis, mostly because I'm too self-conscious, but because it is a gift from Tate, I put it on. I did throw a black bathing suit cover-up on over top, but it doesn't hide much. I definitely don't fill out the top of the bathing suit as nicely as The Beast does, but I don't look half bad either.

I get to the end of the dock just as Tate gets a bite on his line. He reaches for the pole and pulls it back, but whatever has the other end of his line has a strong hold and pulls him within inches of the edge of the dock. Ryan jumps up and gives Tate a hand, but as they both proceed to pull back, the fish removes itself from the hook and the line gives way as they both sprawl backwards.

I watch the next event in slow motion. As Ryan falls on his back, Tate falls onto his side and his right leg sweeps Ashleigh's legs out from under her. She hits the edge of the dock with a soft thump before I watch her red bikini go tumbling over the side and into the water.

The rest of the guys are laughing hysterically and some even rush to Tate to give him a quick high-five before she surfaces. I help Tate to his feet as Ryan pulls a very angry Ashleigh out of the water and back onto the dock.

"You idiotic little cretin," she yells pointing a finger at Tate and charging toward him.

I step between her and him and cross my arms over my chest. She tries to push me out of the way, but I don't budge and hold my ground. I'm not about to let her yell at Tate or call him names. I am not someone who starts fights, but I will stand up to protect those around me. And I think to myself in this moment that I would probably stand up to anyone to protect Tate.

Before I can think of anything to say, Ryan interrupts my confrontation.

"It was only an accident, Ash."

He stifles a laugh. Ashleigh shoots Tate and me a look of pure hatred before plastering her fake smile on her face and turning to Ryan. She sashays back up the dock and toward the house to get dry clothes and we are finally rid of her presence.

"I like you more and more, cutie," Zac says to me with a playful grin. "Weathers isn't used to anyone standing up to her, especially another chic, and I think she may have met her match!"

The guys continue to tease me, and Alex even begins calling me Rocky, though I tell him I have never been in a fight before. I get the feeling that none of them are too fond of Ashleigh and basically put up with her presence more than enjoy it. I notice that Tate has been more quiet than usual, and I am worried that he may have gotten hurt when he fell. He shakes his head when I quietly ask him a few minutes later but announces to the rest of the group that he's going to head inside for a bit. I start to follow him, but something about his body language tells me he wants to be alone, so I stay behind and let him go. I watch him walk slowly to the house before I turn back to the rest of the guys.

I find Ryan staring at me with a crooked grin on his face. He nudges me with his elbow and nods his head towards the direction of the house.

"You got a thing for my brother, don't ya?"

Internally I think it's funny to hear him say that because Tate had asked me the same thing about Ryan just the night before.

"Tate's awesome, but, no, I don't *have a thing* for him. Ashleigh looked like she might try and kill him. What was I supposed to do? And why didn't any of you men" — and I make a motion with my hands to form air quotes as I say the word 'men' — "help him out?"

With that, Zac and Ryan give me a playful push in an attempt to push me off the edge of the dock. I pretend to get hurt, but when Ryan comes closer to make sure I am okay, I push him off the dock completely. He hits the water with a loud splash. Zac bends over at the knees laughing hysterically and I do the same thing to him. He ends up doing a belly flop into the water. The next thing I know, Alex has grabbed me by the waist and we half jump, half fall into the water with the rest of the guys shortly following us. We come up laughing and splashing each other. As much as I enjoy spending time with Tate, it's nice to think that the rest of the group has accepted me, too. I look around, thinking to myself how fun it is to be considered "one of the guys."

Six

"Ayla, can you give me a hand with this spreadsheet?"

Jessica picks up her head from her desk and calls over to me. There are only few hours left of our first week of work and I am helping the event director, essica, organize our task list for the charity event.

I am pleasantly surprised at how much I like Jessica when I first meet her. She is only six years older than me and is still in college while working full-time or Ryan's dad. She is young and fun and lets us work hands-on with the charity vent. I have only been working with her a week and I already feel like I am earning so much.

She appoints me as one of the team leaders, which really pisses Ashleigh off nd makes it that much more fun for me. I am in charge of the event design and m working with Tate, Jesse, and a few others on creating a theme for the event nd tying it together with all of the small details. There are other teams in charge f marketing and promotion, entertainment, and sponsorships. Jessica oversees the ntire project and all of the team leaders report to her.

I find out when we all go for dinner after work that Jessica has a girlfriend amed Leah. I don't like the way Leah treats or talks to Jessica, but I don't know er well enough to say anything like that to her. Plus, she's my boss, so I just let it o.

When we head back to the house in Ryan's car a few hours later, Ashleigh ts in the front seat with her hand on Ryan's arm, while Tate and I sit in the ackseat. Ashleigh is having a conversation with Ryan about Jessica.

"I can't believe your dad actually hired her. Besides the fact that she's a giant yke, she doesn't have a clue what she's doing!"

Ryan doesn't say anything, so I interrupt.

"Actually, I think Jessica does a great job and she's a good leader. I think Mr. Gematti picked the perfect person."

Ashleigh's head snaps around and she glares at me in the back seat.

"You would like her. You're probably a lesbo yourself. I bet you made it worth her while to elect you as team leader!"

Ryan slams on the brakes and Ashleigh flies forward.

"What the hell, Ash?! Just because you don't like Jessica doesn't mean you have to yell at Ayla. Stop being a bitch!"

Ashleigh turns around and pouts with her arms crossed over her chest.

"Besides, what does her being a lesbian have to do with anything?" Ryan continues. "Who cares what bad decisions she makes in her personal life if she can do a good job?"

I feel Tate tense up in the seat beside me and before I can say anything to Ryan myself, I hear Tate mutter under his breath.

"Sounds just like dad."

Ryan looks at me in the rearview mirror first, then at Tate.

"What did you say, Tate?"

"You sound just like dad! I've heard him say that exact thing before. A bad decision?! Why do you think it's a choice at all?!"

I try to make eye contact with Tate, but he continues to stare out the window.

"Are you kidding me, Tate?! Are you really going to argue that being gay is okay? It's wrong and you know it! It goes against everything in the Bible and it's completely unnatural!"

Whoa.

I have yet to witness this side of Ryan and I am shocked by it. I like to keep an open mind about people in general, regardless of race, gender, or who he or she loves or is attracted to. Hearing Ryan say the exact opposite out loud makes me feel sick to my stomach.

I have been raised Catholic and I've heard all of the arguments from a religious standpoint, but I don't agree with any of them. I think people forget that most religions are supposed to be based upon love, understanding, forgiveness and acceptance.

Tate's voice is really low, so low I have to strain to hear the next few words.

"No, I don't think it's wrong or unnatural."

"Oh, dad will just love that! You better keep that to yourself or you'll start World War III!"

Ryan pulls into the driveway and hops out of the car, slamming the door. Ashleigh is still pouting, but follows Ryan into the house. Tate makes no move to get out and keeps staring out the window toward the dock. I unbuckle my seatbelt and move into the middle of the backseat. I sit there quietly for a few minutes because I am not sure if I should leave or stay. I decide to stay and slip my hand in his hand.

"I don't think it's wrong or unnatural either."

Tate squeezes my hand but continues to stare out of the window. We sit like this for a few moments before he turns around with a smile on his face like nothing is wrong at all.

Ryan and Ashleigh go to a friend's party, so Tate and I are on our own. We call Jesse and he comes over to hang out at the house. We try to watch a movie in the game room but end up down at the dock instead because none of us want to be inside. I am sitting in between the two at the edge of the dock. We swing our legs like little kids while eating Twizzlers. We were going to brainstorm ideas for the charity event theme but end up spending most of the night sharing stories and joking with each other instead. By the time Jesse gets in his car to head home my stomach hurts from laughing all night.

I flop down in one of the chairs in the family room and let my legs hang over the side. Tate is lying down on the couch opposite me. Cora walks in and motions to Tate with a head nod toward the kitchen. Tate gets up and grabs another Tupperware container off the counter before coming back into the living room. He sets it down on a table near him and we both say goodnight to Cora.

When she leaves, I look at Tate and then at the Tupperware and then back at Tate. He pretends not to notice and tries changing the subject instead.

"We should probably head to bed. It's getting late and we need to get an early start tomorrow if we're taking the boats out."

Not wanting to push him, I let the Tupperware go—again. I make my way upstairs to get ready for bed. I realize that I still have Tate's sweatshirt on, so I walk back down to the second floor to give it to him. When I get to his bedroom, I hear him talking to someone on the other side of his closed door.

"Yeah, I'll be there in a little bit. I'll leave in a few minutes."

There are a couple seconds of silence and then I hear him say three words that make my heart sink.

"Love you, too."

I flinch inwardly at the realization that hearing Tate say this to someone else makes me jealous. Maybe I do have a little crush on Tate and am just now realizing it. I decide to leave the sweatshirt folded up on the floor outside his door and tiptoe back toward my room. I am halfway up the stairs when I hear Tate's door open. I listen to the sound of him walking quietly down the hall and to the first floor. I jog up the rest of the steps to my window and see Tate walking out the front door of the house. I watch him disappear down the long driveway with the Tupperware container.

I sit at the window a long time after Tate disappears from sight. I try to figure out my feelings for him and realize that I am more hurt that he is hiding something from me than anything else. I have only known Tate a little over a week, but we have become so close so fast that it seems much longer than that. One of the things that I love most about our friendship is that I feel like I can tell Tate anything. It makes me sad to realize he may not feel the same way about me.

I try to convince myself that maybe he was speaking to a relative or a close friend, but I can't erase the sound of his voice when he said those words. I can't figure out why he is hiding her from me, but I'm not sure if I should talk to him about it or just let it be. I decide to let it be for now. If Tate doesn't want me to know about her, then there must be a good reason behind it. I don't want to force him into telling me.

I come up with a million different scenarios that night while lying in bed. Maybe she's not popular and he's afraid to admit he's dating her. Maybe she's older and it's illegal for him to be dating her. Maybe it's one of the guys' younger sisters and he doesn't want anyone to find out.

I count the scenarios like sheep until I fall asleep. I dream that I am following Tate through the woods, but no matter how hard I try, I can't catch up to him. I keep calling for him, but he won't look back. I get the feeling that he is in trouble and I want to help him, but he won't respond and no matter how fast I run, he is always just out of my reach.

Seven

We take Mr. Gematti's cabin cruiser and bow rider out to a small island about two miles from the Gematti's house. The Gematti family owns the island as well. There is a pavilion with charcoal barbecue pits, tables and a bathroom, along with a few canoes, kayaks, a shed with a bunch of equipment and even a small building with a kitchen in it. The guys camp out here all of the time and we pack enough stuff with us to stay overnight. We get to the island, unload our stuff and Tate asks me if I want to take a canoe out.

I'm sitting opposite Tate in the canoe, trying like hell to act like I know what I'm doing and failing miserably. I have an oar in my hand and I'm trying to mimic everything Tate is doing to propel us forward, but I keep getting mixed up and we end up spinning in circles. Tate's dimple is out, and I am distracted by it and my thoughts from the night before.

"Hellooo in there? Anyone home?"

I realize Tate has been talking to me, but I have no idea what he's said.

"Sorry, I'm out of it today."

I smile at him while shielding the sun from my eyes. He tells me to put the oar in the boat and he'll do the rest. I know that he's wondering what's wrong with me, but I don't know how to bring it up, especially here with all of the guys and Ashleigh not too far away.

I look over at Tate when I realize that we are floating at this point. He stopped rowing and is laying across the bench seats with his legs hanging over into the water. I smile at him and do the same. I look up at the bright blue sky and hear the guys laughing in the distance. I look over at Tate to find he is staring at me.

"What's on your mind, Sunshine? You seem awfully quiet today."

I shrug and smile back at him, but he knows something is wrong right away. I have yet to hide anything from him and even if I try to, he can read my every thought in the expressions on my face. He attempts to move closer to me, but I yell out as the boat dips back and forth with his movement. He freezes in place but looks at me with an evil grin.

"Don't you dare!" I yell with a laugh.

I sit up quickly and slow the rocking boat by putting a hand on either side of the canoe.

"Well, that's the first real smile I've seen all day!"

Tate proceeds to rock the boat back and forth until I scream. Tate laughs loudly and I think to myself how much I love the sound of his laugh.

We end up lying on our backs on the bottom of the boat. I jump down here because I am terrified we are going to flip over, but Tate stops rocking immediately when I do. He lies down next to me so our arms and legs touch.

He grabs my hand suddenly, kisses my fingers and puts my hand, still entangled with his own, on his chest.

"Did you come down to my room last night?"

Surprised by the question, I suck in a long breath of air before I respond.

"Yes," I smile at him sheepishly, "but you sounded like you were on the phone, so I didn't knock. I left your sweatshirt by the door and went back up to bed."

I turn to face him, leaving my hand with his on his chest, but using the other to prop up my head.

"I watched you leave last night, too."

I look at his face to gauge his reaction, but he only shrugs.

"I have a friend named Jake whose father passed away last year, and his mother has some... issues. He spends a lot of time taking care of her or alone, so I visit him a couple of times a week. Cora always makes some food for me to bring to him. He eats a lot of fast food and takeout, so he loves when I bring him anything Cora makes."

"Oh."

I am a complete idiot.

Here I am thinking he's running off to hang out with some girl and feeling jealous when he's only helping a friend.

Tate's voice interrupts my train of thought.

"That's what has been bothering you all day? You are a nut!"

Tate smiles the big smile that is slowly starting to make butterflies appear in my stomach the way Ryan's smile does and kisses my forehead.

"What am I going to do with you?!"

I sit up in the canoe, momentarily excited.

"Do you think I could meet him?"

Tate looks confused at first.

"Meet who?"

I laugh at him and shake my head.

"Jake, silly. I'd like to meet him. Would it be weird if I came with you the next time? Maybe I can even bake something for him, with Cora's help!"

Tate seems hesitant, but then grins at me.

"Do you really want to meet him?"

I nod furiously.

"Of course. Why wouldn't I? If he's a friend of yours, I'm sure I'll like him, too."

Tate agrees to take me with him the next time he visits Jake. We sit for another hour in the canoe talking and laughing, but his hand doesn't leave mine the entire time.

Eight

Thankfully, Zac and Jase set up our tent while Tate and I were out in the canoe. I'm not sure I would have been much help anyway. The tents form a large horseshoe shape and at the very end of the horseshoe, Alex has started a bonfire.

Jase and Jesse both have guitars and are singing, drinking and laughing as the sun goes down. Everyone seems to be having a good time and even Ashleigh is joining in on the fun.

Some of the guys invited girlfriends who brought their friends and by shortly after midnight, there are about fifty people on the small island. I lose Tate in the mix of everyone, but am chatting with Ali, Alex's date for the evening, and two of her friends, Sarah and Whitney. They are really sweet but talk a lot about fashion and guys and makeup, so I lose interest in the conversation quickly. I politely excuse myself with a smile and walk to get another drink. Without realizing it, I wind up standing next to Ashleigh who is also pouring a drink for herself.

She smiles at me then quickly frowns when she too realizes it's me standing next to her. She attempts to ignore me altogether, but Ryan walks up behind me and covers my eyes with his hands. I watch her face through Ryan's fingers and think to myself that her dislike of me may have more to do with Ryan's attention than anything else. I tell myself to try and remember this from now on and give Ashleigh a little bit of a break.

Jealousy is a form of flattery, right?

Ryan stands in between us and playfully strings an arm across each of our shoulders.

"I noticed you and Tate were getting cozy in the canoe earlier," Ryan teases me with a sly grin and squeezes my arm.

I roll my eyes at him and he squeezes me tighter. Ashleigh mutters under her breath that I'm "utterly clueless" and stalks off to the tents. Ryan follows her with his eyes but doesn't leave my side.

"What's the deal with you two?" I say pointing in Ashleigh's direction with my thumb.

"She's not so bad when you get to know her, A. I swear! She can be a good time."

Ryan looks at me with a mischievous grin.

"Yeah, I'm sure she can be a great time, Ry!"

I roll my eyes at him again. Ryan picks me up over his shoulder and carries me back to the campfire while I laugh and slap him on the back.

A group is singing around the campfire as Ryan stumbles into the circle with me on his shoulder. He flops down on a log and sits me on his lap. He starts singing the next verse louder than anyone else, so I sing along, too.

In the next few hours, things start to quiet down again. Some of the crowd has left on their boats and some have retired to the tents to sleep for the night. I crawl inside my sleeping bag as Tate unzips the door to the tent that I'm in.

"Hey, Sunshine!"

Tate's eyes look tired or perhaps he's had a few too many drinks.

"Hey! Where the heck have you been all night? I haven't seen you in hours!"

Tate ignores my questions as he unzips the sleeping bag I'm in and pretends to try and get inside with me. I start pinching him playfully and he quickly retreats.

"I was around. I was talking to some friends. I kept trying to find you, but when I did you were talking with a bunch of girls or sitting on Ryan's lap around the campfire."

Tate raises his eyebrows as he mentions his brother's name.

"You were a pretty busy girl tonight."

I can't tell if Tate is teasing me or if he's upset, so I shrug it off.

"Did you have fun tonight at least?"

I crawl back out of my sleeping bag as I ask him.

"I had a blast. What about you?"

Tate reaches for my hand and laces his fingers with mine.

I crawl closer so that I'm within inches of him.

"I had a good time, too."

I look up into Tate's eyes and he looks back, unblinking. I'm not sure if I am feeling brave at the moment or it's the handful of drinks that I've had throughout the night, but I lean in slowly to kiss Tate and stop just short of touching his lips. He puts his hands on either side of my face and whispers my name. I smile and as I do, he kisses me softly. It's a short, sweet kiss, but I feel my heart flutter in my chest.

When Tate's lips leave mine, I pull him back in for another. My kiss is a little more forceful than Tate's and it lasts much longer this time. His tongue plays with mine and his hands move from my face to the back of my head. I come up breathless and realize he's panting softly, too.

Before I crawl back into my sleeping bag, Tate zips both sleeping bags together and crawls in next to me. I fall asleep in his arms shortly after he kisses the top of my head.

I wake up the next morning before Tate does. I quietly wiggle out of the sleeping bag and open the tent to find that I am the first person awake. The campsite is quiet with the exception of the birds singing. I have a pounding headache and try to find a bottle of water in the cooler without making too much noise. I think about the kiss from the night before and I smile to myself.

I'm sitting at one of the picnic tables under the pavilion when I watch Ashleigh emerge from Ryan's tent. Moments later, Ryan emerges, too. He's shirtless when he sits down across from me. He doesn't say a word, but winks with that same mischievous grin from last night. I once again roll my eyes at him but return his crooked grin. I'm positive his night was a bit more intimate than mine was, but at least we both woke up happy this morning.

Ashleigh sits down next to Ryan and offers me some aspirin. I look at her in surprise.

"Just take them," she says without making eye contact.

I thank her quietly as I take the aspirin. Maybe I'm growing on Ashleigh. And maybe she isn't as bad as I think she is, like Ryan said. I swallow the aspirin with a swig of water and then offer her the bottle so she can take hers.

People slowly start to wake up and emerge from the sea of tents. The campsite gets busy quickly as everyone begins to clean up from the night before. A short time later the only tent standing is the tent that I slept in with Tate.

Tate is still sleeping by the time everyone is ready to go, so I unzip the door to wake him up. I can hear his muffled voice underneath the sleeping bag. Giggling to myself as I assume he is talking in his sleep, I pull back the unzipped sleeping bag, ready to pounce on him to wake him up. I see the cell phone to his ear and realize he's on the phone with someone, so I mouth the word "sorry" and start to crawl back out of the tent. Tate grabs my hand and pulls me back down on top of him. He tells the person on the phone that he has to go and quickly hangs up.

"Good morning, Sunshine!"

Tate's attention is now fully focused on me and I suddenly feel shy around him because of our kiss last night. I explain to him that everyone else is cleaned up and we need to start packing our stuff so we can catch up with the group. Tate leans in to kiss my forehead and then we both pack up our clothes, sleeping bags, and lastly, our tent.

The ride back to the dock at the Gematti's house is quick, but very quiet. I think everyone is still half asleep. When we pull into the dock, we all go in different directions, either to start the day or to get some more sleep.

I feel tired, but not ready to head back to bed, so when Tate goes inside to sleep for a few hours, I stay on the dock.

Ashleigh says that she is going to go home to sleep as well and invites Ryan to come with her. Ryan shakes his head and says he is going to stay on the dock with me instead. I see the green monster flash in Ashleigh's eyes once more and I know that the amiable Ashleigh I saw this morning won't be back for a while. She stomps and pouts her way back to her car.

Ryan sits down next to me at the end of the dock, but before long, we are both lying on our backs and talking about the night before and the past few days at work. Our heads are parallel to each other, but our bodies are facing different directions.

Ryan and I are becoming closer as the days pass, too. I may have been inducted into his little family of guys, but Ryan is the reason I am here in the first place. He can read me the way Tate does, and even though I'm still unsure about my feelings for Tate, my friendship with Ryan remains playful. We flirt with each other, especially when it's just the two of us alone.

"You know, Ayla, it's too bad that you and my brother hit it off so well because I think we could have been a pretty good thing together, too."

I can feel the flush start at my shoulders and go straight to the top of my head. Thank goodness Ryan is staring at the sky and can't see how red I am at this moment.

"Yeah, The Beas– uh, I mean Ashleigh, would just love that one!"

Ryan laughs.

"Yeah, I guess that would have made for quite a messy summer, huh?"

"Somehow, I think that anything to do with you and the ladies ends up quite messy, Ry!"

I look at him with a wide grin and wink like he usually does to me.

Ryan spins around so that he is now lying on his stomach and his head is over top of mine and upside down.

"You know me that well already?"

He laughs as I stare into his beautiful, get-lost-in-them eyes.

"But see, that's what I'm talking about, A. I think you are the same way, but just don't like to admit it. You love the attention we all give you. I see the way you act sweet and attentive with Tate. And I've seen you act flirty and sarcastic with Zac and Alex. And it's obvious to me that there's something between us when we're alone together. Sooooo, people in glass houses shouldn't throw stones!"

I'm a little taken aback by this. I guess I never realized that I come across as a flirt. I think Ryan may have meant this as a compliment, but I'm not sure how to take it. It is true that I like the attention from the guys.

But only as friends, right?

And it is true that I've been attracted to Ryan since I met him, but now I think I may have feelings for Tate, also. Maybe I am no better than someone like Ashleigh who pouts the second she doesn't have everyone's full attention.

"Hey, come back to me. I was only teasing, A."

I snap back to reality and realize that Ryan has been staring into my eyes the whole time. Before I can explain what I was thinking about, Ryan leans down and kisses me. I'm so surprised by the kiss that I flinch and end up biting his lip. Ryan laughs into my mouth but doesn't pull back. The kiss doesn't last long, but as soon as it ends, I immediately feel guilty because of Tate, and the fact that I was hoping Ryan would kiss me.

Ryan must read my thoughts in the expression on my face because he begins to apologize. He rolls back onto his back so we are both staring up at the sky again.

"Shit, I don't know why I did that. I'm really sorry. I wasn't thinking. I shouldn't have done that, A, especially because I think my brother really likes you."

"Stop apologizing. I kissed you back, didn't I? I don't know how I feel about anything at this moment, but I can't help feeling guilty because of Tate."

I don't know what else to say, so I stop talking. I look back at the house and up at one of the windows of Tate's bedroom. The curtains are still closed, so I guess that he is probably sleeping.

Ryan follows my gaze to the house.

"Listen, we can pretend it didn't happen, okay? It'll just be between the two of us."

Ryan looks back at me. I nod at him in agreement, but deep down I'm not sure I want to forget it.

I'm not sure how I feel about anything lately.

Nine

I walk alongside Tate, but he flinches anxiously every time I get close enough to touch him. I want to reach out and hold his hand, but he seems distant today and I don't want to push him. I ignore the wave of guilt every time I think about kissing Ryan, but I don't bring it up to Tate because mostly I still don't know how I feel about it.

Tate stops abruptly in front of a small brick house with a fence around it. The whole house is smaller than Tate's garage, but it looks fairly well-kept and the grass is freshly mowed.

I'm holding a tray of chocolate chip cookies and balance it in one hand as I try to reach for the gate. Tate beats me to it and holds the gate open for me. He steps aside to let me walk through and then jogs past me to the front door. He quickly knocks twice then stuffs his hands in his pockets. He doesn't make eye contact with me and he seems nervous.

A guy with spiky dark hair answers the door. He has on a muscle shirt and dark jeans, a leather cuff on his wrist and he's wearing eyeliner that is thicker than mine. My first thought is that he must be in a band. I smile at him. He returns a wide smile and as I introduce myself, he wraps me in a bear hug that lifts me off the ground and spins me around. I throw my head back and laugh, thinking how Tate greeted me the same way the first time I met him.

"Hi Ayla, I'm Jake," he says as he slowly lowers my feet to the ground.

I catch Tate's huge grin over Jake's shoulder and am happy to see that his smile has returned.

"It's so nice to meet you, Jake! I hope you don't mind me crashing your plans today. I brought some chocolate chip cookies because that's pretty much the only thing I can currently bake."

I grin and look up into Jake's eyes playfully as I hand him the tray of cookies.

"Of course not and this is a treat. Tate doesn't usually get to stop by during the day. And if you bring cookies, you can come anytime you want, with or without Tate!"

He turns to Tate, slinging an arm around Tate's shoulders and laughing.

"Deal!"

I walk to the other side of Jake and put my arm around his waist. Tate gives me a funny look and turns out of Jake's embrace. Jake asks if I'd like to go inside. I nod and follow Jake into the house, with Tate only a step behind me.

We walk into a small living room with one couch and a television. There's a strong smell of stale cigarette smoke that fills my mouth when we walk through the door. I try not to make it obvious that the smell bothers me and quickly follow Jake into the kitchen. There's a round table that has four mismatched chairs around it and Jake and Tate each take a seat next to one another. A deck of playing cards sits in the middle of the table and Tate immediately starts shuffling and dealing them. I sit down across from Tate and next to Jake and watch them play. I have never been good at any card games, especially ones where you have to bluff because it's always immediately obvious to everyone else when I'm lying.

Jake opens the plastic wrapped around the tray I brought and eats an entire cookie in one bite. He grins at me with a full mouth of cookie crumbs and gives me thumbs up. He finishes a couple more this way before completing his hand. I haven't seen his mom anywhere but notice that there is a room at the end of the hallway with a closed door. It sounds like there may be a TV or radio on very low behind the door.

We sit around the table for another hour playing cards — me learning to play while the boys teach me — eating cookies, and talking. I learn that Tate and Jake go to school together, but Jake is a year older than both of us. Jake is very open about his mother's problems. He shares stories of receiving phone calls in the middle of the night to go pick his mother up at a bar or, even worse, the police station. I feel sorry for Jake, but he doesn't seem to want sympathy. He simply accepts that his mother has issues and that she isb't able to get better. He talks about it very matter-of-factly. The only bitterness that Jake shows is when he mentions his older brother Sean. Sean is nineteen and no longer lives with them. Jake feels like Sean abandoned them.

It's fun to watch Tate and Jake interact. I can tell that they are very close and have been friends for a long time. They seem comfortable around each other. Tate's earlier mood has vanished, and he seems to be having fun.

At the end of the next hand, I look up at the clock and realize that it's time to head home for Sunday dinner.

"Tate, we better head back before Cora finishes dinner. Jake, why don't you come with us? It's kind of like an open house on Sundays for dinner."

I realize before I finish the sentence that it is something I shouldn't have said, although I'm not sure why. Tate's face scrunches up and Jake lets out a sarcastic laugh.

"Is that so? Thank you for the invitation, Ayla. Tate has never invited me on a Sunday."

He spins around to face Tate with a grimace and Tate begins to stutter, but Jake puts his hand up to stop him.

"I have to take care of mom anyway. No big deal. Thanks for the invite, Ayla."

He hugs me briefly and heads back to the closed door at the end of the hallway.

"Later Tate," he says over his shoulder without looking back.

I look at Tate with wide eyes.

"I'm sorry. I thought because he likes Cora's cooking…"

The end of my sentence trails off as I bite my lip nervously. Tate grabs my hand and leads me out of the kitchen and out of the front door.

We start the three-mile walk back toward the Gematti's house, but Tate still hasn't said anything and hasn't let go of my hand. I squeeze his hand to try to get him to look at me.

"It's not your fault, Sunshine."

Tate picks up his head, but still won't meet my gaze.

"Look, there's something I haven't told you about Jake."

Tate looks straight ahead but doesn't let go of my hand.

"Jake's not very well liked at school. There are a lot of kids that make fun of him, Ryan and some of the other guys included. Dad wouldn't like me hanging out with him, which is why I usually sneak off at night to. I actually told dad that I was taking you shopping today. He has no idea where we were, and I'd prefer to keep it that way."

I can't imagine why anyone would dislike Jake. He made me feel comfortable around him right away, as if we've been friends for years.

"But… why? I don't understand, Tate. Did Jake do something to make them all dislike him? Is it because of money?"

I can't imagine Ryan not liking someone because they weren't as well off as his family is. He welcomed me with open arms and while my family does well, we are far from the financial surplus that the Gematti family has. I can imagine Ashleigh not liking him for this reason, thinking of some of her comments to me, but not Ryan.

"Not necessarily money, although he does get made fun of for that, too. His older brother, Sean, has a bad reputation around town because he's always causing trouble at school or getting caught up with the police for one reason or another. When I started high school, people judged Jake because of his brother…"

This time it's Tate's turn to trail off. He takes a gulping breath and stops walking to face me.

"Sometimes people make fun of the way Jake dresses or some of the things he says or does. There's more to it than that, though, Sunshine. Jake is openly gay at school."

I think he's going to continue, but Tate stops abruptly.

"Okay… so what? That's it?! People don't like Jake because he's gay?!"

I put my hands on my hips in disbelief. Slowly things start to fall in place in my head. The small argument in the car between Ryan and Tate about Jessica and Ryan's comments about how Mr. Gematti feels about it. I realize now that the conversation was about a lot more than just Jessica and her relationship.

"It doesn't bother you that Jake is gay?" Tate looks at me incredulously.

"Of course it doesn't! Why would it?"

Tate seems shocked, but I don't understand why. I know that people in high school can be cruel and judgmental. I've seen it at my own school many times, but I'll never understand the reasons behind picking on someone or not liking someone because they are different. I can't stand the thought of Jake being picked on or disliked simply because he is gay.

I look up and notice that Tate is smiling at me. He still hasn't let go of my hand.

"You're amazing, you know that?"

He tucks a strand of my hair behind my ear. We continue on our walk and chat the rest of the way home. Tate tells me how Jake doesn't let the teasing bother him at school. He tells Tate that this is who I am and if they don't like me, it's their loss. I quietly am jealous of Jake because I wish I could be more like that, especially at school. Tate tells me that he feels ashamed that he hides his friendship with Jake from his other friends and family. He tells me that Jake understands, but that sometimes he's hurt that Tate hides it.

I nod my head sadly at Tate and realize that my invitation to dinner, as innocent as it was, hurt Jake's feelings. I make a mental note to bake him more cookies in the near future.

By the time we arrive at the Gematti's house, I've learned that Tate has been friends with Jake for almost two years now, but that his father and brother have no idea. The only person that Tate has told, other than me, is Cora. It makes me sad and a little angry that Jake isn't joining us tonight for dinner. I don't understand and it's sad to me that they are missing out on knowing someone like Jake because they won't give him a chance.

The entire time at dinner my thoughts are on Jake. Tate can tell I'm distracted, but I don't think anyone else notices. I wish I could find a way to talk to Ryan about it without betraying Tate's trust, but that isn't possible right now.

I excuse myself after dinner and head up to my room lost in thought. I change into sweats and crawl under the covers even though it's a warm summer night. I'm not sure why this is bothering me so much, but I have a nervous feeling in the pit of my stomach that I can't quite explain. Perhaps the feeling is disappointment in people who I care about or sympathy for Tate's friendship with Jake or just the simple fact that I am uncomfortable with hiding things. Maybe it's a little bit of everything. Regardless of what the feelings are, I can't sleep.

After tossing and turning for a few hours, I creep back down to Tate's room only to find he isn't there. I assume he went back to Jake's to apologize for earlier. I feel bad that he didn't come get me first. Maybe he was worried that I'd get him in trouble with Jake again.

Me and my big mouth.

I'm standing in Tate's bedroom doorway when I hear a voice behind me.

"Can't sleep either?"

Ryan's question makes me jump about a foot in the air. He laughs as I turn around with my hand over my now-pounding heart.

Ryan is wearing nothing but a pair of shorts. Even his bare feet are sexy and I despise naked feet. I self-consciously pull at the bottom of my tank top to cover the skin that is showing above my sweatpants.

"Where's Tate?"

Ryan looks past me to Tate's empty room.

"Uh, I'm not sure. I came down here to see if he was awake."

I stop mid-sentence because not one good excuse comes to my mind. It just keeps yelling Jake's name over and over again and I can't complete one rational thought.

"Where the hell would he be on a Sunday night without you?"

I shrug and smile and walk Ryan down the hall away from Tate's room trying to distract him.

"So, you can't sleep either?"

I look up into Ryan's eyes and smile at him, trying to bat my eyelashes the way I've seen Ashleigh do a million times before. It miraculously works and Ryan temporarily forgets about Tate.

"Yeah, I'm working on some ideas for the charity event and was heading to the kitchen for a snack. You game?"

I nod and follow Ryan downstairs as he runs over some of the ideas he has been working on. Ryan makes two glasses of chocolate milk and hands one to me as I sit at the island. He offers me a cookie and when I shake my head, he begins to eat it instead.

We have been in the kitchen for a half hour when the front door opens and closes quickly. Ryan pops his head out and calls to Tate. Tate comes around the corner very slowly with a bunch of sunflowers in hand.

"Trying to be romantic, huh? Caught red-handed, buddy!"

Ryan slaps Tate on the back and laughs as Tate makes an elaborate gesture of handing the flowers to me. I blush crimson as Ryan says goodnight to the both of us and catches my eye to wink at me on his way out of the room.

Tate pulls a vase out of the cabinet and turns to me once he is sure that Ryan is upstairs and out of earshot.

"The flowers are for you from Jake. His backyard is full of them. He says he feels like a jerk for walking out the way he did earlier. I told him about our conversation on the way home and I apologized to him about dinner."

Tate fills the vase with the sunflowers and carries it in one hand while offering his other arm to me. I link my arm through his and we walk upstairs to my room where he puts the sunflowers on the side table for me. He tucks me in, kisses my forehead and retreats to his own room, but I can't help but feel like he's sad for some reason.

Ten

"Here's the final list of sponsors, Ayla. Can you review this and proof all of the signage against this list?"

Jessica hands me two sheets full of sponsor names and I begin checking off the sponsors who are listed on the signage that just arrived from the print shop.

It's the week of our charity event and there are only two weeks left before I return home to New York. Things are in full swing at the office as we get ready for this Saturday's event. In honor of the Chincoteague National Wildlife Refuge, we decided to throw a safari themed gala. It was Jesse's idea, and everyone loved it.

I stand in front of large sponsor signs that look like Safari maps. Across the room from me, Ashleigh and Ryan work on finalizing the guest list and organizing the registration table while Jesse and Tate put finishing touches on some of the large animal cutouts that will be displayed around the room on Saturday evening. Each cutout features animals housed at the Refuge, a way to remind guests that all proceeds benefit the animals directly.

It's hard to believe that I'll be heading back home next weekend. I try not to think about it. My life is so different here and I can't imagine starting school without the guys and especially without Tate. Tate has become my closest friend this summer and the idea of leaving him makes me immediately depressed. I think I may even miss Ashleigh, although I'd never tell her that.

The past couple of weeks Tate, Jake and I have hung out quite a bit. We spend a lot of evenings at Jake's house playing cards, bringing him food, and checking in on his mother, who spends most of her time in her bedroom. Twice, we packed bags and went camping on the Gematti's island when no one else was there. We hang out in quiet places on the beach, making sure to avoid crowds, and we never go into town where people might see Jake with us.

I'm beginning to understand Jake's frustration with Tate. To always have to hide whatever we are doing or see Tate's anxiety of approaching crowds is frustrating for me, so I can't begin to imagine how it must make Jake feel. Sometimes I think Tate is acting like a coward for not telling his father or Ryan, but then I remind myself that Tate feels like he doesn't have a choice.

One night when I bring this up to Tate, he confides in me that his biggest fear of telling his dad is that he will no longer allow him to hang out with Jake and that he feels like Jake needs him. I try to let it go after that conversation, but I can see Jake's frustration growing as summer progresses.

Although Tate and I are pretty much inseparable, things between us romantically haven't evolved. Other than the night in the tent at the island party, we haven't kissed. He holds my hand often, gives hugs freely, and lights up whenever he sees me, but he hasn't made any moves further than that and I haven't either. In the back of my mind, I keep thinking about the kiss between Ryan and me on the dock a few weeks ago and still wonder if Tate saw it. He hasn't brought it up to me, though, so I let it go instead of asking him.

The next week goes by quickly because we are busy getting ready for the gala. On Saturday morning, Ryan and I spend most of the day setting up for the event, along with Ashleigh and Jessica. Tate isn't on the schedule for the morning, so he decides to spend the day at Jake's house without me.

Jessica and I have become very close this summer, and with Tate's permission, I told her about the whole situation between him and Jake. She thinks that Tate is being a little unfair to Jake but understands and appreciates that Tate's trying to be a good friend. Jessica is usually very honest with me, even if it's going to hurt my feelings, but for some reason when I tell her about Tate and Jake, I get the feeling that she is holding something back. She listens when I talk to her about it, but she doesn't say much. For Jessica to not have an opinion on anything is rare, so it makes me pause when she doesn't have much to say about something that she can relate to personally. I assumed she would have some insight for me, but she often stays quiet instead.

"Is it weird that I'm jealous that they are hanging out without me?"

Jessica and I are setting up table arrangements. She purses her lips and shakes her head. There's that look again.

What isn't she saying?

Ashleigh, who needs help with the balloons, interrupts us. She's creating large African trees around the room using wooden cutouts of the base and branches of the tree, and green and brown balloons for leaves. This is another invention by Jesse, who unfortunately isn't here this morning to help assemble them. Jessica and I make our way over to help Ashleigh and the conversation stops there.

Four hours later, the hall looks completely transformed into an African safari. Satisfied with our work, we all head in various directions to get dressed for the evening. Ashleigh rides with me and Ryan to get ready at the Gematti's house because we are all riding together in a large limo, compliments of Mr. Gematti.

I am about to put the last pin in my hair when Tate walks up the attic steps.

"Hey, Sunshine!"

He walks over and stands behind me while I'm in front of the mirror. He whistles at my reflection and I laugh, looking up at him. He places his arms around my waist while I put the last bobby pin in. I turn around in my dark green dress and face him. We lock eyes for only a moment before Tate steps back abruptly to break the embrace.

"You look beautiful."

He smiles and lightly grabs my chin until I return the smile.

Ashleigh and Ryan walk up the steps to my room. I realize it is the first time that Ashleigh has been in here all summer. Of course, she looks amazing. She's in all white, with a brown and green beaded belt that wraps around her waist, showing off her curves. She dons a matching necklace in the same material as the belt and her long blonde hair is curled and flowing down her back.

I catch a glimpse in the mirror of my wavy hair piled on top of my head and start to rethink the updo. As my hand absent-mindedly moves to my head to pull out a bobby pin, Tate grabs it and silently mouths the word no to me. He somehow knows when I doubt myself and always finds a way to make me feel better about it without me having to speak. I'm going to miss this when I'm back in New York. I have gotten used to Tate reassuring me about, well, everything.

Mr. Gematti calls for us from downstairs and we make our way out of the house and into the limo. The rest of the guys are already inside, some of them with dates. I recognize Ali, Whitney, and Sarah from the island party and say hello to them as I get inside. I take a seat, sandwiched in between Ryan and Tate for the entire ride.

When champagne is opened and handed out to everyone, I pass. Tate grabs my drink when I shake my head no and gulps it down quickly before doing the same with his. I raise my eyebrows at him, but he avoids the look and grabs for my hand instead.

The event itself is a blast. Jessica has assigned each of us a small one-hour task throughout the evening so we can enjoy attending the event, too. Tate and I are assigned to help with registration and the hour passes quickly. Afterward, we join everyone in the cocktail room and walk from table to table trying different hors d'oeuvres. It's an open bar and Tate is taking full advantage of it, even though we are both far from 21. I'm not sure if it's the fact that he's a Gematti or because he is wearing a staff tag, but the bartender doesn't even question his age.

Zac and Jackson join us at a cocktail table and Alex finds us shortly after that. I'm talking with Jackson when Tate walks away to get another drink from the bar. I stop mid-sentence to follow him with my eyes.

"Don't worry about him, A. Tate tends to drink a little too much at these things. Scott usually ignores it and it's just some harmless fun."

Zac puts his arm around my shoulders and pulls my attention back to our conversation. After a few minutes, I excuse myself and walk over to the bar where Tate is still standing.

When I am close enough, Tate leans in and whispers in my ear.

"I wish Jake could be here."

Tate's voice sounds sad and bitter.

"I wish he could ride in the limo with us and have fun with everyone. Instead he's at home with his mother while we're all here dressed in suits and ties and eating bullshit food."

I grab Tate lightly by the elbow and look him in the eyes.

"Jake should be here, Tate-I-Am. It's ridiculous that he can't come with us to things like this."

I thought my words would comfort Tate a bit, but instead he looks visibly upset and excuses himself, making his way to the restroom. The guys look at us from across the room, their eyes following Tate.

I shrug at them, walking slowly back to where they are standing. I probably should follow Tate, but I am not about to head into the men's room. I also don't want to send any of the guys in after him if he is upset because he won't be able to explain why.

When cocktail hour ends and Tate is nowhere to be found, I try not to get nervous. I find Ryan in the crowd as everyone makes their way to the dinner tables and ask him to check the men's room for Tate. When Ryan comes back without him, I explain that he was a little tipsy and took off in the middle of cocktail hour, but that I haven't seen him since.

Ryan shrugs it off saying that it was typical of Tate to disappear at these events.

"Don't worry A. You can be my date for the evening."

He smiles wickedly as he offers me his arm. I shake my head at Ryan with a grin and walk arm and arm with him to the dinner table. I sit down, but check the door every couple of minutes waiting for Tate to walk back in. His seat next to me remains empty for the entire dinner and when music and dancing start, Tate is still nowhere to be found. Ryan is on the dance floor with Ashleigh. I decide to walk up to them to tell Ryan that Tate is still missing.

Ashleigh rolls her eyes as I finish.

"He does this all the time. He did the same thing at last year's charity gala."

Ryan looks at Ashleigh with a smirk.

"And I'm pretty sure you did, too, remember?"

Ashleigh blushes bright red, a first that I've seen, while Ryan explains to me that both Ashleigh and Tate disappeared at last year's event and everyone else assumed they disappeared together. Ashleigh swears up and down that they weren't with each other, but they both returned to the after party at the same time and in the same cab. Apparently neither Tate nor Ashleigh would talk about it, so after some jokes at their expense, everyone else just dropped it.

My head is spinning.

Tate and The Beast?!

I shake my head and walk back to the table. Before long, Ashleigh makes her way over to me and sits in Tate's empty seat. She looks straight ahead but whispers to me without looking at me.

"Look, don't ask me why I know this, but you can bet that Tate ends up at Jake's house."

My head snaps up at the mention of Jake's name.

"How do you know about Jake?"

Ashleigh looks uncomfortable but continues in a quiet voice.

"I'm not as clueless about things as everyone else around here is. I know you three hang out quite a bit and I can see that you're worried about Tate. If I had to make a bet, he'll be at Jake's house."

I pause for a moment, knowing that Ashleigh reaching out to help me with something is a big deal for her, but my curiosity gets the better of me.

"I don't understand, Ash? I mean, thank you for helping me, but I'm confused. Tate told me his friendship with Jake is a secret. How do you know they're friends?"

Ashleigh laughs sarcastically and shakes her head at me in disbelief.

"Forget it. I was just trying to help you out."

She stalks across the room to where Ryan is manning the silent auction and refuses to glance back at me.

Confused as ever, I make my way outside and grab the flat shoes I had stowed in the parked limo. I leave my heels along with a note for Ryan telling him not to worry about me and that I'd meet them at the after party.

I've walked to Jake's house a number of times before, but never in a tight dress. The walk is longer now that I'm alone and each car that passes seems to be full of young guys honking their horns and yelling things at me as they drive by. By the time I get to Jake's street, I am furious with Tate for leaving me alone. I'm actually talking to myself and cursing as I open the front gate to Jake's house. I walk to the front door, but before I can knock, I hear a fire crackling in the backyard and a laugh that is unmistakably Tate's.

I make my way around the side of the house, my temper boiling and ready to yell in anger. But as I stomp into the backyard and the fire comes into view, so do Tate and Jake. They are huddled close together on a swing near the fire. Something about the way they are sitting so close stops me from saying anything at all. I slink back behind the tall sunflowers and hold my breath, feeling like I'm watching something private. I know it is going to happen before it does, but I stand there with my hand over my mouth as I watch Tate lean in to kiss Jake.

Eleven

The kiss is long and I realize that I am holding my breath. I let it out in one long, quiet exhale. I try to step farther back into the shadows of the flowers.

Things start to replay in my head as I hear Tate's whispered voice saying "Love you, too" into the phone that night. Ashleigh's voice quickly replaces Tate's, echoing "You're so clueless." And then I think of Jessica's facial expressions every time I'd talk to her about Tate and Jake and her odd silence.

Did they know the whole time? How can I be so close to Tate and not realize what's been right in front of my face all along?

I realize that Tate's not only been lying to everyone else by hiding Jake, but he's been lying to me about Jake.

All of the times that the three of us hung out, I never put two and two together. I feel stupid and embarrassed for some reason. I wonder how long they've been… together. I pull the bottom of my skirt up with my hands so that I can make my way to the front of the house without tripping. I can still hear the murmured voices of both of them talking, but as I walk farther away from the house, the voices get softer and lower.

I don't know where to go, but I know I need to think. I check the time and realize that the gala ended almost an hour ago. The after party is being held at the Gematti's house this year, so I walk in that direction.

I walk along the route that I've walked what feels like a million times before. Headlights in the distance behind me start to slow down and I groan at the thought of being honked at or yelled at again. When the headlights stop shortly behind me and I hear a car pull over, I spin on my heels. I recognize the black truck before Jase even gets out. He hops down and walks over to me looking concerned.

"A, what are you doing walking in the dark on the side of the road?"

As Jase approaches, he reaches out a hand to my cheek and I realize that I have tears streaming down my face. I swipe them with the back of my hand and smile at him.

"Oh, don't worry. It's just the wind making my eyes water."

It's not a believable lie because there is not one bit of wind at the moment. Jase lets it go even though he seems concerned and I'm grateful.

"Where's Tate? Did you find him?"

At the mention of Tate's name, I cast my eyes to my feet. When I don't say anything, Jase continues.

"Ryan saw your note in the limo and told us not to worry when we couldn't find you at the end of the night. I had the limo drop me off at the house so I could grab my truck. Hop in and you can ride with me to the party."

I nod slowly, but don't say anything. Jase walks me to the truck. He opens the door, helps me inside and walks around the front of the truck to get in on the driver's side. His eyes don't leave my face the entire time.

He sits in the truck for a moment without saying anything, but he doesn't turn the key in the ignition. I stare straight ahead silently thankful that I somehow missed the limo passing with everyone in it. I'm much happier that Jase found me walking alongside the road instead of having to explain what I was doing here to everyone. There would be too many things I couldn't explain and I am already moments away from losing it.

Jase clears his throat but continues the silence. I think to myself how cute he looks when he doesn't know what to say. I know he can tell that I'm upset, but that I don't want to talk about it. Instead of speaking, he holds his hand out to me. When I look up at him to smile, he slowly pulls me into the middle of the bench seat in the truck and puts his arm around my shoulders.

"You sure you're okay?" he asks softly.

"Um... I will be."

I lean back to look at him and attempt to smile again. He takes his arm from my shoulder to start the truck. We pull back onto the road and head towards the Gematti's, but I don't move from the middle seat.

When he stops the truck at the house, I can hear music and voices down at the boathouse. The long dock is lit up with colored lanterns and they continue across the backyard. I tell Jase that I'm going to change and then I'll be back outside. He momentarily looks as though he may try to follow me inside but decides against it and simply nods instead.

I run up both flights of stairs and flop myself face first onto my bed. I wait for tears to come, but they don't. I realize that I'm angry and upset because finding out that Tate has been lying to me since we met makes me confused about our friendship. I feel betrayed by my closest friend and even more confused about the kiss in the tent at the island party.

I lie in bed for fifteen minutes, but then decide I should change and go back outside before anyone starts to worry. I throw on a pair of jeans, silently daring Ashleigh to say something to me about it. I find the rest of my outfit, but leave my hair pinned up and make my way down the stairs. At the bottom step, I almost run face first into Tate.

I take a startled step backwards. I can tell by the familiar look in his eyes that he has had too much to drink.

"Heya Sunsssss-shiiiiine," he slurs as he reaches out his arms to wrap me in a hug.

I duck under the embrace, completely avoiding it and brush past him without a glance backward. I hear the strangled noise from his throat as his confusion steps in and it's almost enough to make me turn around and apologize. Instead, I let the anger resurface and then continue down the stairs to the first floor and out the back door to the party.

I lock eyes with Jase right away and walk toward him. He's talking with Alex, Austin, Ace and Jesse, but as I approach, he steps away from the circle and meets me halfway.

"Hey, you alright?"

Jase's newfound concern for me is adorable and if I were in a better mood, I'd probably be flattered.

I nod, give him a hug and whisper thank you in his ear before I break the embrace. We walk back to the guys together.

"There's our girl!"

Ace squeezes my shoulder once I get close enough.

They begin filling me in on the rest of the night that I missed and before long I am laughing with them. I notice Tate talking to Ryan across the backyard but try not to make eye contact. I watch as Ryan glances toward me, but I purposely avoid meeting his eyes, too. I groan inwardly as they begin walking toward us.

I excuse myself from the group, making my way to the ladies' room before Ryan and Tate approach. I see Tate's hurt expression this time and it tugs at my heart. His gaze doesn't leave me the entire time I'm walking to the house and I can feel it on my back as I walk inside.

Once I'm in the bathroom, I grasp both sides of the sink and look at my reflection.

"Why are you being so mean, Ayla?" I ask myself out loud. "Just go talk to him and stop making this into your issue. Tate obviously doesn't feel comfortable with a lot of things in his life and he needs you as a friend right now. Stop being selfish and go be a good friend."

"Who are you talking to?!"

Ashleigh's voice on the other side of the door snaps me from my personal pep talk. I open the door and find Ashleigh with her arms crossed and tapping her foot. I don't know what my expression says to her, but the minute she sees me, her arms drop to her sides and she doesn't say anything at all. I half smile at her as I walk past and while it looks like she wants to say something to me, she stays quiet and walks into the bathroom instead.

Outside the guys are still huddled around the cocktail table. Tate makes eye contact right away and I smile a weak smile at him. The same weak smile is returned, but before I can make my way to him, Ashleigh's dad stops to thank me and congratulate me on a job well done. He asks if I'll be returning next summer and when I shrug, he tells me that there will always be a job for me whenever I do return. I smile, give him a hug and thank him once more.

When I return to the guys, Mikey, Zac and Jackson have joined the group along with Ashleigh. We decide to head down to the now empty dock and have a drink together. The rest of the after party is slowly wrapping up, but Mr. Gematti leaves the lantern lights on for us.

Down at the dock, Tate stands next to me, but we have yet to say anything to each other. Everyone is sharing stories from the summer and before long every last one of us is laughing. Ryan tells the guys about me falling into the water when I first met him in New York and everyone, including Tate, finds it hilarious. Even Ashleigh laughs at that one, most likely because she enjoys the vision of me making a fool of myself in front of Ryan.

Jesse announces that we should meet here next Friday so we can celebrate the end of summer together before I have to leave the next day. Silence follows at the realization that summer is almost over.

"Don't worry, she'll be back!"

Tate assures everyone else but smiles directly at me.

"Why are you so sure?" I ask, jokingly. "I haven't even been invited back yet!"

Ryan laughs, turning to me as he does.

"I think that may have been your invitation, A."

"Yeah, you don't really have a choice in the matter. You have to come back! If you don't, we'll drive to New York and drag you back here," Zac teases me, handing me a drink.

I smile and raise my glass to his, my mood lifted from earlier.

The guys all leave to go home at the same time, but Jase makes sure to ask if I am okay one more time before he leaves, too. Tate tries to talk to me, but I chicken out and head to my room instead. I'm slowly getting ready to go to bed even though I'm not the least bit tired anymore. I hear a soft knock at the bottom step. I peak my head around to find Tate staring up at me.

"You've never knocked before. Are you going to start now?"

I smile at him despite the flips my stomach is making. Tate looks up at me in an attempt to smile, but the smile doesn't quite meet his eyes.

"You've never been mad at me before tonight."

Tate sounds sad and I know it's bothering him that I'm shutting him out. He walks slowly up the steps and before I can say a word, he tries to hug me and apologize. I put my arms out, stopping the hug.

"Do you even know why I'm upset, Tate? Do you even know what you're apologizing for?"

Tate nods his head, looking ashamed.

"Sunshine, I'm so sorry that I left you at the event tonight. I had too much to drink and our conversation about Jake made me upset. Before I knew what I was doing, I was heading to Jake's house. I didn't intend to do it, my feet just led me here. I didn't mean to make you worry."

I put my hand up to stop him.

"You think I'm only mad because you left me at the gala? First of all, why wouldn't you tell me, of all people, where you were going? I was really worried, Tate."

Tate nods.

"When I talked to Ryan earlier, he said you spent most of the night looking for me and worrying. I feel awful about it."

I cross my arms in front of me.

"Well, you should feel awful. Do you know how I found out where you were? Ashleigh told me, Tate."

I let that sink in for a moment.

"Ashleigh?!"

Tate looks at me in shock.

"What did she say exactly?"

I shake my head at him.

"You are unbelievable. That's all you have to say?! How does Ashleigh know about Jake? Perhaps you shared that with her when you two disappeared at last year's event together?!"

My voice is beginning to rise now, but I can't help getting loud when I'm angry. I'm on a roll, so I don't slow down.

"And guess what else? After Ashleigh so kindly informed me where you were, I went to Jake's house."

Tate's eyes fall to the floor and he doesn't say anything as I continue.

"Yup. I walked all the way there, alone and angry, because I was worried about you. And you know what I saw when I got there? I saw you two… you were by the fire out back… and I saw you… I saw you kiss Jake, Tate!"

By the time I finish the last word, all of the color has drained from Tate's face. He looks scared, surprised, and sad all at the same time. Now that I'm not bottling anything in anymore, the anger seems to leave my body. I'm no longer mad at Tate, but ashamed at myself for confronting him with anger. I want to reach out and hug him because he still hasn't said anything. My eyes fill with the tears that wouldn't come earlier.

He continues to stare at me wide-eyed for a few moments longer and then his legs give out and he sinks to the floor. I wait for him to say something, but he doesn't say anything.

I stand over him for a moment but seeing him like that breaks my heart. I lower myself to the floor and hug him tight. I run my hands through his hair a few times and whisper in his ear.

"Hey, we're going to be alright, Tate. This doesn't change us. Nothing changes that. I'm just upset because you lied to me. I thought you could trust me with anything. This entire summer I thought I was helping you keep a secret about Jake, but tonight I realized I was really helping you keep a secret about yourself. The worst part is that you were keeping it from me the whole time."

Tate doesn't speak, but he wraps his arms around me to hold me closer. We stay like this in silence for a while and then Tate finally finds his voice.

"I'm so sorry, Sunshine… for everything. I was so worried that you wouldn't understand or that you'd hate me or be disappointed in me. I know you've only known me a month, but you are so very important to me. You are the closest person to me, even closer than Jake, and I was afraid that I'd lose you. I couldn't bear the thought of it. Please don't hate me for keeping it from you. I can't lose you, Sunshine. I just can't."

Tate's head rests on my shoulder. I pull his face back so I'm staring into his eyes.

"Tate, you will never lose me. We can get mad at each other, but that doesn't mean we aren't going to be friends. Just please don't ever lie to me again."

"I promise, never again."

I kiss his forehead lightly.

"And just so you know, you are the closest person to me, too. I've never been able to talk to someone the way that I can with you. That's why it made me so upset to find out that you were keeping something from me. I don't want you to feel like you have to hide anything from me, ever. I love you, Tate-I-Am."

I help him to his feet, and we lay side by side on my bed, staring at the ceiling. We stay up the rest of the night and talk easily, the way we always have. He tells me about how he met Jake and that they started dating in secret over a year ago.

I make him tell me about last year's charity event and he explains that when he left the event to spend some time with Jake, Ashleigh disappeared around the same time to meet up with Jake's older brother, Sean. They ran into each other in the hallway of Jake's house later that night and Tate realized that Ashleigh was leaving Sean's room at the same time that Ashleigh realized that Tate was leaving Jake's room. Not surprisingly, Ashleigh freaked out, but she was apparently more concerned with not wanting anyone to find out that she hooked up with Sean. Tate was scared that Ashleigh would spill his secret the first chance she had, so they made a promise to each other never to speak of what happened that night to anyone. As evil as Ashleigh can be sometimes, she has kept Tate's secret for fear of anyone else finding out about hers. I now have a better understanding of why Tate avoids confrontation with Ashleigh at all costs and why he gets so worked up when she is mad at him about anything.

As the hours pass, we talk about his relationship with his dad again. He admits to me that he wants to be closer with his father, but he's worried about the day when his dad finds out the truth. He feels ashamed of his feelings for Jake because of his father's beliefs. He also admits that it breaks his heart to know that he will never make his dad proud and he thinks that deep down, his father and Ryan have always questioned it, but neither will ever say anything to him about it. I ask him if he thinks he's just being sensitive because it's something he's worried about, but internally I wonder if Tate's right. I think about Ryan's excitement whenever he mentions Tate having feelings for me and Ashleigh's comments about Tate the first day that I met her. Mr. Gematti does seem to encourage Tate and me to spend a lot of time alone together, which I never took notice of before now.

I bring up our kiss in the tent and how confused I am by it, now more than ever. For the first time since I met him, Tate turns bright red. Tate explains to me that he was confused by it, too. It was something he hadn't planned on, but that it felt right at the moment. He tells me that he knew I was special from the first moment we met and that sometimes he is confused by his feelings for me. He admits that part of him wants to be "normal" and that he can picture himself with me because I make him feel loved. When he starts to apologize at how unfair to me that all sounds, I laugh it off.

I tell him how special he is to me, too, and how surprised I was at how we connected right from the start. I can also understand how important it is for him to be accepted by his father. My dad's approval has always been a driving force in the decisions I make. Tate tells me about a few conversations he's had with his father about me since I came to stay with them and how it's the first time in his life that he can remember his father trying to make conversation with him instead of the other way around.

Tate is quiet for a few moments as we stare at the ceiling above us.

"Sunshine, I don't know how to tell if I'm in love. Sometimes I think about being with Jake and it makes me happy, but it scares me, too. Everything about my relationship with him scares me. I don't want to jeopardize any relationships I have with my family and friends, but I don't want to be without Jake either. I know it sounds selfish, but I'm not comfortable with anyone else knowing, especially because I'm still trying to figure out how I feel."

"I understand that, Tate-I-Am, but you have to look at things from Jake's perspective, too. I can't give you much advice on the love front, because I've never been in love myself, but I think at the very least you should figure out how you feel for Jake's sake. I can't believe how unaware of everything I have been. Jake must think I'm an idiot!"

Tate and I both laugh together, but he tells me how much Jake likes me. He explains that Jake wanted to tell me the truth, but Tate made him promise he wouldn't say anything.

Finally, with the sun peeking through my little circle windows, we fall asleep side by side, with Tate holding my hand.

Twelve

The next day, Mr. Gematti calls me downstairs shortly after a soft knock on the front door. I walk to the door to find Jase standing there with his hands stuffed in the pockets of his jeans. He looks at me, smiles and asks if I am hungry. I'm starving, so I nod and smile back at him.

Jase drives me into town in his black truck that saved me from the long walk home last night. We sit across from each other at a booth and eat pizza and talk. I tell him that he has to come to New York to try "real" pizza someday and Jase lights up at the mention of this. He doesn't bring up anything from the night before, but I can tell he is curious about what happened.

I am trying to decide how to tell him what happened without betraying Tate when Tate and Ryan walk in the pizzeria and hop into our booth with us. Tate plops himself in the booth next to me and uses his hip to move me over. Across from me, Jase moves over as Ryan sits down next to him. I see a momentary flash of frustration in Jase's eyes, which quickly disappears as he calls to the waiter to order more pizza. I roll my eyes at Jase who winks back. After we finish our pizza, we all head to the Gematti's for Sunday dinner festivities. Jase and I don't get another minute alone for the rest of the day.

On Monday night, I walk with Tate to Jake's house like I've done numerous times this summer, but tonight is a little different. This time I know that Tate and Jake are dating, and Tate keeps looking at me anxiously. I smile at him, trying to reassure him silently that tonight will be no different than the last dozen or so times we've hung out at Jake's house.

When we arrive at Jake's, he opens the door and we immediately walk to the kitchen as Jake begins dealing cards out in front of us. Tate seems to relax a bit and we play a few rounds of poker.

Finally, Jake clears his throat.

"A, I'm sorry you had to find out the way you did," Jake says as he puts his hand of cards face down on the table.

I laugh out loud in spite of the nervous look on Tate's face. I shrug off Jake's apology and tell him about my trek to his house on the night of the gala. I tell both of them how I walked in on their private campfire, but only after the very long walk alone that night. I exaggerate a bit, but Tate and Jake are laughing hysterically by the time I finish. We end up laughing most of the rest of the night.

At one point, Jake leans over and places his hand on Tate's on the table. It's a simple gesture, but I take notice of it and smile to myself. Tate, almost instinctively, begins to pull back, but then catches my eye and lets his hand still. He smiles back at me.

When Tate gets up to use the bathroom in between hands, Jake confides in me that he wishes Tate would be more open about his relationship with him, but that opening up to me is a good start and hopefully a sign of progress. I'm pretty positive that Tate isn't any closer to telling anyone else, but I don't share this with Jake. His face looks so hopeful at the moment that I don't have the heart to say a word.

The next night we walk to Jake's house again, but I don't have plans to stay. Tate doesn't know this yet. Once we get to Jake's house, I tell both of them that I have other plans tonight and that they'd be spending the evening alone. Tate looks at me in surprise and begins to protest, but I put my "don't mess with me" face on that he knows so well by now.

"You both need some time alone, and while I love spending every second with you guys, you've had me as an unknowing third wheel for way too long. I have plans and I'll be just fine, so don't worry. Tate, I'll meet you back here in a few hours and we can walk back home together."

Without waiting for a reply, I spin on my heels and start walking in the opposite direction of the Gematti's house. I turn once to wave. I see the surprised look frozen on Tate's face, but Jake says something to him I can't hear, and they walk inside after a quick wave.

I may have fibbed a bit about having plans, but I did have a destination. Not too far down the road is Jase's renovation house. Jase's dad bought a "fixer-upper" that is only two miles from Jake's house. Jase spends most weeknights working on the house into early morning while the rest of the guys are out partying. He had shown all of us the house earlier in the summer and the plans him and his father had for it. Jase calls it an eight-year renovation plan and is trying to do most of the work himself without his dad's help.

When I make my way down the long driveway to Jase's house, I can see a few lights on, so I know he is inside working. I start to get nervous and think that I should have called him first.

I am standing on his front porch, which Jase has just finished rebuilding, with my arm in the air trying to decide whether or not to knock, when the door opens and a light goes on above me. The entire porch is bathed in light and I am suddenly blinded. I can't see anything in front of me but can make out Jase's silhouette in the now open doorway.

The light above me turns off quickly and I hear a surprised voice.

"A?! What are you doing here?"

Jase pulls me by the arm inside the front door. My eyes begin to get used to the light again and I blink a few times before my gaze rests on Jase's face. He's wearing jeans, a baseball hat and a tool belt with no shirt. I have never noticed how muscular Jase's arms are before now and I feel myself immediately start to blush.

"Sorry I blinded you!"

We both laugh before he asks if I'm okay. Regaining my composure, I shrug off the momentary blindness and try to ignore the floating spots that are dancing in my line of vision.

"I hope I didn't scare you. I was with Tate not too far from here and he's hanging out with some friends tonight, so I thought I'd come visit. I hope I'm not bothering you."

Jase shakes his head at me.

"A, you are never bothering me. I'm just working on some demolition in the soon-to-be kitchen, but I could use a break. C'mon in."

I know Jase is too nice to turn me away even if he wanted to, but from the smile on his face and the look in his eyes, I think he is happy to have me here.

He walks me into the kitchen where he is tearing out cabinets. The place is a mess, but he overturns one of the cabinets and puts a cooler on top. He pulls out two sweet teas and hands one to me as he puts his shirt back on. He reaches out for my hand and leads me out to the front porch and over to a wooden swing where he sits down. He motions for me to do the same.

I admire the swing as I sit down next to him.

"Did you build this? It's beautiful!"

Jase's eyes never leave mine as he nods.

"Just put it up last night."

I pull my legs underneath me and Jase rocks us slowly back and forth while we drink our tea. We sit quietly for a while, staring up at the sky.

"Listen, I want to thank you for the other night. I – well – it was a weird night for me and I'm not sure what I would have done if you hadn't pulled up and saved me, my knight in shining armor. I wanted to thank you Sunday, but the guys came before I could."

I still haven't decided what to tell Jase about what really happened, but I want to make sure he knows that I appreciate how sweet he was that night.

Jase locks eyes with me and my breath catches in my throat. He reaches for my hand.

"You'll tell me about it when you're ready. I'm glad you are safe, whatever happened. People drive too fast on that road at night."

We sit on the swing for a while longer and Jase tells me about the rest of the plans for the house. He points to different places on the property from our seat on the swing and then gives me another tour of the house to show me the most recent projects he's been working on. I love watching how excited he is about all of it and I can't help but get excited with him. He has a detailed vision for the house and when he talks about it, I close my eyes and try to see what he sees.

At the end of the tour, I look at my watch and realize that I've been here for over an hour already.

"Jase, I'm so sorry. I don't want to monopolize your time. You need to get some work done. I've already been here for an hour!"

Jase shakes his head at me.

"That's okay, A. This has been one of the best nights in this house since I bought it."

He winks at me and I start to feel those damn butterflies waking up once more. Trying to hide any visible signs of them, I grab a crowbar from the woodpile in the kitchen and steal his baseball hat to put it on myself.

"Put me to work then!"

Jase laughs at me as he shakes his head.

"No way. It's filthy in here and I'm not making you help."

I pout at him and put my hands on my hips.

"But I want to help," I whine. "Besides, I can handle getting a little dirty!"

The smile doesn't leave Jase's face or eyes, but he takes the crowbar from me and shows me how to safely pry off pieces of the cabinets. He puts me to work doing that while he cuts the wood into smaller pieces and carries it out to a pile in the back of the house. Jase is trying to reuse all of the pieces from the old house to create furniture and fixtures for the renovated house.

We spend two hours working together like this. Even though I am dirty and covered in wood shavings, I enjoy every second working alongside Jase.

By the time I meet Tate back at Jake's house a few hours later, I'm covered in sawdust, but smiling from ear to ear. I spend the next two nights with Jase working on the house with him while Tate hangs out at Jake's house.

Friday morning comes all too quickly, and with that, the realization that I'm going home tomorrow. I'm packing my clothes into my once-empty suitcases. It feels strange to pack up my life here. I leave out an outfit for our little dock party tonight and an outfit for tomorrow's long ride back home. I managed to acquire way too much stuff to squeeze back into the two suitcases I came with, so Tate gives me his own to fill, too.

By the time Tate comes up the stairs to check on me, I'm sitting on top of one of the suitcases trying to get it to close. He hops up with me and we manage to get the zipper shut. We're both sad about me leaving, but neither one of us is brave enough to talk about it. We keep laughing it off or making jokes but haven't had a real conversation about it yet.

When the suitcases are both zipped, Tate looks at me with sad eyes.

"I love you Sunshine, you know that?"

I nod, a faint smile forming on my face.

"Of course I do, Tate-I-Am. And I love you, too, but I know you know that."

I sit down next to him on the bed. He shakes his head.

"You have to come back. Deal?"

I don't miss a beat.

"Already have it on my color-coded calendar."

This makes Tate laugh out loud. He grabs my hand quickly and pulls me into a tight hug. After a few seconds, I try to pull back, but Tate doesn't let me go. When he finally does, I can see his eyes are red and full of tears.

"Hey, none of that," I say as I wipe a single tear from his cheek. "We're going to be okay, me and you. I just know it. And Tate, I'm only ever a phone call away."

I lean in and kiss his cheek before I drag him by the arm to the kitchen where Cora is making us breakfast, and where another goodbye is waiting for me. For someone who hates saying goodbye, I am going to have to say a lot of them in the next twenty-four hours.

Thirteen

I'm on my back looking up at the sky. There are endless stars in the sky tonight and not one single cloud. I think to myself how much I'm going to miss how clear the sky is here.

I can hear the guys' voices down the dock a bit but can't make out a single word. I'm at the very edge of the dock pouting and feeling sorry for myself. Not only am I sad that I will only be here for one more night, but it's starting to dawn on me that everyone else will still be together after I leave — for school, parties and hanging out. The group is already talking about the big party they are throwing next weekend for Labor Day, which I'll be back in New York for. I walk away in the middle of the conversation and sit by myself for about ten minutes or so.

"Well, this is kind of appropriate, don't you think?"

I look up to see Ryan's smiling face looking down at me.

"What's appropriate?" I ask as Ryan lies on his back next to me.

"That our summer started and ended at the edge of a dock!"

We both laugh and interlink arms. Ryan sits up and pulls me to a sitting position as Tate approaches. He sits down next to me so I'm in the middle. I link my arm through Tate's and the three of us are now connected.

"Is that a private party down there or can we all join you?" I hear Alex's sarcastic smile in his voice as he yells down the dock to us.

Before any of us can respond, I hear the pounding footsteps of Zac running down the dock at full speed.

I yell out just as he jumps over our heads and into the water. He tries to splash us when he resurfaces. I turn my head just in time to see a bright green water balloon fly by my face and watch as it hits Tate in the side of the head. The balloon explodes on impact and I'm on my feet before Tate realizes what hit him. Another balloon, this one neon pink, soars overhead, but it manages to hit Zac in the water. He thinks I threw it in the confusion and hops up onto the dock to grab me in a very wet hug. I cover my face with my hands as we are pelted with ten different balloons, all glowing in the dark, before Zac decides to jump overboard with me still wrapped in his arms.

I hit the surface of the water and Tate is pelted next. He shuffles backward, protecting his face, and falls into the water. I hop up on the dock, behind Alex, Jackson, Jesse, and Ace, who are the ones who started the attack.

Jase makes eye contact with me from behind one of the posts of the dock. We both make a run for the buckets full of water balloons and manage to steal one of the full tubs before our attackers realize it's gone. We make a run to the roof of the boathouse and find a spot to start launching the balloons toward the dock. Tate and Ryan follow us up on the roof and manage to concoct a slingshot.

I throw the first balloon in the slingshot, while the boys hold either side. Jase helps me line it up and pull back. As soon as we let go, I know the shot is on target. It hits Alex in the side, catching him off guard with the force of the hit and knocks him into the water. Jase turns to me and we high-five.

Zac, Austin and Mikey manage to steal another tub of balloons with Alex overboard and they make a run for a spot on the beach.

The three groups are now in an all-out battle, with only Ashleigh on the sidelines. She made her way to the beach when the ambush started and is sitting in the sand cheering for one person and one person only, Ryan.

Before long, the water balloons run out and a truce of peace is made. We return to the dock soaking wet to shake hands.

I check the clock as we walk past the boathouse and see that it is 2am. I leave for New York in four hours.

By 5am, everyone begins to leave. I say sad goodbyes to Mikey, Austin, Jackson, Alex, Jesse, Ace, Zac and even Ashleigh, who surprises me with a hug and teary good-bye. It is now just Tate, Ryan, Jase and me left at the house. Tate and Ryan leave to carry my suitcases from my bedroom, which leaves Jase and me alone on the back porch.

"I don't know what I'm going to do without my construction partner," Jase says with a smile that doesn't match the sadness in his eyes.

"Don't you start!"

I tease him and poke him in the side.

"I haven't cried once yet and really don't want to start, but if you look at me like that again I will."

I look down at my hands instead. Without saying another word, Jase wraps his arms around me as Tate and Ryan walk outside and place my suitcases at our feet. He kisses my cheek lightly, before heading to his truck.

I hear the car that is taking me home pull into the driveway shortly after Jase leaves. I swallow the lump in my throat and walk slowly to it with Tate and Ryan on either side of me.

I turn to Ryan first. He kisses my face as I hug him and he promises to visit New York before next summer. I release Ryan when I'm sure that I won't cry and jump into Tate's arms.

"I love you, Tate-I-Am," I whisper into his ear.

He hugs me tighter.

"Hey, this isn't a goodbye, silly. It's just a see-you-later. And don't think the drive to New York is going to keep us apart!"

Tate loosens his hug before finally letting me go completely. I back away and smile at them both before getting into the backseat.

The car pulls out of the driveway and I look back as Ryan and Tate wave to me. Ryan puts his arm over Tate's shoulders and whispers something in his ear. I stare at them until they become tiny dots in the distance, then finally turn around and face forward toward New York.

Fourteen

"Sunshine!"

Hearing Tate's voice through the phone makes me smile.

I have spent two summers in Virginia now and am only two months away from spending my third with the boys. Tate still calls me almost every day and I speak to Jase and Ryan once a week. The rest of the guys have made it a tradition to call me every Friday night as a group. My dad hasn't been too happy with all of the time I spend on the phone, but other than that, he really likes the guys.

They came to visit last spring and I brought all ten of them to my family's Palm Sunday dinner. They got to meet my very large, crazy, Italian family and share in one of my family traditions. Dad had the chance to grill them about their futures and ask a million questions. By the end of the week, he got to know them well. Mom is pretty much in love with each one and asks me daily if I'm dating any of them.

"Tate-I-Am! It's so good to hear your voice!"

I look at myself in a gown in the full-length mirror in front of me.

"So, how are you making out? Are you nervous or stressed? I'm sure you look amazing!"

I silently shake my head without responding audibly.

"I'd like to beat up the person who came up with the idea of prom. I mean, really, who wants to get dressed up in a big puffy dress and heels and spend the night dancing?"

Tate laughs into the receiver.

"I don't know, Sunshine… just about every other girl in America!"

I roll my eyes, but laugh, too. It is my first prom and I have been talking to Tate about my reservations for the past few weeks. The night is finally here, and

I am ready to go, but I snuck inside after pictures to call Tate. My date is a good friend of mine who invited me because we were the only two left in our large group of friends without dates.

I spend a lot of my time back home in New York wishing I was in Virginia. I have a great group of friends here at home, but there's always a part of me that is still with the guys. I miss all of them when I'm home, but I especially miss Tate.

I speak with Tate for ten minutes and he manages to make me feel more comfortable that quickly.

"You are my best friend, Tate-I-Am, and my heart. You know that?"

"And you're mine, Sunshine."

I don't even have to be in the same room as him to know that Tate is smiling from ear to ear on the other end of the phone.

I hang up and head out to where everyone is still taking photos. I find my date and smile at him.

Maybe this won't be as bad as I thought.

"Just keep smiling…"

Tate's advice replays in my mind. And that's just what I do.

Fifteen

"My summer started already!"

Ryan's voice teases me on the other end of the phone.

I still have a full month before my school year ends, but most of the guys are in college this year and begin their summer break this week.

A pang of jealousy hits me, knowing they'll have a whole month of fun without me before I join them for the summer.

"I don't know if I can make it another month. Going to prom without all of you there was bad enough. Now I have a whole month of school to get through while you guys all enjoy the beach and parties."

"A, I can hear you pouting from here. That's Ashleigh's job, not yours!"

He manages to get a laugh out of me and I'm in a better mood.

"Just think about all of the fun we're going to have this summer and this time around you're here for the whole thing!"

The first summer I only spent a month with Ryan and his family because I didn't meet him until the middle of July. Last summer, I was only able to spend five weeks because of a family vacation that my parents had planned. This year, I am spending all of July and August in Virginia. The guys have rented three houses along a secluded part of the beach for the summer and invited me to stay with them. I can't wait, but I just have to get through the next five weeks first.

Ryan and I talk for another couple of minutes while he tells me about the big Fourth of July party he has planned for my first weekend with them. We say our goodbyes and I tell him how much I miss him.

A few days later, I receive a large flat package in the mail. I tear open the box to find a thick pad of white paper with a red number on each page and a handwritten note next to it. It is a countdown until I leave for the summer and each day I tear off a new sheet. Each number has a note from one of the guys underneath it.

The first page lists 40 and underneath it, Ryan has written, "... days until you have to cook all our meals for us so start learning to cook now. Love, Ryan."

The second sheet lists 39 and underneath is written, "... days until I whoop your butt in beer pong. Love, Zac."

And it goes on from there. Each one of the guys have at least one note and a few of the pages have notes from all of them as it gets closer to zero. I laugh at the thought of them trying to come up with the little notes and passing the pad of paper around.

I run downstairs to show my mom, who gushes over the thoughtfulness of it. I walk to my room, trying to decide where to hang it and finally put it on my ceiling.

This way, it is the last thing I see each night and the first thing I see each morning, a constant reminder of the countdown to the best and worst summer of my life.

Sixteen

"Have fun, baby," mom tells me as I hug her from inside the car through he window.

"Have fun, but behave," my dad adds.

I smile at dad and give him a tight squeeze before leaning back inside the window. I think mom is having a hard time letting me go for the entire summer, o I am trying to hide how very excited I am from her. I always miss my family when I am in Virginia, but the countdown is finally at zero and I have been ooking forward to this summer for months now.

Even though I've made this trip twice before, this time seems to take the ongest. I can't wait to see all of the guys and give them hugs. I can't wait to jump nto Tate's arms. I can't wait to see Ryan's famous smile. I am even looking forward o seeing Ashleigh. I also can't wait to see Jase.

After hanging out with Jase alone a few times the first summer, I realized had a crush on Jase that developed into full-blown feelings by the end of the econd summer.

Things are a little complicated because everyone assumes that Tate and I are dating, including Tate's father. In an effort to not disappoint Scott, Tate lets his dad, long with everyone else, believe that I am his girlfriend. I was upset at first, but I hink it makes Tate feel safe about his secret. Mr. Gematti seems to have a better elationship with Tate now and Tate insists it's because of me. Somehow, me being Tate's "girlfriend" brought him and his dad closer together.

It does make my own love life difficult, though. Once rumors started preading that Tate and I were dating, no guy would come near me for fear of he wrath of Tate's older brother and friends. My relationships with the rest of the ;uys in our group are the same, but they all assume I'm dating Tate, too. It doesn't lways bother me, except for when I am with Jase.

I think Jase may have feelings for me, but I'm not sure. The problem is that, like the rest of the guys, Jase would never act on those feelings out of respect for Tate, not to mention that Ryan is Jase's best friend.

Ashleigh started to come around a bit last summer when she realized I wasn't trying to steal Ryan away from her. We still have our moments, and she will forever be nicknamed The Beast between Tate and me, but I did spend some time alone with her last summer. We went shopping a few times and spent a few nights having dinner while the guys were having "guy nights." I realized how silly it is to battle with Ashleigh over a guy, even if that guy is Ryan. And once I got past some of our differences, we manage to even have fun together.

It has been almost two years and I have yet to tell anyone about Tate's secret – well, except for Jessica.

Jessica and I became closer last year after I got into a fight with an ex of hers. We were at a party and her ex-girlfriend decided it was a good time to talk about their problems. I was trying my best to stay out of her business, but when she pushed Jessica to the ground, I couldn't keep my mouth shut. We ended up on the ground, throwing punches and pulling hair while Ryan, Zac and Jase tried to pull us apart. In the end, Jessica appreciated me sticking up for her because she said no one else ever did. I truly earned my nickname "Rocky" that night from Alex and the guys laughed about it for the rest of the summer. While I had been completely embarrassed that I got into a fight the next morning, Jase was the one who made me feel better about it. He told me that he was happy that I didn't get hurt, but I should never be embarrassed about standing up for someone else. That's something that my dad would have said to me. My father has never condoned violence, but he's always told me to stand up for myself and others, if given the opportunity.

Memories from last summer start flooding my mind as I sit in the backseat. I think to myself about the many nights Tate and I snuck off to Jake's house, and how even though Jake and Tate are dating, they never make me feel like they'd rather be alone. Sometimes, it almost seems like Jake feels like the third wheel when we're together. I think the fact that everyone thinks Tate and I are dating really bothers Jake, but like me, he keeps it to himself. I did confide in Jake one night that I have a crush on Jase, and I think that made Jake feel better somehow.

The last night alone with Jase comes to mind and I flush at the memory. It was the first time I thought that Jase may have feelings for me, too. We were at his renovation house and he made dinner for me in his completed kitchen. It had taken him a full year, but the new kitchen was finally done. After dinner, he showed me the inside of one of the cabinets. It had our names carved in it. I stared at it trying to blink back tears, knowing exactly where the piece of wood had come from.

Jase had carved our names into a large weeping willow tree during one of the nights we spent working on the house. By the end of the summer, it caught some kind of disease and needed to be taken down. Jase had cut out the carving from the tree and installed it inside the kitchen cabinet.

"This way, you'll always be here with me, even when you're back in New York," he said when he showed it to me.

I wanted him to kiss me right then and there, but he didn't. I think he wanted to kiss me, too, but we both let the moment pass.

This year is going to be different. I plan to keep Tate's secret, but I want to figure out a way to tell Jase how I feel. I talked to Tate about it last week. When I admitted that I had feelings for Jase, Tate was quiet for a long time. He finally told me to tell Jase everything if it would make me happy. He did make me swear on everything that is important to the both of us that I would make Jase keep the secret to himself.

I am a different person this year. I am 17 and becoming a young woman in many ways. I have more confidence than I have ever had before, and I expanded my wardrobe, with the help of my mother, beyond jeans, tank tops and sneakers. I even talked mom into letting me buy a few bikinis, a secret we both kept from my father.

I am much more comfortable speaking my mind now and I am determined to do well at Scott and Paul's company this summer. I have a great idea for the charity event and can't wait to share it with Jessica, who I know will love it as well.

"Miss Ayla, we're here."

John's voice drifts into my thoughts from the driver's seat. I look up to realize we are already in the Gematti's driveway. The last hour flew by, even if the beginning of the trip was painfully slow. Before I can respond, John begins unloading my suitcases from our car into the back of Tate's green truck.

All of the boys have already moved into the summerhouses on the beach, but Tate decided to wait for me at the Gematti's house so I can say hello to Cora and Scott first. Mr. Gematti is waiting for me in the driveway with Tate, who is impatiently tapping his foot trying to wait for me to get out of the car. The second my door opens, Tate wraps me up and spins me around. My heart skips with excitement thinking about spending the whole summer with him.

I laugh and convince Tate to put me back on the ground just as Cora comes out of the house. I give Mr. Gematti a warm smile as he kisses me hello and pats me on the back.

"You make sure these boys treat you well this summer and if you have any issues, any at all, you call me right away. We're only a few miles down the road from you."

He looks at Tate when he mentions the boys treating me well, who only smiles back at him.

"Something tells me she is going to be taking care of all of them, not the other way around," Cora says with a hearty laugh as she hands a large basket to me and then one to Tate.

The smell from the basket makes my mouth water.

"Just a few goodies to hold you over until Sunday dinner," Cora says to me with a wink.

The only way that Mr. Gematti has agreed to let us stay at the summerhouse is if the three of us promised to spend Sunday dinners at his house each weekend.

"Okay, okay. Go, because I know you both can't wait to get out of here," Mr. Gematti says with a smile in his eyes.

I hop into the passenger seat of Tate's truck after thanking John and glance back at Tate. He is hugging Cora one last time and as he breaks the embrace, his father pulls him into another one. I think Tate is as surprised by it as Cora and I are, who exchange raised eyebrows and smiles with each other.

Tate hops into the driver seat and we both wave as we pull out of the long driveway.

"Holy shit, what the hell was that? He hasn't hugged me like that since I was a little kid!"

I can tell by the goofy grin on his face that Tate loved every second of it. Something deep inside me flickers with happiness knowing that Tate is happy. He turns to me.

"And holy shit, you look hot!"

I playfully punch him in the arm and tell him to shut up.

"No, really Sunshine, you have always been beautiful, but there's something different about you this year."

I smile at Tate, knowing he can read my every thought.

"I feel that, too. Is that weird?"

I turn my head to the side in question as Tate pulls me into the middle of the bench seat so I am closer to him. I put my head on his shoulder.

"Mind if we make a pit stop?"

"Jake's?" I ask, but already know the answer before Tate nods yes.

"Of course not!"

The sad part of the summer is that Jake can't stay with us at the summerhouse, too. Besides the fact that Tate would never let that happen, Jake also won't leave his mother alone all summer in the house by herself. Sometimes I feel bad for Jake, who just graduated from high school, but instead of thinking about college like most kids his age, took a job down at the docks to help support his mother. I have always admired him for the way he stands by his mom. I'm sure this won't be easy for him, knowing we are all living together and partying all summer with his boyfriend while he stays home and takes care of his mom and has to hide his relationship. I don't know how he does it and stays positive about everything.

I hop out of the truck at Jake's house before Tate's truck comes to a complete stop. Running through the gate, I meet Jake halfway up the walkway and jump into his arms. He throws his head back laughing and we catch up quickly.

Tate gives him a shy hug – Tate still seems uncomfortable with Jake's affection even in front of me – and the three of us head around back. Tate and Jake take their usual seat on the swing and I walk through the towering sunflowers trying to give them some privacy. Jake's sunflowers are gorgeous this year and I noticed on the drive over here that the sunflowers all over town seem to be flourishing. Tate mentioned it had something to do with the early summer they had here. Before long, Jake and Tate join me by the flowers and Jake proceeds to cut a bunch for me to take to the house. Sunflowers have become my favorite flower and Jake never misses an opportunity to give me a bunch when I'm here.

"Well, I think we should get going because the guys are all anxious to see Sunshine," Tate says pointing a thumb my way.

Jake nods and hands me the sunflowers after giving me another hug.

"Take care of my boy for me when I'm not around," he whispers into my ear.

"Always," I whisper back.

I let him go and make my way to the truck so Tate can say goodbye.

It is just before dinnertime and my stomach is growling. I open one of the baskets from Cora and grab a homemade biscuit she has stowed in there. It is heavenly and I have finished the entire thing by the time Tate and Jake make their way to the front of the house. I roll my window down and throw the Ziploc bag of biscuits to Jake who catches them midair.

"You have to take these, otherwise I'll eat the whole bag."

Jake smiles and winks at me.

Tate gives Jake one more hug and then hops back into the truck. He starts the engine and we are on our way to the summerhouse, leaving a sad-looking Jake on his front walk alone.

Seventeen

The summerhouse is only a few miles down the road from Jake's house, so it doesn't take long for us to get there. Tate's truck pulls into a stone driveway that sits to the side of a brown and white house with a large deck that wraps around to the back. I can see a built-in hot tub on the second floor of the deck from my seat in Tate's truck. I sit there stunned for a few seconds and then my excitement takes over. I hop out of the truck, momentarily forgetting about my bags, and race Tate to the front door.

I beat him there with a squeal of excitement.

"The grand tour, Sunshine!" Tate says in a deep voice and bows as he takes my hand.

He leads me through the entryway to an enormous open room that houses a beautiful kitchen and a massive dining room table. There are windows all the way around the room that look out onto the Chesapeake Bay.

Through the windows, I can see a stone patio with wicker chairs facing out toward the bay. Tate leads me through to the "great room" as he calls it, which is basically a living room and game room combined. It has a couch, two futons, a foosball table, a tv, a piano and a couple of comfy chairs that I try out right away. The stone patio continues out the windows of the great room and I can see a garden outside. There are two bedrooms downstairs, each with a queen size bed, dressers and their own bathroom. Tate has already claimed ownership of one of these bedrooms and tells me that Jesse is staying in the other. I am disappointed to find out that I am not going to be staying on the same floor as Tate, but he tells me not to worry because the best room was saved specifically for me.

He shows me to the main staircase that leads upstairs from the dining area but drags me to the wood paneled elevator to get to the second floor.

"We have an elevator?!" I squeal again, jumping up and down like a little girl while Tate laughs.

On the second floor there are two master bedroom suites, complete with master baths. One of the suites belongs to Ryan and the other is mine. I look at Tate in awe. I feel guilty taking such a large room, but before I can get an argumentative word out, Ryan's voice behind me cuts me off.

"All the guys agreed this should be your room. So, no arguments!"

He drops one of my suitcases he grabbed from Tate's truck and pulls me into a quick hug.

Jesse follows behind him with another suitcase and duffle bag. He drops them at his feet before hugging me, too. I don't even have time to share my excitement with him about staying in this beautiful house all summer because we all hear a voice from the first floor that is unmistakably Alex's.

"Dinner's here!"

We run down the stairs, my stomach now growling, and I am greeted by the rest of the guys. I make my way to each of them with smiles and embraces before making a plate to eat for myself.

"This house is incredible!" I gush to Jase who gives me a lingering hug as I put my plate down next to his.

"You haven't even seen the rest of it," Tate interrupts me and spins me by the arm out of Jase's embrace.

He half leads, half pulls me out to the patio. I let out a gasp as I realize that the grass surrounding the front, sides and back of the house leads way to a long strip of private beach. There is a 40-foot dock in front of a two-story boathouse on one side of the beach. On the opposite side of the house is a two-story, two-car garage. Straight ahead is a second dock, this one about 100 feet out into the bay.

The guys follow us outside, excitedly pointing out different things. Ryan informs me that we are on a private harbor and the sandy beach I see is ours alone all summer. Across the harbor are a few summer rentals that include a house that Ashleigh is renting with some friends.

The boathouse is home to Ace, Jackson and Zac who each have their own bedroom on the second floor and an open, shared living room. Each of their bedrooms has a door to a full wrap around upper deck that faces the bay. The garage has been converted into a guesthouse with four full bedrooms where Austin, Alex, Jase and Mikey are all staying. They have a small kitchen, two bathrooms, a large central living room, and floor to ceiling windows on the second floor that have great views of the harbor. I have a feeling most of our meals will take place inside the main house, which makes me happy. Even if we are living in different buildings on the property, we'll still eat our meals together.

We walk up to the second story deck of the main house, which is home to the hot tub, and I tease Ryan that it conveniently stands right outside his bedroom.

From here, you can see both ends of the stretch of beach and beyond. The deck wraps around to the front of the house and has an entrance to my bedroom as well.

I keep shaking my head in disbelief and promise myself to take plenty of photos. I know mom will want to see it all, even though I also know that she'll have me describe it all in detail tomorrow when I call her.

After a second round of dinner and a lot of catching up and laughs, we all head to our prospective rooms. I'm slowly unpacking my suitcases when Tate flops on my bed, pouting.

"What could you possibly be pouting about or are you just practicing your favorite 'Beast' face?"

I shake my head at Tate as I continue hanging clothes in my new closet.

At the mention of Ashleigh's nickname, Tate's wide grin returns. I tried to stop using the nickname as much after Ashleigh and I became better friends last year, but I knew it would trigger one of Tate's dimple-filled smiles.

"Everyone is going out tonight and leaving us behind!"

Tate's forehead scrunches in frustration.

"Really? On my first night back?"

Now it's my turn to pout. Tate and I are only seventeen, not old enough to get into any of the bars or clubs yet. Everyone else in the group is at least eighteen this summer. I was hoping that Tate and I wouldn't be left behind much, but it's my first night and it's already happening.

Trying to be positive, I suggest to Tate that we stay in and have a movie night. Tate doesn't seem happy with that answer and is frowning when Jase walks in my doorway and knocks softly on the open frame.

I look up at him and smile from ear to ear. Jase leans against the doorway and starts making small talk with me, but Tate interrupts us both.

"So, Sunshine, I have plans tonight, too. That's what I came up here to tell you. I probably will be back late, so you'll have to figure out something to do tonight on your own since everyone else is going out."

Tate starts to back pedal out of my room. Momentarily confused, I stare at him puzzled.

"What? You're leaving me now, too?!"

As Tate takes an additional step slowly backwards, he is now out of Jase's eye line. Realizing this, he gives me an evil grin, thumbs up and then quickly disappears down the hall. I know immediately that he is headed to Jake's house in hopes that Jase will take the opportunity to hang out with me alone.

I just love Tate.

I smile nervously at Jase.

"I was thinking of staying behind and working on the house tonight if you want to join me?" Jase asks, as if on cue.

"Absolutely."

This time, it's Jase's turn to smile from ear to ear.

Eighteen

"So, how'd it go with you and Jase last night?"

Tate sings to me as he flops on his stomach on my bed. I am already in the same position, flipping through some magazines. I have been up for a few hours already, but everyone else is still asleep in their rooms. I can tell by Tate's hair that he has just woken up a few minutes before.

"It was fine," I shrug at him and continue turning the pages of the magazine.

Tate nudges me with his shoulder, so I look at him. There are creases of worry in his forehead and I realize he's wondering if I told Jase last night.

"No, I didn't tell him yet. It wasn't the right time and I didn't know how to bring it up or where to start. We ended up sanding and finishing some furniture at the house. It was fun spending time with him, but nothing exciting to tell."

Tate can sense my disappointment.

"Just tell him and get it over with. We'll both feel better about it once you do."

I know that Tate is nervous about Jase's reaction to his secret and I immediately feel guilty about making him feel this way.

"I don't have to tell him if you're really that uncomfortable by it, Tate-I-am. I don't exactly know how he feels about me anyway. He probably still thinks of me as one of the guys."

Tate rolls his eyes at me and shakes his head.

"You, my friend, live on a different planet sometimes."

He punches me playfully on my arm. I hop on top of him while he's still lying on his stomach and tickle him until he begins to yell and tries to throw me off.

"You love birds want to keep it down? Some of us are trying to sleep!"

I look up to find Ryan standing in my doorway, his hair disheveled and without a shirt. I blush, hop off of Tate and throw one of my pillows at Ryan, who dodges it in one quick move.

"It's nearly noon and we're wasting the day away inside because all you guys want to do is sleep. I'm heading to the beach!"

I grab my beach bag and head past Ryan and down the stairs. I'm nearly to the sand before I realize that Tate is only a step behind me.

A few moments later, Ryan joins us, and he and Tate begin to throw a Frisbee back and forth. I put on my headphones to block out the world around me, lay on my towel and go somewhere else. The sun is strong today and I can feel its warmth dance across my skin.

I let my mind wander to last night.

I am helping Jase sand a rocking chair that he is working on for a new customer. My stomach is in knots as I work beside him. I have never felt this nervous around him before. I keep dropping things and sound like an idiot every time I speak. I also notice that every time I get close to touching Jase, he seems to tense up and back away. At first, I think I am being too sensitive, but when our hands brush momentarily and Jase immediately pulls away from me, I realize that I'm right. Maybe I am wrong about Jase having feelings for me. I decide not to bring up anything about Tate tonight. It feels awkward to bring it up out of the blue and I think that I may have misjudged Jase's feelings for me. Maybe I made it all up in my head. I am starting to reconsider telling Jase about Tate at all.

There is one moment where I feel it, the electricity between us that seems to begin anytime we are close enough to touch. I felt the same thing last year when Jase showed me the cabinet with our names hidden inside. We are cleaning up for the night and getting ready to head back to the summerhouse. Jase is telling me a story about his customer and leans in to pull a piece of wood shaving out of my hair. His fingers and palm lightly brush my cheek and it's as if a current goes through my body. I flush immediately, and Jase, realizing his hand is still resting on the side of my face, flushes too. He pulls his hand back, continues his story and finishes putting away his tools. I wonder to myself if Jase felt it too or was it just me?

A noise on the beach makes me pick up my head and pull my headphones from my ears. By now, most of the guys have made their way out of the houses and onto the beach. Some are drinking beer and sitting around me on towels. Some had joined in the Frisbee throwing, which now evolves into a game that looks like a cross between Frisbee and football. Alex is sitting closest to me, and after offering me a beer that I decline, fills me in on their night last night.

"We have to get you a fake ID, kid. You missed a good night!" Alex says as he takes another swig of beer.

"Tell me about it. At least tonight we'll all be together for the party," I say, referring to the big 4th of July party Ryan has planned at the house.

He has a bunch of girls coming over after dinner to help him decorate, a deejay to play music and lights, and a professional coming to shoot fireworks off from the water. I don't even want to know what that costs, but I'm sure Mr. Gematti paid for it.

"I think the whole town may be coming to this thing. Casanova over there throws a party and no one wants to miss it," Alex says with his sarcastic grin, nodding his head at Ryan.

I laugh out loud and nod in agreement. I can feel the excitement building. This is going to be the biggest party I have ever attended. All of my thoughts about Jase disappear as I sit with Alex and Jackson talking about tonight's festivities.

Shortly after we finish a dinner of hot dogs and hamburgers which Tate and Ryan made, a group of ten girls show up on our front porch laughing and giggling. Ryan lets them in, and they bounce around him talking nonsense. Some of them are carrying boxes of decorations with them and Ryan asks a few of the guys to help them with the rest. I elaborately roll my eyes at Zac, Jackson and Alex, who laugh in agreement before I make my way upstairs to shower and get ready.

Normally, I would have been excited about decorating for a party or, well, for anything for that matter, but not with those girls. I should be used to the way girls act around Ryan by now, but it still annoys me. I can never picture myself acting dumb or falling all over myself to get a guy's attention. I guess that's one of many reasons why I've always been more comfortable being friends with guys over a group of girls.

Stepping out of the shower, I pull out a short, white sundress that I bought with my mom specifically for the party. I have red sandals to wear, along with red flowers for my hair and a bright blue necklace. I clip a few pieces of hair back with the flowers but let the rest of it curl around my shoulders and down my back. For whatever reason, the hair gods have blessed me with a good hair day today and I silently thank them as I stare in the mirror.

Not half bad.

I put finishing touches on my makeup and make my way down to the kitchen to find a drink before heading outside. I am surprised to see that there are a number of people outside already, even though the deejay hasn't even finished setting up yet.

A loud whistle makes me spin around and I find Tate and Jesse standing behind me.

"Damn, A!" is all Jesse says, but Tate has already picked me up and is spinning me around in his arms when Zac, Jackson and Alex walk in.

"Pre-Game!" Zac bellows and his voice echoes through the empty house.

Jackson and Alex have already begun to line up small plastic shot glasses on our dining room table. Most of the guys have been drinking since before dinner, so I have a feeling things might get out of hand tonight. I briefly consider not drinking so that I can make sure nothing bad happens as Zac pounds two very large bottles of Jameson on the table in front of the cups. He pours large shots, which are probably closer to two full shots, into each of the twenty-two cups that are lined up before him. Zac hands one to me and when I try to protest, he shakes his head.

"There are two for each of us," he informs me as I look past him to the rest of the cups lined up. "We each have two shots to do to start the party, but we all have to be together to do it. I don't want to hear any excuses. No babysitting for you this summer, A. We're all big boys and you are going to have a good time tonight, right?"

I smile at Zac and take the shot from him. Before I can answer, he glances around the room.

"Where the heck are the rest of us?" Zac asks as he silently counts only six.

"Ace and Austin went to pick up their ladies but should be back any minute. Ryan is outside mackin' it with the decoration bobble heads and I have no idea where Jase or Mikey ended up."

Jesse shrugs as he finishes, locking eyes with me as he grins. I laugh out loud as Zac calls outside for Ryan. Ace and Austin walk in with their ladies on their arms. Zac politely escorts the girls outside and points them in the direction of food and drinks.

"Only us," he says, looking at me.

Mikey and Jase come through the front door with another keg, bringing it through the house and out to the back deck before joining us back inside.

Zac gathers everyone around the table and hands us each the first shot.

"Cheers to the start of the summer with my best friends."

We all raise our glasses for Zac's toast and take the first shot at the same time. I immediately want to spit mine back out, but pride makes me swallow it instead. It burns from the second it hits my mouth, down my throat and continues to burn in my stomach. I wrinkle my nose and Tate laughs at me, but nods in agreement.

Zac hands out the second round of shots and my mouth waters at the thought of having to do another.

"And this one, my friends, is to help us have one craaaazy night tonight!"

I tip back the second shot and again I can feel the burn down to my stomach. I haven't eaten much all day, so I already feel the fuzzy effects in my head. I decide to lay off the drinking for a little bit as we all agree to meet down at the docks at midnight before the fireworks.

Zac opens the back door and lets the ladies in again. I watch Austin and Ace's girlfriends quickly return to their sides. I also watch some of the decoration crew make their way inside and begin to hang on the arms of some of the other guys. They all know to stay away from Ryan now, because the first person through the open back door is Ashleigh. After kissing Ryan, she makes her way over to me to say hello and offers an awkward hug. At least she is trying to be friendly now. We make small talk for a few minutes and then Tate calls for me from the back deck.

I meet him at the keg and hug him tightly.

"How do you always know when I need you?" I whisper in his ear.

He hugs me back and whispers softly.

"I'm your soulmate, duh. That, and I could see you two through the glass windows from here."

I shake my head at him but am grateful he always has an eye out for me when we're together. It's nice knowing someone always has your back, even from a distance.

Tate hands me a red Solo cup filled to the brim with foamy beer. I hesitate for a second, remembering my vow to slow it down only moments before, but then decide to take the beer anyway. Tate walks me to the beach, and we drink and dance and hang out with a group of people that I don't know.

I hear my name screamed while in the middle of dancing in the large group. I turn around just in time to catch Jessica as she jumps in my arms. We're both tipsy at this point, so we end up jumping up and down and squealing, just like all of the girls I usually make fun of. Jessica introduces me to her date, Stella, who hands us both a drink before giving me a lingering hug.

Tate disappears as I start to dance with Jessica and Stella. At the end of one song, I slip away from both of them, who are now very focused on each other anyway. I head toward the house, but don't see Tate anywhere. I meet up with Jackson at the keg, who hands me another full cup of beer. I stand and talk with him for a couple of minutes before Alex pops up behind me with a drink in each hand. He does a silly dance and swings me around in a circle, careful not to spill any of his two drinks.

I shake my head at him and laugh but notice Jase walking toward the garage out of the corner of my eye. Excited at the chance of having a moment alone with him, I fill another cup and excuse myself from the group to bring Jase a drink.

"Don't forget — midnight — dock," Alex yells to me over the railing of the deck as I smile and nod over my shoulder.

I watch Jase go inside the garage and open the front door to follow him, which is no easy task with two drinks in hand. I walk up the stairs to see Jase looking out one of the large windows across the room with his back to me.

"Hey there!"

It's out of my mouth before I can pull it back, because as I say it, Jase takes a step sideways and I realize there is a girl standing behind him facing him. I couldn't see her on my way up the stairs because Jase was blocking her, and they were very close to each other. I don't know if I interrupted a kiss or just talking, but they obviously came up here to be alone. I don't need a mirror to know that I am red from head to toe. The heat creeps up my neck and across my face as the girl shoots me a look that could kill from dark green eyes.

"I — am — so — sorry!"

I stutter before putting the beer I brought for Jase down on the table next to me.

I spin around on my heels, and half run, half fall down the stairs and back out the front door.

I am such an idiot.

I walk quickly to the front of the house and to the front deck. Everyone else is around back. I chug the rest of my drink and hoist myself up on the railing.

"A–"

Jase's quiet voice surprises me so much that I almost fall. I manage to catch myself and regain my composure.

"Shit, Jase, oh please go back to that girl so she doesn't kill me. I'm sorry. I didn't realize– I thought you were alone– I just wanted to bring you a drink."

I'm babbling now and must be bright red again. Jase smiles as my heart flips and walks up the porch steps, stopping at the top, but not any closer.

"Don't be sorry. That was really sweet of you."

Jase stands in the same spot on the top step for a moment but looks unsure of what else to say. He glances down at his feet and I sense that he feels awkward around me. This realization feels like I got punched in the gut. Tears form in the corners of my eyes before I can stop them.

"Don't be upset."

Jase takes one small step closer. I swipe a single tear with my finger and smile.

"I've obviously had too much to drink, so don't mind me. I'm an idiot."

I hop off the railing and try to walk past Jase, but he grabs me by the arm to stop me.

"A, talk to me. What's wrong?"

Jase now has a hand on each of my arms while I face him, staring straight into his eyes.

"Nothing. Really. It's nothing."

I try to smile and laugh it off. Jase lets go of my arms and I step back so I'm leaning against the front door. I look down at my feet, suddenly embarrassed.

"A– that girl, she means nothing, you know? I just met her tonight. Besides, you and Tate are together—"

Jase trails off, leaving that God-forsaken sentence hanging in the air. The lie that Tate lets everyone believe because it's easier than telling the truth. Suddenly, I'm angry.

"Why does everyone assume Tate and I are a couple?! He's my best friend, but he is not my boyfriend! It's fine if you hang out with other girls, Jase, and you don't owe me an explanation, but I'm so tired of hearing–"

"Wait, you and Tate aren't together?" Jase interrupts me.

I look up at him, surprised, but still angry.

"No, we're not together, and that's the point I am trying to make—"

Jase interrupts me again.

"So, you're one hundred percent single at this very moment, right now."

I look up at Jase, frustrated that he doesn't seem to be listening to me.

"That's what I said, isn't it?! But you're not listening–"

Before I can finish my sentence, Jase kisses me. It's a forceful kiss and a hungry kiss that pushes me against the front door. His hands are around my face and then lifting me off my feet and wrapping my legs around him and then back to my face.

The electricity that I felt last night from being close is nothing compared to his. Every cell in my body seems to come to life and I can feel everywhere, while hearing and seeing nothing around me. Right now, in this moment, it's just me and Jase, and he's kissing me the way I've wanted him to for almost two years now.

When we finally separate and my feet are back on the ground, I have tears in my eyes again. I look up into his as he wipes at the corner of my eyes with his thumbs.

"Do you know how long I've wanted to kiss you?" he asks, never looking away from my eyes.

I don't respond because I'm still working on remembering how to stand, let alone figure out how to speak again.

"Since that night you showed up on the front porch and surprised me two summers ago. I wanted to kiss you right then and there but wasn't sure I'd ever be able to stop."

Jase smiles and kisses me again, very softly on the lips. And again. And again. My thoughts are slowly starting to make sense, and I think I remember how to speak again.

"Jase," I whisper.

"A," he says between kissing my neck and ear.

"Can we go somewhere– else?"

I feel him startle, tense up, hear him cough and I smile as I realize how that sounded.

"No," I clear my throat, now slightly embarrassed. "Not that. I need to talk to you about some things and I want to make sure that no one else is around. There are things I need to tell you– so you understand."

Jase pulls his head back to look at me again.

"Understand what?"

I reach up and lightly touch the side of Jase's face.

"Everything."

I sigh and grab Jase's hand as I lead him to his truck. He lifts me inside and gets in the driver's side. He pulls me across the seat, just like he did two summers ago, and I lean into him as his truck pulls out of the driveway. We end up at his renovation house and on the front porch swing.

He looks at me expectantly but kisses me softly again before tucking my hair behind my ear. His hand travels to my hand and he holds it, kissing it every few minutes while I take a deep breath and begin to tell him what I came here to.

"That night, two summers ago, when you found me on the side of the road, I was leaving Jake Oliver's house. I went there looking for Tate, because Tate, him and I had been hanging out together for most of that summer. I was really angry at Tate for leaving me at the gala and by the time I got to Jake's house I was even ngrier. I heard them in the backyard, but when I walked around back... I found Tate kissing Jake."

Jase's eyes shoot to mine in surprise. I hear him let out a long breath of air, but he doesn't say anything, so I continue.

"I spun around and headed back to the Gematti house, which is when you found me and rescued me in your truck. I didn't tell you what happened that night because I hadn't talked to Tate about it yet. That same night, I confronted him, and he admitted to me that he realized he was gay almost two years before that. He didn't tell anyone, including me, because he was worried how we'd all react. He's terrified of Ryan or his father or any of you guys finding out. He has been dating Jake in secret for almost three years now. I'm one of very few people who know and now you are, too. You have to promise not to tell anyone, Jase. You have to."

Jase lets out another long breath and doesn't say anything for a minute.

"Wow. I don't really know what to say. You are the only one besides Jake that knows, A?"

"Well, actually, no. Jessica knows, and now you do. Cora knows, too. And believe it or not, Ashleigh knows."

"Ashleigh?"

Jase looks at me again in surprise.

"Remember that night of the gala the year before I met all of you, where Tate and Ashleigh disappeared, but swore they weren't together?"

Jase nods.

"Well, technically, they weren't together, but they were at the same place."

Before I can say anything else, Jase interrupts me.

"Sean! I knew she had a thing for him."

I nod.

"Yeah, she hooked up with Jake's brother Sean that night while Tate was with Jake. They ran into each other in the hallway and swore each other to secrecy."

Jase shakes his head.

"I'm surprised Ashleigh kept her promise."

"Think about it. Would she chance ruining her relationship with Ryan, who hates Sean? Tate is scared to death of her because she has that over his head, but I don't see her ever telling anyone for fear of Ryan finding out."

"I guess you're right. I can't believe Tate's been keeping this a secret for so long. But now I understand why Tate lets everyone think you're his girlfriend, especially Ry and Scott. I just wish you told me sooner."

Jase reaches over to pull me closer to him on the swing. He rests his chin on the top of my head and we rock back and forth in silence for a few moments. Finally, Jase speaks into the top of my head.

"This feels like a big sacrifice on your part, though. How long are you supposed to keep up the lie? And you're lying to people you care about. I don't think that's very fair of Tate."

I feel awful as Jase says this because I've felt the same way at times but haven't admitted it out loud. I would do anything for Tate and feel the need to defend him when Jase says this, even though I secretly agree. I pull away from Jase and sit up again as I shrug.

"It's a small lie so that he can be happy, so that he can have a better relationship with his dad, and so that everyone can love him for the Tate that he is instead of disliking him because of who he's attracted to."

Jase momentarily lets go of my hand.

"I think you should give people the benefit of the doubt, A. Sure, some people are going to have a problem with it, but you just told me and it doesn't change the way I feel about Tate. I just think it's selfish of him to involve you. You guys are both lying to the people you love, but he gets to be with the person he cares about, even if it's in secret. In the meantime, you are supposed to play the part of his girlfriend, but for how long? And what about what you want?"

Jase's forehead is full of lines of concern and I'm starting to feel sick to my stomach.

"I don't think I'm explaining this right, Jase. My point wasn't to make Tate out to be the villain here. He's a victim in all of this."

Jase reaches for my hand again.

"Okay, but you're avoiding my question. What about what you want?"

Jase kisses my hand and looks straight into my eyes once more.

"I want you," I whisper.

Jase kisses me and I can feel his smile on my lips.

"I want you, too. But how can we be together if everyone else we both care about thinks you and Tate are dating? That's the only thing that's kept me from kissing you the past two years and why you haven't told me how you feel about me until now. How fair is that for us?"

My stomach is in knots now and I don't think the alcohol I've consumed has anything to do with it. There's a nagging voice in the back of my head that keeps telling me I shouldn't have told Jase. The voice sounds a lot like Tate's.

"A, I will do anything you want, and if you and Tate want me to keep this secret, you know I will. You have my word. But if I have my choice, I want to be with you, and I don't want to have to hide it from anyone, especially our friends."

I nod slowly.

I want that, too.

I say this to myself but feel guilty for thinking it.

"Don't you think Tate feels the same way? What about Jake? I know he wants everyone to know, but Tate feels like he has to hide it— like he doesn't have a choice."

Jase shakes his head at me.

"But that's my point. He does have a choice. It's his decision to not tell people."

Jase pauses for a moment as he stands up from the swing. He looks at me with his arms crossed.

"I don't know what the right answer is, A. All I know right now is that I want to go back to the party, hand in hand with you. And I want to dance with you and kiss you without caring who sees. Instead, we're going to go back to the party and act like none of this happened because everyone else there thinks you are Tate's girlfriend. Right?"

I look down because I can't meet his eyes knowing he is right. I want to go back to the party hand in hand with Jase, too. I want to run up to Tate to tell him about my first kiss with Jase. I want to fall asleep tonight in Jase's arms, but I know none of that will happen because I can't bear the thought of hurting Tate. When I don't speak, Jase takes that as my answer.

"Right."

Jase turns away from me and walks to the truck. I hop off the swing to quickly follow him. When I catch up to him, my voice is just above a whisper.

"When you kissed me on the porch, that was the best moment of my life. I want to be with you, Jase, but it's complicated."

Now Jase's voice sounds angry. He throws his arms up in the air.

"So, you're telling me you want to be with me, but that you can't be with me?"

I flinch and shake my head furiously.

"No, that's not what I meant at all. Nothing I am saying tonight is coming out right. I want to be with you and I'm hoping we can figure this out together. I understand if you don't want to, but I care about you more than you realize. I feel like no matter what I do, I hurt one of you. I don't know how to make you both happy but being with you is what I want."

I put my face in my hands because my head is swimming with alcohol and a thousand different thoughts of Tate and Jase. When I look up at Jase, the anger has left his eyes and in its place is concern. I'm on the verge of tears again and silently vow to keep my drinking in check in the future because I hate being this emotional.

Jase slowly pulls me closer to him, the anger and fight in him now gone. He takes my hands from my face and wraps my arms around him before encircling me with his. He takes one hand and tips my chin up so he can kiss me again. He puts his head on top of mine and rests it there for a few minutes before opening the passenger side door for me. I don't want to go back to the house. I want to stay here with Jase but remember our promise to meet at midnight on the dock with everyone else. A quick glance at the clock tells me that we only have twenty minutes to get back to the party before anyone realizes we aren't there.

Jase leans over to kiss me once more from the driver's seat before starting the truck. This time I move to the center on my own. I wrap both arms around him and stay that way until we pull into the driveway at the summerhouse. He still hasn't said anything as he pulls the keys out of the ignition and gets out of the truck. I do the same and grab for his hand before we walk back to everyone else. He starts to speak, but someone I don't recognize yells to Jase that Zac has been looking for us.

Without a word, we turn and walk slowly, side by side, our hands brushing each other's ever so slightly.

Jase is right. We should be able to walk into the party holding hands, but Ryan would notice right away. Ryan would ask about Tate and me, and it would snowball from there. Tate has never let me down and I feel obligated to protect him. It feels like the right thing to do. But if helping Tate keep his secret ends up hurting Jase, is it the right thing? I'm suddenly unsure of what the rest of this summer will bring, but it may not be as much fun as I thought.

Zac brushes past me with Jager in hand this time and yells over at us.

"There you two are. Docks. Now!"

Jase and I make our way down the long dock, pushing through the enormous crowd. A group of people has formed around Zac, but he manages to make enough space for the eleven of us to form a circle. I stand between Ryan and Tate, with Jase on the other side of Ryan. Zac hands out the plastic shot glasses, once again filling them too much as he does.

We raise our glasses, waiting for Zac's toast.

"Here's to the end of one hell of a night!"

Zac's deep voice carries over the crowd around us.

I lift my glass higher and nod with a secret smile thinking of Jase before I take the shot. The burning returns and I cough this time. I can feel the burn in my nose and my head feels light and dizzy.

The fireworks start over the water and the crowd oohs and aahs. There are people cheering and yelling all around us. I look up to see Ryan kissing Ashleigh and Zac kissing Jase's girl from earlier. The other guys are either lip-locked with girlfriends or random partygoers. All I can think of is how much I want to run into Jase's arms to kiss him.

Instead, Tate grabs me with both hands on either side of my face and kisses me straight on the mouth. He laughs and lifts me up over one of his shoulders, so I now have the perfect view of Jase's back, walking away from all of us toward the garage with his head down.

Nineteen

"That was some party last night, huh?"

Tate's voice rings through my ears, sounding louder than it actually is.

I groan in response and put the pillow over my pounding head. I'm still in bed, but Tate slept next to me last night. He could tell something was bothering me when I went inside shortly after our midnight toast. I didn't want to talk about it, so he didn't push it. I remember hearing him come into my room a few hours later and get in bed beside me, but I must have fallen right back asleep.

I roll over to find Tate holding out a bottle of water and two aspirin, which I take without question. He takes two himself and finishes the now half empty bottle of water I hand to him.

"Sooo?"

Tate tosses the empty plastic bottle on the floor.

I groan again.

"So what?"

I roll back over and place the pillow on my face again. Tate laughs at me.

"Cranky this morning, huh? So, where did you and Jase disappear to last night?"

Tate begins poking me in the side, which normally makes me laugh, but this morning just annoys me.

Everything from last night comes flooding back. I had a dream of Jase walking away from me with his head down, but when I tried to follow, Tate pulled me in another direction. Even though Tate has no clue about any of it, I wake up angry with him this morning.

When I ignore his question and poking, he gets under the covers with me and tries to pull the pillow away from my face.

"Tate, please just leave me alone. I don't feel well."

"You need to drink more water. You'll feel much better after you eat, too. Come on, get up and I'll make you some breakfast."

I don't even attempt to move and a few minutes later Tate leaves my room. I hear the door quietly close behind him and I immediately get up and get in the shower. I let the warm water wash away last night's makeup and memories. I stand under the showerhead with my face upwards for what seems like forever but is probably closer to fifteen minutes. Every time I think about Jase kissing me last night, my heart skips a beat and a smile makes its way across my face before I can help it. I touch my fingers to my lips at the memory, but the vision of Jase walking away from the party last night quickly replaces it. I let tears fall down my cheeks that had been waiting to escape since last night. I know that there is something special between me and Jase. Something inside me changed when he kissed me last night, but nothing changes the fact that Tate is my heart. He understands me the way no one else ever has. I know he loves me, and he has always been there for me, so how can I not be there for him now? I wish I could make Jase understand that.

I turn off the water and step out of the shower onto the tile floor. The bathroom is full of steam and the way it tingles on the surface of my skin mimics Jase's skin brushing mine. I suddenly feel like I can't breathe and rush out of the bathroom into the cooler air of the bedroom. I get dressed quickly and head downstairs.

The smell of bacon hits me in the face when I reach the top step and my stomach growls in response. I can see Tate in the kitchen cooking from the stairs and I smile instinctively. Ace, Jesse, and Austin are all at the dining room table eating pancakes. They look up at me when I walk in the room. I wave to them as I walk by, but they all share the same hungover look that I am sporting this morning. I walk over to where Tate is cooking bacon and making scrambled eggs. He grins widely at me and points to a platter with a mountain of pancakes.

"Cora would be so proud," I say to him playfully.

He takes an exaggerated bow and I duck under his arm and wrap my arms around him in a tight embrace. He follows my lead and kisses the top of my head before turning his attention back to his crackling bacon. I start making a plate for myself that I pile high with pancakes.

"Do you want me to make you a plate, Tate-I-am?" I ask him while licking syrup from my fingers.

"Nah, I ate already, Sunshine. You took too long to get up!"

I laugh and roll my eyes at him.

"Some of the guys headed out to get some more groceries for the house, but Jase is still in bed. Why don't you make him a plate and bring him some breakfast to wake him up?"

Tate's wicked grin is back, and his dimple is out. I shake my head at him with a smile and make a second heaping plate. Tate adds some freshly made bacon to both and sends me outside with a tray of pancakes, bacon and orange juice. I walk across the yard carefully balancing the tray and make my way upstairs to the second floor in the garage.

I place the tray down carefully on a table in the living room. There are clothes and shoes strewn everywhere. A few empty cups are scattered across the floor. It smells like gym socks and stale beer.

Jase's bedroom door is open a crack, so I peek inside before opening it all the way. Jase is facing away from me in nothing but a pair of shorts. The muscles in his back and shoulders move ever so slightly with every steady breath. They make my stomach jump and I take a shaky breath in before walking fully into the room.

Jase's room looks nothing like the rest of the place. His clothes from the night before are folded over the chair near the door. There is nothing on his floor but a few trade magazines and a baseball hat. The window is cracked slightly so there is a cool morning breeze blowing the sheets on the other side of the bed. I sit down lightly on the edge of the bed, trying to decide how to wake Jase up without startling him.

I'm just about to lean in to do so when my eye catches a photo on his desk. It's a black and white picture of me that Jesse had taken at a barbecue on the island last year. I'm sitting on top of a picnic table and laughing. I remember when that photo was taken. All of us were gathered at the picnic tables waiting to eat and Alex had made some sarcastic remark that made me laugh out loud.

I get up from the bed and walk closer to the desk. There are building plans and rough sketches all over the desktop. My photo is the only one in the room. I pick it up to take a closer look.

"Sometimes when I can't focus or can't figure out what I want to do next with a plan, I look at that picture. Your smile makes everything else in the world disappear."

I look over at the now wide-awake Jase. He's sitting on the edge of the bed and throws a t-shirt over his head before heading into the bathroom. He squeezes my shoulder as he walks by.

I head out to the living room while Jase is in the bathroom and set up the small table for us to eat at. I grab two cups from a stack of clean plastic cups that didn't make their way to the floor and fill them with orange juice. Thankfully, Tate has thrown silverware and napkins on the tray because I somehow doubt there are any stashed here. When Jase comes out of the bathroom, he sits across from me. He smells of Irish Spring soap.

"Not exactly breakfast in bed, but–"

I shrug and look up at him.

"Are you kidding? Breakfast at all is amazing. I figured I'd slept so late there wouldn't be anything left."

"Well, Tate saved a bunch for the both of us. I had trouble waking up this morning, too."

At the mention of Tate's name, Jase casts his eyes toward his plate. I shovel in a large mouthful of pancakes in an attempt to keep another stupid comment from rushing out of my mouth.

I was worried things would be awkward between us this morning, but we chat easily and laugh the way we always have. The only difference this morning is that Jase reaches out for my hand as he takes his first bite and doesn't let go of it the entire time we eat. His thumb grazes the tops of my fingers continuously until we take our last bites.

I clean up the now empty cups and plates, piling everything back on the tray. Jase grabs my arm as I walk by him and pulls me down onto his lap. He kisses me quickly and the kiss tastes like syrup. I lay my head in the space between his chin and shoulder and we curl together on the couch while he grabs for my hand again.

"I thought a lot about our conversation last night," he whispers so low that I have to strain to hear him. "I didn't sleep much. I kept playing our conversation over and over in my head. A, I'll do whatever you want me to do. I'll say whatever you want me to say. I'll act however you want me to act. It shouldn't be all or nothing on my end. I want to be with you, A, and if that means helping you keep a secret in the meantime, then I'll do it."

He kisses me again and this time it's longer, deeper and sweeter. When he finally pulls away, it's my turn to speak.

"Listen, I know this isn't going to be easy, for either one of us, but especially for you. And I don't disagree with everything you said last night. I just need to help Tate through this, and I don't know any other way to do that just yet, but I'm working on it. And what happened last night, between us, I have been waiting and hoping for– well– a very long time. I can't explain the way I feel around you, the way you make me feel. You make everything in me come to life. What you said before, about making everything else in the world disappear, I feel that too."

The last part comes out just above a whisper because we both hear the door downstairs open and close at the same time. I hop up to grab the breakfast tray from the other side of the couch and Jase starts picking up around the room.

Alex and Mikey come bounding up the stairs and flop on opposite sides of the couch.

"Did you recruit some help to clean this place up?" Mikey says to Jase and nods toward me.

"The only two neat freaks in the group. You two should have roomed together to save us all the headaches," Alex says to Mikey as they laugh and high five each other.

I throw an empty plastic cup at Alex and it bounces off his forehead. This makes Mikey double over in laughter as Alex hops over the couch. He grabs the sprayer from the kitchen sink and starts soaking me with water while I shriek and run to every corner of the room. It doesn't matter where I try, the sprayer reaches each corner of the small living room. By this time, Jase and Mikey are laughing hysterically at my expense, so I decide to stand still, shrug, and let the water run over me. My hair is now matted to my face and dripping down my back, so Alex finally concedes. He shakes my hand in a truce, but I am already silently planning a way to get him back.

I grab the breakfast tray and head towards the house, leaving all three guys behind.

Twenty

Jessica and I stop after work to grab a bite to eat and work on some ideas for the charity gala at the end of the summer.

"So, what's this great idea you have for the charity event?"

"Well, since we are doing a Broadway theme for the gala this year, I was thinking of having some of the actors from the North Street Playhouse do live performances at various times throughout the event."

The North Street Playhouse is a non-profit organization that provides live theatre year-round. Since Mr. Gematti is a huge supporter of anything to do with the arts, he decided to make the North Street Playhouse the charity for the annual benefit event.

"Oh, A, I just love that idea!"

Jessica claps her hands together across the booth from me and I laugh.

"Good, because I already called them to see if they'd be interested and the director loved it."

I can tell by Jessica's eyes that she is already somewhere else, envisioning the event in her mind down to the tiniest detail.

"What if we brought in an audio visual team so that they can show clips of various Broadway shows throughout the evening, even if they are silent, and then show live feeds of the North Street Playhouse performances on those same projection screens?"

Now it's my turn to be excited. This is why Jessica and I have worked well together since the first day. We feed off each other's ideas and energy. The final result is always better than I could have imagined.

Jessica and I finish our food, writing down ideas as we go. As I'm waving goodbye to her as she pulls away in her car, I catch a glimpse of Jake. He is across the street in a small art gallery and hasn't seen me yet. I smile to myself and start to walk across the street until I realize that Jake is talking to someone beside him. As my eyes focus, I notice that Jake is holding this person's hand.

Excitement pounds through my veins at the vision of Tate doing something with Jake in public. I jog across the street with a goofy smile on my face and open the door to the gallery. A small blast of cool air conditioning blows through my hair as the curator smiles at me from behind the front desk. I smile back as I make my way over to Jake, who is now standing in front of a sculpture in the middle of the room. They are no longer holding hands, but my heart sinks as I see a guy with sandy brown hair standing close to Jake.

"Hey!" I say instinctively loud, before I can think better of it.

Jake spins around on his heels with a large smile on his face until his eyes settle on me. Brown-haired guy does the same, but his smile never leaves his face.

"Hello," he says in response with a questioning look on his face.

Jake won't even make eye contact with me.

"Hi, I'm Jake's friend, Ayla. It's nice to meet you–"

"Matt."

Matt finishes my sentence before Jake can. He shakes my hand and I notice his palms are soft and sweaty.

"You're Tate's girlfriend, right? Jake has a picture of you three in his bedroom at home. He's told me so much about both of you."

I manage a tight smile at Matt.

"That's funny, because I haven't heard anything about you at all."

Matt laughs and puts his arm around Jake's shoulders.

"He's keeping me a secret I suppose. You don't want to share me with the world, do you, Jakey?"

Jakey? Ew, gross.

I think I am going to be sick right then and there, but I manage to swallow the nauseous feeling back.

Jake finally finds his voice and manages to squeak out a response.

"Right."

He still won't meet my eyes even though I am burning holes through him with mine.

"Matt and I have to get going, Ayla. It was nice to see you. We'll catch up later."

And with that, Jake pushes a confused Matt out of the gallery. I stand with my mouth hanging open and my hands on my hips for a good five minutes before I make my way out of the gallery and back out onto the street.

Jase's truck is parked and waiting for me across the street. He waves at me from the driver side window before sending me a questioning look and nods toward the art gallery. I hop into the passenger seat and quickly tell Jase the whole story without taking a breath. It comes out as one long, angry run-on sentence.

Jase, who's always so levelheaded, grabs my hand.

"A, give Jake the benefit of the doubt. You don't know what was going on there or who exactly Matt is just yet. Why don't you talk to Jake before you say anything to Tate? Give Jake the opportunity to talk to Tate himself."

I nod, looking down at our linked hands and think of Jake's hand interlocked with someone else's. I try to imagine how it would feel to find Jase holding hands with another girl and I instantly get jealous, angry and hurt all at the same time.

"How would you feel, Jase, seeing me holding hands with someone else? If Ryan had seen that, wouldn't you want him to tell you?"

Jase is quiet for a moment and looks out through the windshield when he answers quietly.

"I do know how that feels. I watch you hold hands with Tate every day, A. I've also watched you do more than just hold hands with him."

Jase turns back to face me again as he says the last part. I put my head down.

"But that's different, Jase."

My voice is low because I realize I'm a hypocrite. Jase scoots me closer to him.

"I know it is, A. But everyone else around us doesn't. No one else but me, you, Tate and Jake know that. You can't get angry about something that Jake is doing when you are doing it yourself. You don't know what that was all about until you talk to Jake."

I look up into Jase's eyes and realize he's right, even though I hate to admit when I'm wrong.

"You're right. You're always right."

Jase smiles at me and shakes his head with a laugh.

"I'm making sure I get that one in writing," he says as we pull out onto the main road.

I lean into Jase with his arm around me and close my eyes. I know deep down Jase is right but keeping a secret from Tate doesn't feel right. I'm starting to get tired of keeping all these secrets from people I care about and realize that Jase has been right about everything.

Twenty One

"Bombs away!"

This is all I hear before the sound of water hitting the patio block out back and then an aggravated female shriek.

Alex and Jackson have concocted some kind of bucket drop from the roof, so that when someone on the patio walks by, they drop a gallon of water on top of their unsuspecting victim.

An evil grin makes its way across my face because I know the only other girl who is here at the moment is the one from the party two weeks back, the one who was in the garage with Jase and then kissing Zac down at the dock later the same night. Today, she is clinging to Ace, and Alex and Jackson have been waiting to douse her with water all afternoon.

"What are you smiling at?"

Tate comes up behind me while I'm washing dishes and gives me a hug from behind. Before I can answer, I hear another splash of water and Ace's voice yelling curse words in response. The sound of Ace's southern angry drawl is almost as cute as his happy one. I laugh out loud and Tate, who now realizes why I was smiling, laughs with me.

Tate immediately grabs a dishtowel and begins to dry the dishes as I wash them. He starts chatting with me about his day and asks me how Jessica is. I stumble over my words, remembering the art gallery and Jake holding Matt's hand.

"She's– uh– she's– good."

I smile weakly at Tate.

"Okaaay."

Tate looks at me questioningly, expecting me to add more, but I stay quiet instead.

"Uh-huh. What's up, Sunshine?"

I shrug and smile back at Tate.

"Nothing at all. I'm just somewhere else tonight."

"Does this have anything to do with Jase? You don't seem to want to tell me anything about him lately."

Tate looks sad as he says this and I realize that I have been keeping things from him lately, and more than just what I saw between Jake and Matt earlier. Before I can say anything in response, Alex and Jackson run down the stairs and into the kitchen.

Alex tosses me two empty buckets, as Jackson yells at me as they run by.

"Fill them!"

And then they are gone, running out the back door. I put the buckets in the sink and turn on the water without questioning it. Seconds later, Ace comes running down the stairs with a Super Soaker water gun that is so big, I'm not sure I could have even picked it up. He yells something as he runs by that I can't quite make out and then he is gone out the back door behind them. I look at Tate, who is laughing again, but I can still see a sadness in his eyes. He helps me pull out the full buckets and agrees to carry them back up to the roof for the boys.

Tate makes his way up the stairs, slowly balancing a bucket in each hand. I watch him disappear from view and I can hear yelling down at the docks. I look out through the back windows and see that an all-out water war has erupted and most of the guys have joined in. Ace's lady friend is nowhere in sight and I assume she left when the shenanigans took over.

I grab two sweet teas from the fridge and head upstairs to find Tate. He's sitting on the railing on the back deck watching the water war and smiling to himself. I walk up behind him and hand him the bottle of tea over his shoulder.

"You're not going to join in?"

Tate shakes his head at me in response.

I sigh deeply, shake my head, too, and climb on the railing next to him. We sit there in silence for a few moments, watching the guys in the distance, and then I blurt it out.

"He kissed me."

Tate spins around to face me with his ear-to-ear grin.

"When?!"

"The 4th of July party."

My smile mimics Tate's.

"Tate, you wouldn't believe it. I walked in on him and Ace's lady friend from today. I'm not sure what they were doing, but they were up in the garage alone. I was so embarrassed and went flying down the stairs and to the front of the house. I didn't even realize Jase was behind me until I got to the front deck."

I smile, flushing at the memory.

"And he kissed you?"

"Well, there was some conversation prior to it."

I laugh.

"But, yeah, then he kissed me. And it was—"

I trail off trying to find the right words to describe it to Tate.

"—like you're just waking up for the first time?"

Tate finishes my sentence. I look into Tate's eyes and grin.

"That's a really perfect way to describe it."

I lean my head on Tate's shoulder.

"Is that what it was like for you when you kissed Jake for the first time?" I ask cautiously.

Tate is quiet for a moment.

"Not right away. When Jake kissed me for the first time, I was still dealing with feelings I didn't really understand. I liked it, but I was angry at myself for enjoying it. I was mad at him for kissing me, but I also wanted him to do it again."

I nod, knowing that Tate still deals with some of these feelings even now.

"Is it still like that for you now when Jake kisses you?"

"Not always. Not when we're alone. When it's just me and Jake, or the three of us, I don't have those feelings. I can shut them out because when it's just us, I'm not ashamed."

I pick my head up off Tate's shoulder and grab either side of his face with my hands. I pull his face close so that our noses touch.

"You listen to me, Tate-I-Am. At no point in this life should you be ashamed of yourself, ever. If anyone ever makes you feel otherwise, then they don't truly know the person you are. I know you better than you know yourself, Tate, and I have never been ashamed of who you are, ever."

Tate lowers his head so that our foreheads are now touching instead.

"Sometimes I feel like you should be. I'm a coward, Sunshine."

He says something else, but it's inaudible. I realize that there are tears in his eyes, so I wrap my arms around him and hug him.

I hate that someone I love so much, hurts so much. There's a part of me that worries that Tate hates himself and that makes me hate the world for making him feel this way.

Tate lets me keep my arms wrapped around him for a while, but then pulls back. He smiles at me and swipes at his eyes with the back of his hand.

"So, tell me more about Jase and this kiss."

I laugh at his obvious change of subject but start to tell Tate the details of the past two weeks. I even tell him about the conversation Jase and I had the first night, in regards to my relationship with Tate. Tate's eyes glaze over for a bit through that part, but he is smiling again by the time I finish the details about breakfast the following morning. I can see the hesitant look in Tate's eyes, so I quickly reassure him.

"But don't worry, Tate. Jase won't say anything to anyone else. His only issue with any of it has nothing to do with you and Jake."

"I understand, Sunshine. I guess I've been a little selfish in wanting you all to myself in some ways. I love the way you light up around him, but it makes me jealous, too."

I take a sip of my tea and put my head back on Tate's shoulder.

"I understand that. I've felt the same way with you and Jake at times."

Tate turns his head toward mine.

"Really?"

I can tell without even looking that he is smiling.

"Of course. It's hard to let go of someone you love to share them with someone else. I've always said this to you, but you and I are destined to be in each other's lives. We're soulmates and I think that's obvious to everyone around us, which is why we make Jase and Jake jealous, too."

I hear a low laugh from Tate and relax a bit knowing he's in a better mood. I decide not to bring up Jake and Matt in an effort not to depress Tate any more today, but my heart sinks as the image of them in the art gallery returns to mind.

Twenty Two

The crackling of the fire has me mesmerized and I sit in a trance with my legs folded under me. It's Sunday night and we have just returned from a delicious dinner that Cora made for us at the Gematti's house. The boys decide it is a good night for a fire on the beach, so I sit while they collect wood and get the fire started.

Tate sits on one side of me, toasting a marshmallow over the fire. Jase is on the other side of me, close enough so that our arms and legs are touching, but nothing else. He purposely brushes his hand on my leg or arm any chance he gets, and it sends waves of electric current through my body.

It's a warm night and even warmer as the fire takes off. There's a breeze from the water, but other than that, everything around us is mostly still. The quiet is peaceful and it seems to put everyone in a tired daze.

I want so badly to crawl into Jase's lap, tuck my head into the small space between his neck and shoulder that I seem to fit perfectly into and drift off to sleep.

Tate offers me the marshmallow, which I take with a smile. He offers a second one to Jase who has the makings for a S'more. Tate pops a third, un-toasted marshmallow in his mouth and smiles with it inside his cheek. I laugh. Tate always knows how to make me laugh.

Jase squeezes my knee discreetly as he gets up and heads inside to get another drink with Ace and Jesse. Ryan and Ashleigh are on the other side of the fire across from Tate and me. The rest of the guys are dispersed at the docks, on the beach closer to the water, or inside the house.

I still haven't told Tate about Matt and keeping it from him is making me sick to my stomach. I know that Tate has seen Jake since then, but he hasn't said anything to me about it, so I'm assuming Jake hasn't told him yet either.

Jase still thinks I should talk to Jake directly about it, but it's hard for me to find a time when Tate isn't around to talk to Jake. I hate secrets and always have, especially one like this. Tate can sense that I've been on edge around him, but I haven't been able to bring myself to tell him the truth for fear of hurting him.

Maybe I'm the one who is the coward.

"Wanna take the canoe out?"

I blurt it out in a moment of courage. Tate pops another marshmallow in his mouth.

"Sure!"

We row out about a half-mile from shore and then stop and float with the current.

"Okay, spill it. What's on your mind? You've been acting half zombie all night."

Tate leans back in the canoe with his hands folded behind his head. I look down at my hands, not able to look Tate in the eye.

"Right. I hate that you can read me better than anyone."

"Spill it, Sunshine!"

Tate's lazy crooked smile makes me pause, but for only a second.

"Okay, forgive me for not telling you this before, but I saw Jake with this kid Matt at the art gallery downtown and they were holding hands and he called him 'Jakey' which was totally gross and the whole thing was weird, but I was scared to tell you because I didn't want to hurt you and I was going to talk to Jake about it, but I haven't had a chance to yet and I hate keeping anything from you."

Phew.

I take in a long breath because that all came out in one run-on sentence with no pauses in between.

Tate's smile has left his face and he carefully moves in the canoe so that he is closer to me. He reaches out for my hand, so I take it and look up at him.

"Hey. You don't ever have to be scared to tell me anything, Sunshine."

His voice is soft, but he doesn't sound as upset or angry as I thought he would be. I tilt my head to the side to look straight into his eyes, but he avoids it.

"You already know about Matt, don't you?"

I realize my mouth is hanging open, so I close it.

"Yes, but I didn't know you knew. Jake doesn't know I know either. I, uh, followed him one night after he thought I left. He went downtown to a bar and after an hour, the two of them left together. I've seen them together a few times after that."

Tate looks at me and shrugs. I crawl closer to Tate, trying not to rock the canoe too much.

"Why haven't you said anything to Jake, Tate?"

"Because I already know what he'll say, A. I know that he's just trying to prove a point."

Tate stays quiet for a few moments but reaches out to hold my hand again.

"Listen, we had a big fight a few weeks ago about you."

I raise my eyebrows in surprise, but let Tate continue.

"You know those things that Jase said to you the night he kissed you? That it's unfair that I let everyone think that you and I are together? Jake feels the same way. He hates that we can't be together in public and that I won't even be seen with him in front of our friends. He hates that I have a 'fake' relationship with you and that it's unfair to him that you and I go out with friends and have fun while he stays at home in hiding. He loves you, A, but you make him very jealous. It's my fault that he feels that way, but I'm not ready to do what he wants to fix the situation. I know in my heart that him taking Matt out in public is a slap in my face. I'd be a hypocrite to get angry or upset with him about it. He knows that it will eventually get back to me, so I'm just choosing to ignore it."

I tug at Tate's hand and he looks up at me.

"Well, to be fair, you're not ignoring it, Tate. Technically, you're kind of stalking Jake and avoiding confrontation."

Tate smiles over at me.

"Why don't you tell me how you really feel," he says with a short laugh. "Is that your way of politely telling me I'm a coward, Sunshine?"

I shake my head at him.

"I don't think you're a coward, Tate, but I do think you need to talk to Jake."

Tate's smile leaves his face again.

"Why? Why do I need to talk to Jake? I've told Jake how I feel. He knows that I'm not ready for that and he doesn't have the right to force me into it by bringing someone else into the picture. That's not fair."

I pull Tate closer to me, but he pulls back.

"Hey, you don't even know if that's Jake's reason for all of this."

"Of course I do, Sunshine. I know Jake a little better than you do, okay? He's angry with me and this is his way of proving his point."

Tate moves away from me to the other side of the boat. I throw up my hands.

"Okay, you're right. I'm sorry, Tate. I hate that you can't seem to make yourself happy. It's like you don't think you deserve to be."

I look across the water to see the fire in the distance, still flickering strongly.

"Yea, well, maybe I don't."

Tate puts his head down and rows us back to shore. He heads down the dock after pulling the canoe out of the water, leaving me standing there alone. I slowly follow him back toward the fire, where Jase is sitting with Ryan and Ashleigh. Tate reaches the fire before I do but keeps walking past it without stopping.

"Where are you headed, brother?" Ryan yells to Tate as he walks by.

Tate stops in his tracks but doesn't turn around.

"A walk."

Then he continues walking again. I reach the fire and stop, watching Tate's back. He stops in his tracks again, turns around and heads back toward me. He reaches me and in one motion wraps me in one of Tate's signature bear hugs that lifts me off of the ground. He doesn't say a word but kisses the top of my head as he returns my feet to earth, spins on his heels and is off in the opposite direction again.

"What the hell was that all about, A?" Ryan asks me puzzled.

I shrug in response and shake my head. It's not a complete lie because I'm a little lost as well. I sit down next to Jase who gives me a worried look and squeezes my knee again. He hands me a drink as Ryan and Ashleigh get up and walk toward the house. It's now just me and Jase and the fire. Everyone else has either gone inside or headed out for the night.

"Was that about the Jake thing?"

The sound of Jake's name on Jase's tongue sounds awkward for some reason. I smile at him, despite feeling upset.

"Sort of. Apparently, Tate knew. It all seems a bit complicated to me, but I think Tate is still working things out. He's still trying to figure out what he feels and how he feels about what he feels."

I shrug once more. Jase wraps his arm around me and pulls me closer to him as I shiver with a sudden breeze.

"I think he's pretty lucky to have you. I think we all are."

I climb into Jase's lap when he says that, tuck my head under his chin and drift off to sleep as the fire dies out.

Twenty Three

Someone shaking my shoulder startles me awake and I sit up. Jase, who must have also fallen asleep, wakes up when I do.

My eyes focus on Tate's solemn face and I shake off the sand from my clothes as I stand up. Jase hops to his feet, too, and with one look at Tate's face, says that he's going to head inside to bed.

"You don't have to do that, Jase," Tate mumbles, awkwardly avoiding his eyes.

Jase places his hand on the small of my back, kisses my shoulder and then looks straight at Tate.

"You two have some time together. I'm beat anyway."

He smiles and starts to walk past Tate, then thinks better of it, steps back in front of him and looks him straight in the eyes.

"Tate, regardless of what anyone else thinks, I love you like own my little brother and would do anything for you. When Ayla shared with me what she did, it didn't change the way I feel about you. It just made me sad that you felt like you couldn't tell me yourself. You're my brother, Tate, and that will never change."

Tate looks up at Jase, momentarily stunned. Jase gives Tate a quick, slightly awkward hug and heads in the direction of the garage. I want to run after Jase and jump in his arms to thank him. Tate stands still for a moment, tears forming in his eyes. He opens his mouth to say something, but nothing comes out and he closes it again.

"You okay?" I ask him, taking a step closer and placing my hand on his shoulder.

Tate looks down at his feet, then back up at me before he speaks.

"I wasn't expecting Jase to say anything like that. It caught me a little off guard."

Tate's voice is low and full of emotion. I wrap him in a tight hug.

"He just wants you to know that he loves you. We all love you, Tate."

I can feel him nodding into my shoulder. He pulls back from the hug to look in my eyes.

"I went to talk to Jake, except when I got to his house, Matt's car was in the driveway. I almost knocked on the front door, but then lost my nerve. I sat on the curb across the street from his house for almost an hour before I headed back here. Matt was still there when I left."

I frown at Tate, but for the first time am at a loss for words. I don't know what to say to comfort him. I link my arm through his and we walk toward the dock at the end of the beach in silence. When we reach the dock, I sit at the edge and let my legs swing back and forth. Tate does the same.

"What's going on in your head, right at this very moment?" I ask him quietly.

"I'm angry, and hurt, and kind of want to beat Matt's ass..."

I laugh and shake my head as Tate continues.

"...and am a little relieved all at once."

I raise my eyebrows in surprise.

"Relieved?"

"Yeah, I know. Weird, right? All I keep thinking in the back of my head is that maybe Matt is better for Jake. Maybe he's more of what Jake wants, more than I can be for him."

I sigh.

"Tate! Why do you do this? Why do you think you don't deserve anything good in your life or anything that brings you happiness? I've seen you with Jake. I know how you two feel about each other. How can you say that Matt is better for him?"

"Because, Sunshine, I'm not sure I ever want to tell people about 'it.' I live in fear every day that someone is going to find out, or worse, my dad or brother find out. I don't want to be like this or feel this way. I don't want anyone to know about it, so how can I try to be with someone like Jake who wants to shove it in people's faces?!"

Tate looks distraught and it almost breaks my heart in two.

"I don't know what it's like for you, Tate-I-Am. I'm not going to sit here and pretend that I do, but the best advice I can give you is to figure out what you want — what you really want and not what anyone else wants for you — and go for it with everything you have in you."

"I guess that's what I've been trying to figure out. It's hard to take everyone else out of the equation because that all affects how I feel — about myself, about Jake, about all of it."

"Should it, though? Should other people's opinions affect what makes you happy?"

Tate pulls away from me.

"It's easy for you to sit on the other side of things and tell me what I should and shouldn't feel, A. It's not that easy for me. Of course other people's opinions are going to affect what makes me happy. Who cares if I'm happy with Jake if that relationship makes me lose everyone else in my life that I love?!"

Tate stares out over the water, shoulders tense and visibly agitated.

I look down at my hands in silence because I'm not sure what else to say. Everything that comes out of my mouth seems to sound wrong to Tate and I only want to see him happy. There's a part of me that knows he's right. I know that I would and do let other people's opinions of me affect my happiness and the decisions I make. It's hard not to. I don't know what the right answer is for him and I don't know what to say to him anymore. So instead, I say something that I know will bring a smile to Tate's face. A sort of routine we have when either one of us is sad or angry or just have had enough with life at the moment.

"Let's run away together, tonight. We'll pack our bags and disappear to some remote island and grow old together instead."

Tate is still looking out on the water, but I can see his dimple in the moonlight so I know he's smiling.

"Yeah, I'll take care of hunting and fishing and you can plant a garden."

I smile, knowing the routine of this conversation now by heart, and knowing that, at the very least, I made him smile again.

"You better take care of the garden, too. We both know how not-green my thumb is. I'll cook the food and I can build us a hut or something."

Tate laughs out loud.

"With all the skills Jase has taught you, right?"

Tate turns to me, smiling from ear to ear. I smile back at him and nod and we lock eyes.

"You don't have to babysit me, you know. If you want to go join Prince Charming in bed, be my guest. I'm good now."

I don't even hesitate.

"No, I'm right where I want to be. Prince Charming will be there tomorrow."

Tate doesn't say anything in response, but he scoops me up in his arms and sits me in between his legs with my back to his chest. We sit like this, Tate's arms wrapped around me, until the sun comes up.

Twenty Four

It's Friday afternoon and everyone in the office seems to be ready for the weekend a little early. It's only two weeks out from the big charity event, and Jessica is trying her hardest to keep people motivated and focused. It isn't working. The large windows looking out onto the water from the office isn't helping. There are crowds of boats tied together and if the office is quiet enough, you can even hear the party boat music from here.

Jessica, who has been trying to have a staff meeting to get updates on the event, throws her hands up in the air.

"Alright, I give up. You're all spending more time staring out the windows than listening to each other. Everyone go and enjoy the weekend. But be ready on Monday to hit the ground running!"

There are shouts of excitement and fist bumping all around. I smile at Jessica and mouth "thank you" to her as I head out of the conference room.

I walk to the parking lot behind Tate and we both jump in his truck. We head straight for Jase's renovation house, knowing that he is working on the house today.

Tate has been hanging out with Jase and me a lot more in the past week since he's trying to avoid Jake and the whole situation with Matt. Any time we're not with the larger group, the three of us are together. It's fun for me because I get to spend time with the both of them. I think Tate enjoys it, too, but I also think he misses spending time with Jake. I'm not sure how Jase feels about it. He's a good sport with just about anything, but I think he misses alone time with just the two of us. I don't want Tate to feel left out or spend time alone, so I include him in everything we do. I'm sure it's frustrating for Jase, but I know Tate would do the same for me. In fact, he did do the same for me when Jake, Tate and I were inseparable my first two summers here.

Tate has the music blaring and the windows down. We're both singing at the top of our lungs. He's in a great mood today, but he keeps grinning at me with a mischievous look in his eye and it's making me nervous.

We pull into the long stone driveway that leads to Jase's renovation house. He's working on building a stone fireplace in the sunk-in living room. It's too hot to be doing that kind of project in my opinion, but Jase doesn't seem to mind. He tells me that working on the house relaxes him.

Tate hops out of the car and heads to the front door with me right behind him. We don't knock, knowing Jase won't hear us over the noise of the saw he's using. I step into the living room first.

Jase's back is to me and he's wearing nothing but work jeans, a baseball hat and a pair of work boots. He has headphones in his ears, so he hasn't heard us come in and he's nodding his head slightly to the music. His back is shiny with sweat, which only illuminates the muscles that move as he works with the stone. I stop in my tracks at the sight of him and my mouth falls slightly open. I always love to watch him work and today is no exception.

I've never been as physically attracted to someone as I am to Jase. It's as if there is an invisible force pulling me toward him when we're together. I momentarily forget Tate walked in with me, and when I regain my composure, I blush and look over at him. He raises his eyebrows at me and shakes his head but laughs.

"I'm going to hit the head. I'll be right back."

He turns to leave, and I know he's leaving me alone with Jase on purpose.

I walk up behind Jase, who is still unaware that he's no longer alone. I wait until he moves away from the saw, then step up to his back and kiss his right shoulder while wrapping my arms around him. He startles and pulls his headphones out, but I know he is smiling without seeing his face. He spins around within my embrace, lifts me off the ground and kisses me full on the mouth. I haven't kissed him like this all week, and I realize in this moment how much I've missed it.

When he starts to pull away, I put my hands at the back of his head to stop him and continue the kiss. I wrap myself closer to him and refuse to let go. He smells of stone dust, soap and a little bit of sweat all at once. It's intoxicating and for the first time in my life, I wish Tate wasn't here.

Oh shoot, Tate.

I hear him clear his throat somewhere behind me and I feel the blush in my cheeks return. Slightly embarrassed, I put both feet back on the floor and look up at Jase, who couldn't look happier, before turning to face Tate.

"You guys got out early today?" Jase asks, looking at Tate.

Tate nods and walks into the room with three bottles of lemonade in hand. He offers one to Jase and then hands one to me but doesn't miss the chance to wink at me. I'm now red from head to toe and can feel the heat from my cheeks as they burn.

"Hope you don't mind. I kind of helped myself to your cooler in there."

Tate throws a thumb towards the kitchen at Jase, who shakes his head.

"Not at all. Glad for the break. I was getting ready to head out of here soon, anyway."

Jase puts his arm around my waist to pull me closer. Tate chugs the lemonade and swipes at his mouth with the back of his hand.

"So, should we head back to the house to get ready for the island tonight?"

Ryan has planned another party on his family's island. This one should be much smaller than the 4th of July party, but I am looking forward to it. Tate and I help Jase clean up a bit and then we all pile in Tate's truck to head back to the house, leaving Jase's truck filled with stone parked at the renovation house.

When we get to the summerhouse, I make my way to my room to take a shower and get dressed. After showering, I throw on a dress, put my hair up in a messy twist, and head downstairs.

The guys are gathered in the kitchen and laughing as I hit the bottom step. I check the time and realize we still have four hours before the island party begins.

"What do you guys want to do for dinner?" I say to no one in particular.

Jase's eyes jump to my face as I enter, and his immediate grin makes my stomach flip-flop. Tate interrupts before Jase can get a word out.

"Oh, I have something planned."

He winks at me and makes a motion to the both of us to follow him. Jase looks at me in question, but I shrug, grab his hand, and follow Tate back outside and into his truck.

I'm between the two of them, but I can feel Tate's excitement radiating off his skin. I look at him knowing that I can get it out of him if I can just catch his eyes, but he avoids the gaze. I know he's been planning something by the silly grin on his face. I also realize at this moment that he's still wearing his work clothes and hasn't showered yet.

"Hey, what did you do while Jase and I were getting dressed? Why are you still in work clothes?"

I'm becoming more curious as the seconds pass. Tate shrugs, but flashes me a dimple-filled smile. We are headed in the direction of Jase's renovation house again, so I stay quiet.

Unlike me, Jase loves surprises, so he's enjoying every second of the anticipation. Me on the other hand... I'm hoping for the best. I've never enjoyed surprises. They just make me nervous.

We pull down the long driveway of the renovation house and Tate stops the truck at the front door. The three of us hop out of the truck as Tate leads us up the front porch and inside.

As we hit the doorway, Tate stops in his tracks.

"Shoot, I forgot something in the truck. Hang on one second while I grab it. You guys go inside, and I'll catch up."

I follow Jase inside and down into the living room where he was working on the fireplace earlier. I walk over to the stone and run my hand over the part he's finished. It amazes me the things Jase can create. He can take simple things like stone and wood and make something beautiful from it.

My stomach is growling now and I'm wondering what Tate's plan is for dinner. I'm really in the mood for some of Cora's cooking, but don't want to tell Tate that and ruin whatever his dinner plans are. I'm so hungry that I can almost smell Cora's famous fried chicken.

I hear the sound of Tate's truck on the stone driveway and run to the open front door in time to see Tate furiously peeling out and leaving us behind. I throw my hands up in question as he looks at me in the rearview.

He yells out through the cloud of dust behind him.

"Be back in a few hours. Love you!"

And then he's gone.

Oh, what the hell.

Not that I mind spending alone time with Jase, but I'm starving and now we're stranded here unless we either want to walk or unload the palette of stone from Jase's truck, neither of which I want to do in this heat.

"A, you have to come in here and see this."

Jase's voice travels from the kitchen. I walk through to find him.

"Babe, he left us here. Can you believe him—"

Before I can finish, I see a small table and chairs set up in the open space of the kitchen. The table is set with a tablecloth, candles, flowers, and a card. There are plates of fried chicken and macaroni and cheese, and an ice bucket with champagne and two glasses. I look at Jase and shake my head in awe. I realize Tate's plan all along was to give us time alone. And it was Cora's famous chicken that I smelled.

Jase grabs my hand to lead me to one of the chairs. He pulls it out for me and helps me push it in as I sit down. He sits across from me, all the while holding my hand.

I'm about to dig into the food, but Jase stops me and makes me open the card first. It's a hand-written note from Tate. I read it aloud to Jase in my best Tate voice.

"While I've had a blast the past week with the two of you, I'm sure you'd both like some alone time without me every once in a while. I know you're both too good of friends to admit this, so I've set up a special dinner for just the two of you before the party tonight. I love you both more than words can say (truly, I don't even know how to explain it), and I wanted to do something special to show my gratitude for letting me into your world the past week. I'll be back around nine to pick you up for the party."

I look across to Jase and he has the same look of surprise, appreciation and wonder in his eyes that I feel. Jase opens the champagne, pours us each a glass and makes a motion to toast.

"To Tate," he says and clinks my glass.

"To us," I say.

"To us," he repeats.

His eyes never leave mine as we both take a sip of champagne. I crinkle my nose because I've never really liked the taste of champagne and Jase laughs at me.

We both begin eating, talking about our day. Every once in a while, Jase pulls me in close to kiss me before we take another bite of food. The whole meal is perfect, and I don't want it to end.

As I'm finishing my last bite, I take a final swig of champagne to empty the glass. Jase has already emptied his twice and is on his third. He pours me a second one, but I get up from my chair and walk over to his. I wait for him to put the bottle down and climb on his lap, facing him, and kiss him.

It starts out soft and sweet, but after a minute it becomes something else. His hands go to either side of my face and mine are already fisted in his hair.

The kiss gets warmer and slower, and his hands find the bottom of my dress. He pulls the dress up so it pools around my midsection. His hands are inside the dress touching the bare skin of my thighs and lower back. His thumbs graze my sides. His hands touching my skin make something inside me come alive and my back arches slightly at his touch. He pulls the dress over my head and throws it behind him. He kisses my neck softly, wrapping his arms all the way around my body and pulling me tighter to him. I want him to keep kissing me and never stop. I want him to keep touching me and never stop.

Instead of saying these things, I just whisper the word upstairs into his ear.

Without missing a beat, Jase stands up with me still in his arms. He walks towards the stairs, kissing me the entire time. When he reaches the first step, he uses one hand on the railing and one hand underneath me so that he can take them two at a time. I laugh into the top of his head, and when he hits the top step, he kisses me again.

Still in his arms, I pull his shirt over his head and leave it on the last step. We make our way into the bedroom and Jase lays me down on the jersey sheets on his mattress. He crawls on the mattress next to me and leans over and kisses me again, even slower this time. And then again, even slower. And again. And again.

An hour later, I am wrapped in Jase's arms and wishing we didn't have to go to the party tonight so that we can stay here instead.

I already know that I've fallen in love with Jase, so when he caresses my cheek with his hand and whispers "I love you" against my lips before kissing me, I whisper back, "I love you, too."

We stay like this, tangled in navy sheets, for another half an hour. Neither one of us makes a move to get dressed or even get out of bed so I know we're sharing the same feelings.

When Jase checks his watch and realizes we only have twenty minutes before Tate's back to pick us up, he has to literally pull me out of the bed. I whine and pout every step of the way, which thankfully Jase finds cute.

He dresses me like a little kid, and then I do the same for him, kissing his shoulders before lastly putting his shirt back on. I use a piece of glass down in the entryway as a mirror to fix my hair and go into the kitchen to help Jase clean up our dinner.

When Tate walks in through the front door at nine, no one would have known we spent most of the time upstairs in bed. Dinner is cleaned up, and Jase and I are sitting on one of the counters in the kitchen, drinking champagne and laughing.

Tate walks over to Jase to shake his hand with a smile, but when he's close enough, Jase picks Tate up in a Tate traditional bear hug. I laugh and the second Jase lets go of Tate, I jump in Tate's arms. I wrap my arms around him in the tightest hug I can make and kiss the side of his face.

I whisper thank you into his ear before he puts me back down.

"Glad you guys enjoyed, and sorry for the secret. I figured it would be better as a surprise."

Tate's smile shadows mine and Jase's.

"It was perfect," I say at the same time that Jase says, "Thank you."

"Okay, enough of this mushy stuff. You ready to get your party on?"

Tate grabs my arm, leading me out of the kitchen and to the front door. I look back over my shoulder at Jase, who is right behind me. He is smiling with every part of his body and grins at me when he catches my eye. The three of us head out the front door, back to Tate's truck and are soon on our way to the summerhouse.

Twenty Five

The music is blaring so loudly that I am silently thankful this party is taking place on the island. I thought this party was going to be on the smaller side, but somehow word got out and everyone in town seems to be here.

Jase and I were together at the beginning of the night, but Tate found me in the crowd and pulled me out to an area where people were dancing. I haven't seen Jase since.

The sea of people dancing around us separates Tate and I, and I end up dancing with people I hardly know. My eyes scan the crowd and I find Tate dancing in the middle of a group of girls. I catch his eye and raise my eyebrows at him. He shrugs at me with a huge grin as I laugh out loud. He calls out to me, and I try to make my way to him. Before long, we are dancing together amongst his new friends.

Tate has me by the hand and I am twirling around him when I look up and catch Jase's face in the crowd. He looks visibly worried and is heading straight toward the two of us. He reaches me and Tate, grabs both of our arms without saying anything and pulls us away from the dancing crowd. He hasn't said a word when he finally stops walking and turns to face us. We're pretty close to the water now and far from anyone else, but Jase whispers anyway.

"Jake's here."

Jase stops and waits for us to react.

"What?!" I shriek, a little louder than expected. I look at Tate and he is glancing wildly around, trying to catch a glimpse of Jake.

Jase reaches out for Tate's shoulder and whispers again.

"He's here with a group of guys and it's not going over so well with Ry. Him, Zac and a few of the other guys are headed to the docks to tell them to get lost. I wasn't sure what to do but figured you'd both want to know. I don't know how you feel about this, Tate, but at the very least, I think we should go and stop them before it escalates into something stupid."

Tate shakes his head, not fully listening.

"I can't believe he would come here. I can't believe he would just show up."

I feel nervous tension building in my stomach and take off in the direction of the docks without waiting for Tate or Jase. I know that they both will follow me anyway. I'm pushing through the other side of the dancing crowd when a glimpse of Matt stops me in my tracks.

"Are you kidding me?" I say to no one in particular. "He brought Matt here?"

Tate is right behind me and spots Matt at the same time I do. He doesn't stop walking when I do, though, and continues to walk straight toward them.

Jase follows after Tate, but I jog past both of them because I also notice Ryan, Zac, Alex, and a few other guys I recognize walking in a group towards the docks as well.

Jake is in the middle of four guys, animatedly telling a story, and waving his hands in the air. The beer from the cup in his hand is sloshing over the sides and spilling onto the ground. I can see the look of panic and anger in Tate's eyes and that makes me more nervous than the look of hatred in Ryan's eyes.

Trying to smooth things over, I run into the group around Jake first and give him an exaggerated hug, cutting him off in his story mid-sentence.

"It's so good to see you, love! So glad you guys could make it."

I slap Matt on the back like we're buddies, but he flinches. Perhaps I slapped him a little harder than necessary.

I look up at Tate and Ryan, who are now standing next to each other, only a few feet from Jake and me. I see the confusion in both of their eyes, but don't miss the smile on Jase's face. He realizes what I'm trying to do and steps up beside me with his hand outstretched to Matt's.

"Hey man, nice to meet you. I'm Jase."

He shakes Matt's hand and turns to Jake, nodding at him.

"What's up, Jake? Good to see you. Beer is up under the pavilion and there's some food on the tables. Help yourselves."

Jake doesn't know what to say and I'm positive that wasn't the reception he came here hoping for, but he smiles at Jase as he shakes his hand. He makes a motion to the rest of the group and heads toward the pavilion. He walks right past Tate but doesn't look at him. Matt recognizes Tate and starts to say hello, but Jake grabs him by the arm and pulls him forward. They proceed to have a conversation with each other that I can't hear from where I am standing.

Tate is standing still in front of me, completely stunned, but won't take his eyes off of Jake.

Ryan walks over to me and doesn't look happy.

"What the hell, A? Why would you invite Jake Oliver? And how the hell do you even know him?"

Ryan has never been angry with me before and it surprises me so much that I can't think of a reason that would make sense. I am waiting for Tate to come up with some good excuse to save me, but it's Jase who comes to my rescue instead.

"Didn't you run into him with Jessica downtown, A? At that art gallery or something?"

Jase stands next to me, with Tate still frozen on the other side of me.

"Yea, uh, Jess and I were having dinner and we ran into Matt and Jake outside the art gallery. Jessica introduced me to Matt, and I invited them both without thinking. Why? Is it a big deal?"

This time Zac responds before Ryan has the chance.

"Because he's a faggot, A, and so are all his friends he brought with him."

I notice the way Tate flinches when Zac spits out the word faggot and realize I flinch, too.

"Do not EVER use that word in front of me again, Zac, or you and I are going to have a problem."

I've never spoken to Zac like that before, and I don't think he expects it. He raises his eyebrows and laughs at me until he realizes I am serious.

"Seriously, A? You're going to break out your Rocky personality for saying the word fa—"

"Don't finish that word, man."

Jase interrupts Zac before he can say it again. He walks up close to Zac so they are standing chest to chest and doesn't blink as he stares straight into Zac's eyes. I openly admit to losing my temper from time to time, but it's rare that Jase loses his, so Zac backs down immediately.

"Alright, Alright. Sorry guys. Geez. The freaks can stay."

I shake my head at Zac and point a finger into his chest.

"I love you, kid, but right now I would really love to punch you in the face."

Zac looks at me as if I've slapped him, and Ryan shakes his head at me.

I walk away from the group, making sure to push Tate out of my way as I walk by him. I don't understand why he didn't say anything to defend Jake, or worse, to defend me. I can't comprehend how Tate is so worried about what everyone else thinks that he's afraid to speak his mind.

When I reach the pavilion, I walk over to where Jake and Matt are standing. Jake looks at me with a smile and offers me a sip of his beer. I swat it away, spilling some onto his arm and the floor. I grab Jake by the arm and pull him away from where Matt is still standing.

"What the hell is wrong with you?" I hiss at him.

His smile instantly disappears.

"Well, so much for the warm welcome, huh? You had to swoop in and save him like you always do, right Sunssshhhhiiinnnne"

Jake's face twists in anger and sarcasm as he stretches out Tate's nickname for me.

"You can't always protect him from everything. He needs to grow up and be a man."

I cross my arms over my chest, my temper rising quickly.

"And what was your genius plan here, tonight? To show up, embarrass Tate, rub Matt in his face, and get your ass kicked all in one night? I swooped in there to save you, not Tate, because I'm the idiot who thought we were friends. Apparently, you don't feel the same way."

"I don't need you to be my friend, Ayla. I need you to disappear so I can have my boyfriend back. I need you to leave him alone and leave me alone. I need you to stay out of our relationship because it's none of your business. And I need him to STOP HIDING HIS FEELINGS FOR ME!"

Jake yells the last sentence loud enough so that most of the party turns around and stares at us.

Matt's mouth is hanging slightly open, and out of the corner of my eye, I catch Zac starting toward us, chest puffed out and ready for a fight. I lock eyes with him and shake my head violently at him until he stops in his tracks. He shakes his head back at me, crosses his arms, and stands watching us from a few feet away like a guardian.

I look back at Jake, who realizes that we have the attention of more than half of the party now.

"Sorry everyone," he yells. "The faggot and his faggot friends are causing a scene. We'll leave now so you can get back to your little party and your perfect little lives."

"'Bout time," someone yells from the crowd.

"A, are you going to threaten to punch Jake in the face, too?" Zac yells over to me.

I can't find Tate in the crowd anywhere, which just fuels my anger. I pull Jake's arm so that his face is within inches of mine.

"You are unbelievable!" I say to him through clenched teeth. "How dare you come here and do this. You don't realize how much damage you are doing. Do you think this is going to make it easier for Tate? I have always had your back. Always. I've always stuck up for you, and fought for you two, and tried to help Tate through all of this. We're supposed to be friends, Jake. I thought you cared about him. Why would you do this?!"

Jake pulls his arm away from me.

"Some friends we are. I haven't seen you in weeks! I thought you were special, A. I thought you got us. I thought you got me. Turns out, you're just like everyone else around here."

This really pisses me off because I don't think I am anything like everyone else, but before I can respond, Tate is by my side.

"LEAVE! Don't say another word. Grab your shit and leave. NOW!"

Jake laughs in Tate's face and pushes him in the chest. Tate doesn't budge. Zac, Alex and Ryan are now directly behind Tate waiting for an excuse to start a fight.

"Okay, enough already."

Jase's voice behind me startles me. I didn't realize he was there the whole time. He walks out in between the two groups, physically separating Jake and Tate. He turns to Jake and the guys he arrived with, including a very visibly upset Matt.

"Come on guys, I think it's time you left. I'll walk you down to the docks."

And that easily, Jase dissolves what could have quickly turned into chaos. He disappears down the hill towards the docks with Jake, Matt, and their other friends.

I turn around and look at the boys, all now huddled closely behind Tate.

"You guys make me sick. I want to make it clear that there's something wrong with the way you all think, regardless of how Jake acted tonight. Since when did you all become so close-minded and homophobic?!!"

There's silence all around as the guys in front of me look to their feet. Ryan steps toward me.

"A, you have to understand. Jake's not a good guy. You just don't know him well enough."

I look to Tate, waiting for him to say something, to say anything, but he doesn't. He won't even look at me. So, I stand up for Jake instead.

"Actually, I like Jake a lot. And he *is* a good guy. Perhaps you haven't tried to get to know him."

Ashleigh steps up in what I assume to be an attempt to smooth things over, but in typical Ashleigh fashion, just makes it worse.

"You should see him in school, Ayla. He throws it in everyone's face. Maybe if he wasn't so obvious about it or kept it to himself a bit, it wouldn't be so bad."

Ashleigh glances quickly at Tate and then looks away.

I roll my eyes, realizing I'm not going to get anywhere with any of them. I'm starting to get a better idea of why Tate feels the way he does.

"Enough. ENOUGH! I can't listen to anymore. Are you listening to yourselves? Do you realize how ignorant you all sound?!"

I try to push myself through them angrily when Mikey's voice stops me.

"Not all of us feel that way, A."

Everyone's head turns in unison to Mikey.

"Back at school, a few of the guys on the team are gay. I don't have a problem with it. They still have my back on the field, and that's all that matters to me."

"I'm sure they have more than just your back, Mikey," Alex quips and laughter is heard all around.

"Hey, man, you should stop with that shit. A is right. It's not funny. You miss out on meeting some really great people when you act like that."

Mikey catches eyes with me and I smile at him gratefully.

"Glad to hear someone is making sense."

Jase's voice comes from behind me and I can feel the heat from his body along my back.

"Would you guys feel differently about me if I told you I were gay?"

Now everyone laughs.

"Come on, man, really?" Ryan interrupts him.

"Seriously, that's not believable, dude," Zac follows up.

"I mean it. If I were to tell you, someone who you've known and grew up with your whole life, that I was gay, would it really change how you feel about me? Would it make you not want to hang out with me?"

Alex's sarcastic comments keep coming.

"It would make me not want to shower in the gym with you anymore, man."

A few less laughs are heard this time.

"But no, it wouldn't make me not want to hang out with you. I think it would be weird that you didn't just tell us from the start, though."

"Right, because you guys are so accepting and understanding. You make it easy for people to be open with you."

I lean back into Jase and he puts his arm around my waist.

"All I'm saying is, I think most of you don't feel as strongly about it as you think. What if someone you love is gay? How would you feel about it? Would it change how you felt about them? It shouldn't. And Mikey is right. Your ignorance keeps you from having really amazing people in your life."

I look at Ryan to gauge his reaction, but he's staring at Jase's arm around my waist with a weird expression on his face. I try to catch his eye, but he keeps staring at Jase's arm. He finally looks up, but glances quickly at Tate, and then back at Jase while Jase finishes talking.

There are a few moments of silence before Ryan clears his throat.

"Yeah, okay, we get it. You make some valid points, bro. I guess it's a good thing you act like an old man already so you can teach us a thing or two."

Ryan laughs and throws his arm over Jase's shoulder, pulling him away from me. He walks him over to the cooler and hands him a beer. Everyone else seems to return to what they were doing. The music gets loud again, and before long people are dancing and laughing and drinking like nothing ever happened.

I look over at Tate, but he is staring out onto the water lost in thought. Jase has joined the rest of the guys at one of the tables with his drink in hand. He locks eyes with me from across the pavilion and we share a silent moment together.

Tate walks in the direction of the docks, so I follow a few steps behind him. When he walks to the end of the dock and hops into one of the canoes, I yell out to him.

"Where are you going?"

Tate jumps and looks up at me, not realizing I had followed him.

"Home," he says with a flat voice void of any emotion at all.

I walk over to hop into the canoe with him, but he starts rowing away before I can.

"Hey. Come back. I'll come with you, Tate-I-Am."

Tate doesn't even slow down.

"Nope. Don't need you to. I also don't need you and your boyfriend to make speeches to the group on my behalf. Why don't you go back to him and the two of you can try to stop world hunger or something?"

Tate continues to row off into the dark distance as I stand there in shocked silence. I sit down at the edge of the dock, not sure if I am angry or hurt. It doesn't matter what I do or say anymore because it all seems to piss Tate off or hurt his feelings.

I wish I were back in Jase's bed so I could re-do this night over again. It hadn't gone at all as I had planned in my head. I was so excited for this party, but I ended up fighting with two of my closest friends in one night. I look out onto the water, no longer able to see Tate in his canoe. I let tears fall silently down my cheeks and into the water, wishing he would row back to the dock, but knowing in my heart he was already far away.

Twenty Six

The next morning, I wake up in Jase's bed back at the summerhouse. Jase had found me down at the dock shortly after Tate left, and decided to take me back home. He stayed up the rest of the night with me listening to me vent about Tate and Jake. We finally drifted off to sleep as the sun peeked through the windows.

I look over at him and he's still sound asleep. I crawl out of his embrace, careful not to wake him, and peek out the window. The sun is shining brightly, and I guess that it must be the middle of the day. The boats aren't here yet, which means everyone else is still back at the island.

I write a quick note to Jase that I went to the house to take a shower and get dressed. I leave it on the pillow next to him and walk very slowly to the house. I decide to walk up the stairs to the deck and into my room from outside in an attempt to avoid bumping into a still angry Tate. I am pretty upset and angry about last night myself, but much less so because of talking it out with Jase.

I open the sliding glass door to my bedroom and slip inside, closing the door quietly behind me. I go through my closet, grab an outfit, and head into the bathroom to take a shower. Inside the shower, I let more tears fall.

I can't believe how last night spun out of control so quickly. I hate that I managed to piss Tate off, and I hate that I offended Jake last night, even though he made me so angry. I got a glimpse of how Jake really feels about me, which breaks my heart because I consider him a close friend.

I replay last night's events over in my head for what feels like the hundredth time and get angry with Tate all over again for being mad at me and Jase. Somehow, he turned the two of us standing up for him and Jake into something wrong. Once again, Tate plays the victim even though I think he should be ashamed he didn't say anything himself.

I also cringe at the thought of me telling Zac I wanted to punch him, embarrassed that my temper got the best of me in the heat of the moment yet again. Hopefully, I can apologize to Zac without it becoming a big deal. Knowing Zac, he'll probably just laugh it off, but it doesn't make it any less embarrassing.

I hear a soft knock at the door and wonder if Jase woke up and came to find me. The door opens a crack and even though I can't see through the shower stall because of the steam, I sense it is Tate.

"Sunshine?"

Tate's voice floats softly into the bathroom.

"I'll be out in a minute."

I turn the water off as the door closes again. I groan inwardly because I don't think I'm mentally ready to have this conversation. The torture of having Tate stay mad at me is stronger than my desire to avoid talking about it though, so I open the shower door and step onto the cool tile floor. I dry off quickly, throw on my clothes, and open the bathroom door.

I know right away that Tate hasn't slept by looking at his eyes. They are puffy and red, and he looks exhausted. He's standing with his head down and I keep thinking he's going to start talking, but he doesn't say anything. I'm not about to start this conversation, so I stand in silence as well.

Finally, Tate picks up his head to look at me. He doesn't say a word but walks to me to wrap me in a hug. It's not one of Tate's typical bear hugs. He doesn't lift me off the ground or spin me around. He stands as close as our bodies will allow and holds me. After a moment or two, I reach my arms up around his neck and hug him back.

"I'm so sorry," he whispers softly into my ear.

I don't say anything right away, but keep my arms wrapped around him, so he pulls me tighter to him.

I put my hands in his hair and pull his head back softly so that I can see into his eyes.

"You okay?" I ask him.

"Nope."

He smiles weakly at me.

"Do you want to talk about it?"

I let go of his hair and brush his cheek with my hand. His hand quickly follows and covers my hand on his face.

"I do, but not right now. Later," he says, and nods at me as a reassurance.

I nod back. Pulling out of his embrace, I walk him into my bathroom and turn on the hot water in the shower. I pull his shirt over his head and drop it in

my hamper. As I grab a clean towel out of the linen closet and turn around with
t in my hands, I see that Tate is already undressed and in the shower, letting the
water pour down on his face. I throw the rest of his dirty clothes into my hamper
but leave the towel on the counter for him. I jog down to his room to grab some
clean clothes and leave them next to the towel in my bathroom.

Closing the bathroom door quietly behind me, I try to clean my room up a
bit, and finish doing my hair. When the bathroom door opens again, Tate looks a
little better, but still exhausted.

I walk to him and pull him by the bottom of his t-shirt into my bed. I pull
back the covers, convince him to get inside, and then tuck him in. I lay next to
him, on top of the covers, running my fingers over his arm until he falls asleep.

When he's snoring softly, I get out of bed, careful not to wake him, turn off
the lights, and go back out the sliding glass door. I hop up on the railing of the
deck and sit staring out onto the water, swinging my legs over the side.

I'm sitting in the same spot two hours later when Jase walks out the front
door of the garage. He waves to me and I blow him a kiss, which he returns with a
smile that reflects in his eyes.

"Coffee?" he yells up to me.

"Oh, yes, please!" I yell back.

I watch Jase walk across the yard and into the kitchen downstairs. While I'm
waiting for Jase to make his way upstairs, the sliding door to my bedroom opens
slowly and Tate peeks his head out.

I smile at him and wave him out. He opens the door wider and joins me on
the railing. We chat for a few minutes about how he slept, and he says that he feels
much better. He only got a couple hours of sleep, but he definitely looks better
than earlier.

Jase walks out with three coffee cups in hand. He hands one to me and then
one to Tate. I look at the three cups in surprise, and Jase replies.

"I heard you two chatting away up here, so I figured Tate might need a
cup, too."

Tate doesn't say anything out loud but nods furiously into the cup as he
takes a long swig. I clink my coffee mug with Jase's and mouth 'thank you' to
him before taking a sip myself. We sit in silence as we drink the rest of the coffee,
staring out into the water.

The boats have yet to return home from the island, which means the party
must not have died down until sometime this morning. My stomach reminds me
that I haven't eaten since last night. As I'm finishing my last sip, I offer to make

some lunch. Tate and Jase both happily take me up on the offer. I take the three empty coffee cups with me to the kitchen and leave Jase and Tate alone on the upper deck.

In the kitchen, I turn on some music and take out the ingredients to make Grilled Cheese Triple Deckers — something Tate and I invented last summer. The sandwich basically consists of two grilled cheese sandwiches on top of one another with a different kind of cheese in each layer. It's greasy, but delicious, and the perfect thing to eat after a long night of partying.

I melt butter in three different frying pans and take out the bread and cheeses. I can hear the murmured voices of Tate and Jase on the floor above me but can't make out what they are saying. A few moments later, the grilled cheese sandwiches are done and on paper plates. I load a tray up with the food, napkins, and drinks and head back up to the second floor.

The door out to the deck is open and there's a soft breeze coming through to the inside. The boys don't realize I'm in the doorway, so I pause for a second to listen.

"She loves you so much, Tate. We all do. You just have to cut her some slack here and there. She always puts you first, sometimes before me, and always before herself."

"I know she does, Jase. That's why I hate myself for some of the things I do or say. Sometimes I hate myself as the words are coming out of my mouth because I can watch in the expression on her face how much it hurts her."

"Listen, we all know that A is the type of person that takes care of people. That's the role she plays with all of us, but there are not many people in her life that look out for her or put her first. I know you do that for her, which is one of the reasons she feels like she owes so much to you, but you have to stop putting her in the middle of all of this. I'm here for you. You know she's here for you. We'll both support you any way we can, any way you need us to, but what went on last night is not acceptable. I love Ayla, and I'm not going to allow her to get hurt over and over again."

I slink back inside the door, trying to swallow back tears as Tate responds.

"I know it's hard for you to understand our relationship, Jase, and I truly am glad that she opened up to you about me. I just need to figure this shit out on my own, and sometimes I feel all of this pressure because so many people know now. Last night, I felt A watching me, waiting for me to say something, expecting me to blurt an omission out to everyone and I'm not at a place where I want to do that. That's what Jake wants, and in a way, I think that's what Ayla wants, but it's not what I want. I'm sorry that I involved her in this, and because of that, involved you in this. I wish I could fix that for the both of you, but I just don't know how to."

Jase puts his hand on Tate's shoulder and squeezes.

"In time, all of this will work itself out. I'm not really concerned as much as I used to be about what everyone else thinks because I know how A feels about me and she knows how I feel about her. I just know that a big part of her happiness is based on you, and she doesn't think you are happy. Are you happy, Tate?"

Before Tate can answer, I sneeze unexpectedly in the hallway just outside the open door. Jase and Tate both pick up their heads at the same time and look at me.

I smile sheepishly at them.

"Lunch is ready."

Jase hops up to give me a hand with the tray, but Tate shakes his head at me instead.

"How much of that did you just listen in on?"

"Oh, you know, enough."

I smile at Tate and sit down with my sandwich in between the two of them.

"How much is enough?" Tate asks with a dimple-lined mouthful of grilled cheese.

"Gross. Chew your food buddy," I say and close his mouth with my hand. "I heard enough to know that last night was probably harder for you than it was for me, and that I should have taken that into consideration."

I look down at my plate and continue to eat slowly.

"Listen, Tate, I didn't expect you to announce your relationship with Jake last night, especially in front of that crowd. I'm sorry if that's how I made you feel. I did, however, expect you to stand up more for Jake, or stand up for me, or better yet, stand up for what you think is right. You have to decide for yourself what you're ready to do or say, and I won't push you to do something you aren't ready to do. I did and said what I thought was right, and to have you leave me and talk to me the way that you did— well, it really sucked."

Jase grabs my now empty paper plate, along with his and Tate's and quietly heads back inside with the food tray, leaving Tate and me alone on the deck.

"I'm sorry, Sunshine. And I feel like I've had to apologize to you a lot lately."

"Well, I'm sorry too for not being more understanding. It's hard for me to put myself in your shoes. I honestly don't know how I'd handle being in your position, and I probably wouldn't handle it half as good as you do, but I want so badly for there to be an easy answer to all of this so that we can all live happily ever after like we are supposed to."

Tate smiles and leans in to kiss my cheek.

"You are such a dork. Yeah, I would like a happily ever after too, just not sure how that would work. I do know that rowing away from the dock last night, watching you stare at me with your big sad eyes hurt more than throwing Jake out of the party last night in front of everyone. I spent all night after I got back trying to figure out how I was going to get you both to forgive me."

"Well, to be fair, I think Jake has some apologizing of his own to do. I'm not saying he was completely at fault last night because there were a lot of different things at play, but I'm sure that part of him feels guilty about last night, too. Have you tried talking to him at all?"

Jase walks back out on the deck as I ask Tate about Jake. He stands next to me and puts his arm around me.

Tate looks down at his hands.

"No. I don't know what to do. What if I go there and Matt is still at his house?"

Jase clears his throat.

"Maybe you could give me and Ayla a ride to the renovation house since I have to get my truck?"

Tate smiles a dimple-filled smile at both of us, realizing we'd have to drive right past Jake's house to get to Jase's. He nods his head and the three of us head downstairs and out to the truck.

When we drive past Jake's house, Matt's car is nowhere in sight. By the time that Tate drops us off at Jase's, he is twitching nervously. When I grab for his hand, I can feel his pounding pulse in his fingers. I kiss his hand and hold his chin.

"Listen, be honest about everything you felt last night. Everything. You can't go wrong if you are honest, Tate, but you have to be willing to hear Jake's side of things, too."

Tate kisses me on the cheek once more and lets me get out of the truck. Jase and I stand on the front porch and watch Tate pull out of the long driveway and disappear in a cloud of dust.

Twenty Seven

There's a field on part of Jase's property that is full of sunflowers and purple wildflowers. It's one of my favorite places to be.

Jase had to unload the stone from his truck, but he refused to let me help so I ended up walking through the field of flowers instead. I close my eyes, outstretch my hands, walk through the field and feel completely at peace. I stop, lay down on my back and watch the sunflowers wave in the breeze.

I hear Jase call my name from the house and I yell out for him to come find me. I grab the stalk of the closest sunflower and wave it slightly to show him where I am. Within a few moments, the sunflowers around me move in motion as he walks through the field getting closer.

I sit up, expecting to see Jase's face come into view any second, but instead Jake walks through two sunflowers and looks at me.

I hop to my feet in surprise.

"Oh. Hi!"

Jake flashes a sad smile at me. Now that I'm standing, I can see Tate and Jase at the back of the house. Jase waves to me and I wave back. Tate must have brought Jake here to talk to me.

I look back at Jake, lower myself into a sitting position, and pat the ground so that Jake will sit next to me. He does and we sit in awkward silence for a few moments.

"Sooo—" I finally say when I can't take it anymore.

Jake lets out a long breath.

"Yeah, soooo — last night was interesting to say the least."

I nod.

"Yes it was. Did you and Tate make up?"

Jake looks at his hands.

"Sort of. We talked about last night and a little bit about Matt, but we need to talk a lot more. I wanted to see you first before we did."

Jake turns to look at me.

"A, I am sorry for the way that I acted last night. To show up at the party like that, and then make a scene in front of everyone is not usually my style. I'm sorry that I took my anger out on you. I said things to you that were completely out of line. I wasn't even angry with you. I was angry with Tate and with myself."

I don't say anything, so Jake continues.

"I don't know what I was trying to do last night. I was just tired of being completely ignored by Tate. He hasn't answered a phone call from me in over a week. Neither of you have come to visit. I was angry and hurt and I still am. I had a few too many drinks with some friends and I figured if you wouldn't come to me then I would come to you. I wanted to embarrass Tate, but I didn't think about how it would make you feel or my friends feel. Matt told me he never wanted to hang out with me again after last night."

"Well, I don't really blame him, Jake. And Matt's part of the reason I haven't been to the house to see you, and I know that's the reason Tate hasn't been. I didn't realize he wasn't answering your phone calls, and I apologize for not coming to talk to you myself. That day at the art gallery – I didn't know what to think and when I talked to Tate about it, I was even more confused. I don't really understand, but then at the same time, I guess I do."

Jake nods, but looks away from me and out through the flowers.

"It's beautiful here."

I smile over at him.

"My favorite spot in the world."

Jake smiles back.

"You know, I never really got to know Jase well in school, but he's a good guy. You two deserve each other. I was pretty grateful that he was there last night, and I told him so when we first got here."

I lay on my back and put my hands behind my head, so Jake does the same.

"He is pretty amazing. Jake, I can't believe how much I care about him. I think I'm in love with him."

I can feel Jake nodding next to me.

"I can see that. Does anyone else even know that you two are together?"

"No, and that's a point of contention with Jase. I'm sure you can relate."

I smile over at Jake.

"I still can spend time with him in front of everyone else though because we all hang out together, so I guess it's really not the same for us. I can't imagine how you feel, Jake. At first, I was upset with Jase for not being more understanding, but he's really been amazing through all of this, and I can understand why he feels the way that he does. I feel that way sometimes, too."

"Do you think Tate will ever be okay with being gay?"

Jake's abrupt question surprises me and I'm not sure how to answer. My silence seems to answer the question for Jake.

"I don't think so either. So, what's the solution? Do we continue whatever it is that we are doing and be unhappy just so Tate can stay comfortable? Do you and Jase continue to hide your relationship so that Tate can keep up his lies? And how long do we continue the charade? Look, I don't want to push Tate, but he's fine with where he is right now because it's comfortable for him. He fails to think about what it's like from our sides of things. I'm not sure how much longer I can do this. It's already been three years."

Jake doesn't have to meet my eyes for me to know that he has tears in his. I reach out my hand and rest it on top of his arm.

"Jake, I'm sorry, too."

"What are you sorry for, A?"

"For not trying to see things from your perspective more. I've always looked at things through Tate's eyes. Last night, when I yelled at you — it was all about how it affected Tate. I should have been a better friend for you, too. I was only protecting Tate. I should have done a better job to protect you, too."

Jake shakes his head at me.

"A, it's not your job to protect all of us. I love that about you, but there are things you can't control and things you can't save us from. I'm not angry with you, but I have a lot of built up resentment toward Tate. If you are honest with yourself, you'd realize we are both resentful of the position Tate has put us in. Last night we took that resentment out on each other. We both love him, and he obviously loves both of us. I'm just not sure if he loves me enough. I'm not sure he can love me the way that I want him to, and I think he's realizing that, also."

"Oh, Jake," I whisper and interlock his fingers with mine. "Is there a part of you that resents me? If you were truly honest with yourself?"

Jake turns his head to face me.

"I'm resentful that me and Tate can't have what you and Tate have, but I love you like family, A. I have from the moment we first met. You have a way about you

– you make people feel loved almost immediately. I don't have many people in my life that I know love me, but I have never had to question if you cared about me. You made me feel like your family since the first day we met."

Jake gets up, still holding my hand, and pulls me to my feet.

"Come on, let's go find those boys we left behind."

I follow behind Jake, reaching out with my other hand as we walk through the flowers, trying to find the peace from before, but not quite being able to grasp it.

Twenty Eight

Jase stays behind at the renovation house to finish up the stonework, but only after making sure I am okay and promising me he'd be back for dinner.

Tate drops Jake off at his house, and then hops out of the truck, too. He leaves the keys in the ignition and tells me he'd meet me back at the house and would walk home. I start to question him but see the look on his face and decide not to. I move over to the driver side and start the truck again. Jake gives me a little wave, and Tate smiles weakly at me as I slowly back out of the driveway and head home.

The boats still aren't back, so I walk straight into the kitchen and start making dinner. I fry some chicken cutlets and make that into chicken parmigiana. I am putting the chicken into the oven when Jesse walks into the house through the sliding glass door.

"A, that smells awesome. Do I have time to take a quick shower?"

Jesse walks over to where I am standing in front of the stove and puts one arm around me as he asks the question. I nod at him with a grin.

"I figured everyone will want a shower before they eat. I also planned on everyone coming home starving and thought it would be nice to have the whole group together for dinner."

Jesse kisses my cheek and makes his way to his bedroom. Before long, I hear the water turn on. I notice there are lights on in the boathouse and garage, too. I set the timer for the chicken and walk down to the boathouse first.

Zac meets me at the door and scoops me up in a hug before I can even apologize or tell him about dinner. I laugh into his shoulder.

Zac looks at me and smiles.

"I'm so sorry I lost my temper with you last night."

"So, you don't want to punch me in the face anymore? That's good to hear!"

I shake my head at Zac, knowing he won't let that comment go for a while, but am happy that we can laugh about it and that's he's not angry with me.

"Not at the moment, anyway," I say to him with a smile and shake a finger at him.

Zac laughs and lets me past him. Jackson is in the shower, and it looks like Ace is just getting out of one, his hair still wet.

"Man, I thought for sure you were going to hit Zac last night. I was taking bets that it would happen!"

Ace playfully punches Zac in the arm.

I laugh at the two of them as they continue to jab at each other.

"I've got dinner in the oven boys. When you're done with your showers, come over to the house so we can all eat together."

"Awesome!" they both say at once.

I let myself out and head over to the garage. I meet Mikey halfway, who's on his way to the garage, also. I don't say anything to him but walk right up to give him a hug.

"It was an interesting night last night, huh?" Mikey says as he lets me go.

"You know, you're the second person to say that to me," I reply, looking up at him. "Thank you for speaking up last night. My temper got the best of me as usual, but I appreciate you saying what you did and having my back."

"Always for you, kid."

Mikey grabs my cheek and squeezes like my older relatives always do.

"I meant every word I said, too."

I nod at him as he drops his hand to his side.

"I could tell and thank you. Listen, I'm making some dinner for everyone and it should be ready within the next twenty minutes. Can you let Alex and Austin know? I want us to eat together, if everyone's up for it."

"Of course. I know everyone was talking about how hungry we were on the boats. We'll meet you in the house in a little bit."

"Great, and thanks again, Mikey. Really."

Mikey flashes me a big grin and walks inside the garage, so I head back up to the kitchen. I open the sliding glass door to find Ryan standing in the kitchen alone.

"Smells amazing, A. Looks like you made a ton."

Ryan looks over at me and I can tell that he hasn't slept much. I flash Ryan a warm smile.

"Just thought we should all eat together tonight and figured everyone could use a good meal to soak up all the alcohol."

At the mention of alcohol, Ryan makes a face.

"Don't even talk about it. It was a long night last night. Or early morning, I guess, depending on how you look at it."

Ryan walks to me and, when he is about a foot away, reaches for my arms.

"You pissed at me?"

I pull back and look at him.

"Of course not. I wish I could change your mind about a few things, but I'm not mad at you."

Ryan pulls me into a hug.

"Good," he whispers.

He stands there for a moment like he wants to say something else but doesn't. We stand in silence, and I open the oven to check the chicken. The water I started begins to boil, so I place the spaghetti into the boiling water with some salt.

Ryan sits down across from me on a stool. He puts his head down on his arms.

He doesn't pick up his head when he asks me the next question.

"Are you and Tate okay?"

I'm kind of surprised by this and let out a nervous laugh.

"Uh, I think so. Why?"

"I don't know. Things seemed weird between you two last night. I noticed that you and Jase have been spending a lot of time together, too. Just seems interesting, I guess."

Ryan picks up his head and gives me that same weird look from last night.

"Interesting? What the heck does that mean," I ask Ryan, grinning because I can't help it.

"I don't know, A. Just something I noticed. I know Tate loves you a lot. He may love you more than anyone else in this world. I just don't want to see him get hurt. I hope you realize how much you mean to him."

Ryan looks sad all of a sudden. I can't help but notice the irony of this situation, and while I know Ryan's intentions are good, I also can't help but get a little ticked off.

"What are you asking me exactly, Ryan? Or what are you trying to tell me?"

I put my hands on my hips, which is my universal 'I dare you to say what you're about to say' stance. Ryan immediately backs off and gets up from the stool.

"I'm not trying to start anything, and I definitely don't want to fight with you. I love you, A, but Tate is my brother. Jase has been my best friend pretty much my entire life and I can read him pretty well. He's got a thing for you, has for a while, but I'd like to think that he wouldn't act on it out of respect for Tate. That's all I'm saying."

I open my mouth to fire a response about Ryan being a bit of a hypocrite, but before I can, Jase and Tate walk through the front door together. Ryan doesn't take his eyes off of me, but when Tate walks into the kitchen to give me a hug, Ryan walks up the stairs and into his room.

"What the heck was that about?" Tate whispers in my ear.

"You wouldn't believe me if I told you. Just some more drama for our soap opera that is 'The Life of Ayla & Tate.'"

I shake my head and strain the pasta. Tate, Jase, and Jesse who came out from his room, set the table while I pull the chicken out of the oven. Within the next few minutes, the boys have all convened at the dining room table with the exception of Ryan. The table is full with fresh salad, chicken parmigiana, spaghetti, garlic bread, and plenty of water because no one has the desire to drink anything else tonight.

Zac makes everyone say grace before we eat. When he's finished, I hop up and head toward Ryan's room.

Knocking lightly on the door, I open it slowly when he responds with, "C'mon in."

"Hey, please come out and eat with everyone. I promise that we can talk more about this. There's more to it than I can explain to you right now, but I promise you," and I try to look Ryan dead in the eye, "I would never do anything to hurt your brother. You have my word on that."

I reach out my hand to pull him out of the bed. When he reaches for it, he won't meet my eyes with his, but grabs my hand and lets me pull him up. He lets go of my hand the second his feet hit the floor and walks past me without saying anything. He walks to the dining room and sits in the empty seat next to Jase, where I was sitting only a few moments before. The other empty seat is at the opposite end of the table next to Tate, so I sit there instead.

There's a tension filled quiet that sits in the room like a heavy fog as everyone eats in silence. The only noise is the occasional clink of utensils or water glass as we eat. I have suddenly lost my appetite, so I move the food around my plate with my ork. Tate squeezes my knee under the table, and I look at him. He flashes me a sad smile and I remember that he has yet to tell me about his conversation with Jake. I get the feeling from looking at Tate's face that it didn't go well.

One by one, the guys get up and clean their plates. Because of the night before, no one is in the mood to go out anywhere. Everyone heads back to their rooms shortly after dinner is cleaned up. Tate, Ryan, Jesse, Jase and I are the only ones left in the house. Jase is helping me dry the dishes and Tate is wrapping up leftovers when Jesse says he is heading into his room for the night to catch up on sleep. He thanks me again for dinner before he disappears into his room.

Great, this won't be awkward at all.

I catch Ryan looking over at us washing and drying the dishes together and he shakes his head at me.

"Tate, why don't you and A go do something fun. Jase and I can finish up the dishes."

Ryan stares straight at me while talking to Tate.

"I don't know. I didn't get much sleep last night either. I might just call it a night myself," Tate says, trying to catch my eye, but I won't stop glaring at Ryan.

Jase clears his throat.

"Ry, why don't you and Tate both call it a night. You look exhausted. We can all do something tomorrow when everyone's had some rest."

Ryan finally breaks his glare with me and walks over to the sink in between Jase and I. He grabs the towel out of Jase's hands.

"Why don't you call it a night, man. We're good here, just the three of us. I don't need you taking care of anything."

Jase looks confused and takes a step back from Ryan.

"What's your problem, Ry? Do you have a chip on your shoulder about last night? Why don't you come right out and say what's on your mind?"

"Oh, this is about a lot more than last night, bro."

And as Ryan says the word bro, he shoves Jase backward a foot. For once in my life, I have no idea what to do or say. I stand there in shocked silence. Jase stands up straight, fixes the collar of his shirt and gets about an inch away from Ryan's face.

"I don't know what's on your mind, but whatever you're angry about, I'm not going to fight my best friend."

Ryan laughs in his face, but before he can say anything, Tate stands in between them to separate them.

"Stop! Ry, why don't you take a shower and go to bed. I think whatever it is that has you so pissed off will make more sense in the morning. Jase is heading back to the renovation house tonight, and Sunshine and I are going to go for a walk. Okay?"

Tate has his hand on his brother's chest and as Ryan looks down at his hand he seems to calm down. He takes one look at me and then casts his eyes to the floor. He pats Tate's hand and makes his way to his bedroom, slamming the door a little louder than necessary.

"What the hell?!"

Jase and Tate both look at me at the same time. I feel like my head is going to explode. I don't know whether to scream, laugh or cry. Everything is falling apart at once. So, I do what I always do when I feel like I'm in over my head; I run away. I walk right past Jase and Tate and grab Tate's keys from the counter where I left them. Once I hit the front door, I am in a dead run to Tate's truck. I put it in reverse and fly out of the driveway, kicking stone in various directions. The back end of the truck bucks to the right as the tires squeal. I look in the rearview mirror long enough to see Jase jogging after the truck and Tate standing by the front door with his arms in the air in exasperation.

Twenty Nine

I open my eyes and am immediately confused at where I am. The bright sunshine is making it hard to see, and I sit up quickly remembering I am still inside Tate's truck. Memories from last night come rushing back to me and I groan at the thought of having to go back to the summerhouse. Back to face Tate and Jase after running away from them without a good explanation and I'm sure making them sick with worry. Back to a still pissed off Ryan, who wants to fight Jase because we can't tell him the truth. Back to a depressed Tate, who probably broke it off with Jake last night and needed a friend, but instead I ran off with his truck.

Last night, I fought every urge in my body to keep driving until I hit New York, every bit of flight adrenaline that consumed me trying to convince me running away was the best option. While the thought of driving until I was back home, crying in my mother's lap until I felt better was tempting, I knew that it wouldn't solve anything.

I open Tate's glove box and rustle through some papers looking for the small bottle of mouthwash that he usually stashes there. I find a pack of gum instead and pop a piece into my mouth. I use the rearview as a mirror and fix my hair. You can't even tell I have been crying all night.

Looking around, there are a few other cars parked, along with a few RVs, at the park and ride just outside of town. I pulled over here last night and must have accidentally fallen asleep. I'm sure Jase and Tate are panicking now that I've been gone all night. I sigh heavily, start the ignition, and pull the truck out on the highway, heading to the summerhouse.

When I drive by, Jase's truck isn't there. I keep driving and end up in the direction of the renovation house. On my way past Jake's house, I realize Jase's truck is parked in the driveway there, so I make a quick right and pull in behind him.

Before the truck is even in park, Jase, Tate and Jake all come rushing out the front door. Jase jogs over to the truck and opens the door for me. Thankfully, he doesn't look mad at all, only worried. I don't say a word, but when I look at him I bite my lip, afraid that if I speak I might cry.

Instead of speaking, Jase spins my legs around so they are hanging out of the open door and wraps them around him so he can hug me. Tate and Jake stand in the driveway together watching us.

"I'm sorry," I whisper into Jase's ear, not wanting to let him go.

"Are you okay, A?" Jase whispers back, pulling me in tighter.

"I think so, but I'm not sure."

I pull out of his embrace and smile at him sadly. I reach out one hand and run it through his hair and down the side of his face.

"I'm sorry I brought you into all this craziness. I had no idea what it would become."

Jase reaches up and covers my hand with his.

"Whatever it is, whether it's this or anything else, there's nowhere I'd rather be than right by your side."

I laugh.

"I'm going to remind you that you said that, because I have a feeling it's going to get much worse before it gets better."

Jase lifts me out of the truck, the keys still dangling in my hand. When my feet are on the ground, I let go of Jase and turn around to face Tate.

"I'm sorry I stole your truck," I say to him, not able to meet his eyes.

Tate picks me up in a bear hug before I finish my sentence.

"I'm just glad you're okay. Where did you go last night? We thought for sure you'd end up here or the renovation house."

"Actually, I pulled in at the park and ride and fell asleep. I didn't mean to be gone all night. I'm sorry that I made you all worry. I felt like I couldn't breathe. I felt like I needed some air, like I needed to get away for a bit."

I look up quickly and then back down at my feet. Jake walks over and puts an arm around my shoulders as Tate lets go of me. He squeezes and shakes his head sadly at me.

"You see, Tate. This is what I was talking about yesterday. A is just another piece of your collateral damage. I know you never meant to hurt anyone, but all the lies and secrecy, it's destroying the people and relationships you care about."

Tate drops his head as mine snaps up.

"I'm not anyone's collateral damage, Jake. Listen, I understand you're angry with Tate, and in some ways, you have every right to be, but this is not his fault. We are all a part of this. If anything, I'm just as much at fault as Tate is. And you are, too."

Jake lets go of me and puts his hands on his hips.

"So, when does Tate take responsibility for the fact that because he doesn't want to lose a relationship with his father and brother, he's ruining his relationship with me, and with you, even if you can't see it right now? He's ruining your friendship with Ryan, Jase's friendship with Ryan, and putting stress on your relationship with Jase. Doesn't that all seem very unfair to you?"

Jake walks to Tate and puts his hands on both sides of his face.

"Listen, I know you're terrified, and I'm not saying it's going to be easy, but you need to tell your brother. Things are going to get worse unless you do, and you're putting A and Jase in a very difficult position so they can protect you. It's time for you to grow up now, Tate."

Tate pulls out of Jake's reach.

"I know! Jesus, I know what I have to do. I just have to figure out a way to do it on my own terms. I don't want him to find out from anyone but me, but it has to be at the right time and in the right way."

Tate stomps over to his truck and hops in the driver seat.

"I'm heading back to the house. You guys coming home or going to the renovation house?"

Jase looks at me and then looks at Tate.

"I am going to finish up that fireplace, but why don't you take A with you back to the house."

I know that Jase is trying to give the two of us some time to talk alone, but I can see the concern in his face, and I wonder if he is avoiding going back to the house, too. I hate to admit it, but part of me is worried that what Jake said is true. This thing with Ryan is going to get worse unless we tell him the truth, or some version of it.

Jase kisses the top of my head, shakes Jake's hand, and hops into his truck and leaves. I'm still standing in the driveway in the same spot, staring at nothing.

"You coming, Sunshine?"

Tate's voice snaps me out of my thoughts.

I nod slowly. I hug Jake tight and stay like that for a few moments. I finally let him go and get into the passenger seat of the truck.

As we pull out of the driveway, heading in the opposite direction from Jase's truck and getting farther and farther away from Jake, I feel the pit in the bottom of my stomach growing bigger and bigger.

Something bad is about to happen. I can feel it. If only I had known then how bad it was about to get.

Thirty

"Okay, so tell me what happened again? I want the details. I can't believe I missed the party and all the drama!"

Jessica is sitting across from me in the lunchroom at work. Sitting in front of me is a Cora special and one of my favorites, a peanut butter and banana fried sandwich, but I can't bring myself to take a bite. I haven't eaten much of anything the past few days.

I tell Jessica the details from the party, then the events of the next day from my talk with Tate, to overhearing Jase and Tate, to Jake showing up at Jase's house, and then Ryan and Jase's almost fight. I'm exhausted just re-telling the stories. I also tell her about me taking Tate's truck and the conversation in Jake's driveway.

Jessica looks less excited about the drama when she realizes how upset I am about everything.

"I'm sorry, A. I didn't realize all of that happened. A few people had mentioned that Jake showed up at Ry's party. I didn't realize how much more went down. So, what did Ryan say when you and Tate got back to the house yesterday?"

"Nothing, we haven't seen him actually. He spent the night at Ashleigh's last night, and Jase ended up staying at the renovation house. I haven't talked to either one of them. Tate and I talked a lot, though. He's a mess, worse than me. He feels like it's all his fault, and he feels this pressure now to tell Ryan and he's not ready to do it. I don't want him forced into saying or doing anything he'll regret or later resent us for. I just don't want to lose a friendship with Ryan either, and I refuse to get in the middle of Jase and Ryan. They've been friends since they were little kids. I have never felt so helpless before. I don't know what to do to help him, Jess."

Jessica puts her hand on mine on the table.

"Maybe it's not your job, babe. This is something that Tate has to figure out for himself. I know from personal experience that coming out to your family is no easy task, especially if you know that your brother and father are against it from the start. I know you don't want to hear this, but this isn't something you can protect him from. It's going to hurt him, and you can't do anything about it."

I bow my head, but let Jessica keep her hand on my hand. I let one single tear fall from my cheek.

"How did everything get out of control so quickly?"

Before Jessica can respond, one of the girls working on the sponsorship team comes into the room to ask her a question.

"We better get back to work," Jessica whispers to me and pats my hand.

"We're less than a week out from the event, so I have to get this stuff tied up. We'll talk more later, promise!"

And then Jessica is gone with the sponsorship girl and I am sitting alone in the lunchroom, my uneaten sandwich still sitting in front of me. I wrap it up, drop it in the trash and go back out to my desk where there is plenty of work to help keep my mind off of Tate, Ryan, Jase, and everyone else.

By Friday, my mind is almost entirely consumed by the charity event. I have task lists all over my desk and am working with Jessica to review everything that has to be done tomorrow morning for setup. I am finishing a phone call with the audiovisual team to confirm what we need for tomorrow when Ryan walks over to my desk with the registration list in hand.

Ryan and I haven't spoken much in the last week. He has been spending most of his time outside of work at Ashleigh's place, and at work we keep the talk strictly work-related. We act professional, but every time we have to speak it breaks my heart knowing he is still mad or hurt or upset. I promised him that night that we would talk more about it, but I haven't seen him outside of work since. The fact that I am supposed to be heading back to New York in a week and a half is also nagging me. I can't go back home without resolving this with Ryan, but I don't know how to do that without revealing too much about Tate.

I am also worried about Jase. I haven't seen much of him in the past week either. He spent most of the week at the renovation house, claiming he is trying to finish up a few projects before the summer ends, but I know he is more worried about another run-in with Ryan and not knowing how to handle it or what to say

"Jessica wanted me to give you a copy of this for the files."

Ryan's voice welcomes me back to reality.

"Thanks."

Ryan hands over the stapled pile of papers but remains in front of my desk.

"Listen, A, whatever happened last weekend, let's just squash it. You're only here for a little more than a week, and I don't want to spend it with us not speaking to each other. I'll go talk to Jase, too. Tate and I spoke last night and I obviously overreacted. He explained to me what a good friend Jase has been to him, and that he's been going through some stuff he wants to talk to me about. He also said that if it hadn't been for you and Jase, he wouldn't know what he would have done this summer. I feel like an ass, and I'm really sorry."

I shrug and look down at my hands.

"I would have done the same if I had been in your shoes, Ry, but I hate when you're mad at me."

I smile up at him and he flashes one of his award-winning smiles back at me.

"Good. I know you're going to be working late with Jessica tonight. I'll go talk to Jase when I get out of here, and tomorrow we can all have a good time at the gala together."

"Sounds good," I say.

I watch him walk off in the opposite direction.

I walk to the bathroom and let a few tears of relief fall into the sink. Staring into the mirror, I let out a long breath and hope that things are starting to look up, trying to ignore the pit in my stomach that still doesn't seem to want to go away.

Thirty One

"You look absolutely beautiful. I am one lucky guy," Jase says while walking into my room.

I can see his smile in the reflection of my mirror as I put my earrings on. He puts his arm around me and kisses my neck. I turn around and kiss him on the lips, something I missed doing this past week.

"You look pretty handsome yourself."

I raise my eyebrows at Jase, pulling him in for another quick kiss.

"You guys ready to go?"

Ryan walks through my open doorway. He takes a sideways glance at the two of us in my room together alone, but then shakes his head and smiles instead.

"You look amazing, A," and he walks over to grab one of my arms and spin me around.

"It's just a plain black dress, guys. I mean, really, I could wear a paper bag and you'd all say I look amazing."

I look at my reflection again. My hair is curled, and bounces around my shoulders in a flattering way, thank goodness. I have on a strand of pearls and pearl earrings that I borrowed from Jessica.

I found the dress with Ashleigh and she insisted that I buy it for the gala. It is a knee length cocktail dress with an empire waist and pleated skirt. The top of the dress has black lace overlay, and Ashleigh let me borrow a pair of black pumps that she said would make me just about Jase's height. She winked at me when she said it and I looked at her in surprise.

"Oh please," she had said, "I'm not blind. You two make a cute couple, even if everyone else thinks you're destined to marry Tate."

That was all she had said because one of the other girls she lives with walked in and started crying about her latest boyfriend woes.

I look down at the shoes and smile, realizing that they did make me almost as tall as Jase.

"Perfect kissing height," Ashleigh had said.

We make our way out to the driveway where everyone else is waiting. The guys all make a big deal of how I look when I walk outside, so I spin around jokingly and strut down the driveway like it is a runway. I get a few whistles, but Tate's is the loudest.

The guys all look so handsome that I decide I want a picture of the group. There are some groans, but I make them stand together and set the camera up with a timer so we can all be in it.

"Stop groaning. I don't have any pictures of all us from this summer. I need something to take back with me next week."

With that, everyone stops moaning and poses, as the realization hits us all that yet another summer is coming to an end. The camera flashes, momentarily blinding us, a moment now frozen in time for me to keep.

After piling in a stretch hummer, something Ryan had talked Mr. Gematti into renting, we are off to pick up the rest of the girls at Ashleigh's place and then off to the gala.

Just like the last two galas, Jessica has assigned us all one-hour tasks throughout the event. Tate and I are assigned to a booth selling programs and memorabilia for the event.

"You really do look beautiful, Sunshine. You're glowing tonight," Tate says to me when we are alone in the booth.

I lean my head on his shoulder and the event photographer snaps a picture of us when I do.

"We all look nice tonight. I can't wait to see how that picture from the house turns out."

Tate spins me around to face him once everyone else is out of earshot.

"I'm going to tell him. Not tonight, obviously, but I made plans to take the boat out tomorrow with Ryan and I'm going to tell him."

I'm shocked and I don't know what to say.

"Really?" is all I can manage.

"Yea, I want to do it before you go back, because I want him to know about you and Jase before you do. I'm going to ask him to keep it a secret until I can igure out a way to tell dad, but maybe Ry can help me tell him. Sunshine, I think 'm going to be sick just thinking about it. I just want to get it over with. Tonight :an't pass quickly enough."

Tate leans over and rests his arms on the table at the front of our booth. He uddenly looks exhausted.

Why hadn't I noticed that before?

"Do you want me to go with you tomorrow, Tate-I-Am? I will if you want ne to."

I put my hand on his back.

"I would love that, but no, I need to do this alone."

He turns to me.

"Thank you though, for everything, Sunshine. I love you, you know that?"

I wink at him.

"Love you, too."

I smile at Tate and say something that I know will make him smile, too.

"Hey, want to run away together, tonight, just me and you?"

"Sure, let's hop in the hummer and take it to the coast. We'll swim to some sland and I can hunt and fish and you can cook."

This time, Tate puts his head on my shoulder and the videographer walks ›y while he does. He turns the camera on us, blinking red, which means it has a ive feed to the screens in the cocktail and main event rooms. We both wave to n audience we can't see.

Thirty Two

Once our shift ends, and two other people come to relieve us at the booth, I make my way to the cocktail room with Tate. I spot Jase right away, standing at a bar across the room and talking with Ryan's dad. He looks up at me immediately, as if he can sense my presence, and smiles at me. I smile back but follow Tate with my eyes as he walks to the bar and orders a drink. Nothing new, I think to myself, worried that Tate will be drunk before too long.

I don't try to lecture him as he downs the first drink in a few seconds and quickly orders another one. I know he has a lot on his mind tonight, so maybe this will help the night pass faster for him.

I walk across the cocktail room toward Jase, stopping to say hello and make small talk with some of our event sponsors. By the time I finally reach Jase, cocktail hour is almost over and Mr. Gematti has moved on to talk with someone else.

"Hi, handsome," I whisper into Jase's ear as I walk up beside him.

"Hi, beautiful," he whispers back.

I blush and put my hand on his chest. We chat about our night so far, laughing as we do, and taking advantage of every excuse to touch each other. What I don't see while Jase and I are talking is Ryan staring at us from across the room with that same strange expression he wore last weekend.

As cocktail hour ends, the ballroom opens up and even though I know what to expect, I am excited as I walk into the room. Large spotlights are mounted in the corners of the room to make it feel like a real Broadway show. The large screens that display the live feed from the videographer's camera are playing clips of classic Broadway shows as the rest of the guests file into their designated seats. At every table there is a tall, flowered centerpiece, each themed after a different Broadway show. The famous Broadway comedy and tragedy masks sit at each place setting.

I'm sitting at a large table that was purchased by Mr. Gematti, and in between Jase and Tate. Ryan is across from me sitting next to Ashleigh. The rest of the guys are either seated at our table with us, or at the table right next to us where some of the staff are also sitting.

Tate orders two drinks and lines them up at his plate as Mr. Gematti takes his seat. He looks at the drinks, then at Tate, and shakes his head disapprovingly. He doesn't say anything to Tate, but the look is enough. Tate hangs his head, but it doesn't stop him from continuing to drink them.

As dinner is served, and the short program begins, the screens now go back to the live feed so that the entire room can see the 10-minute skits that the North Street Playhouse will be performing. The lights dim, and the performances start. Halfway through the first one, Tate drops his drink and the glass shatters as it breaks across the floor. You can hear the echo of the glass breaking on both of the video screens.

Some of the liquid from Tate's glass splashes onto the skirt of my dress and my legs before I have time to react. The aroma of Jack Daniels fills the air around the table and Tate hops to the floor to start cleaning it up, along with one of the servers. Mr. Gematti stands up and grabs Tate by the arm, whispering something into his ear that I can't hear. I see a flash of hurt in Tate's eyes as Mr. Gematti pushes Tate toward one of the doors of the ballroom. Tate walks through the door and out into the hallway as Mr. Gematti takes his seat again, nodding an apology to the tables around us. I start to get up, but Mr. Gematti stares at me and shakes his head so I remain in my seat.

As the short play ends, there is applause heard all around. The actors take their bow and head back to their seats, the last performance not happening until after dessert.

The music returns and people get up to dance. Some of the guys are on the dance floor with their dates. Zac is dancing with a woman who could be his grandmother. Ashleigh leads Ryan out to the dance floor and Jase turns and grabs my hand to do the same.

Jase spins me around and then pulls me close as we dance. I smile at him, all the while my mind on Tate and wondering if he is okay. Ryan catches my eye from over Ashleigh's shoulder, but I can't read his expression. I put my head down on Jase's shoulder, so I don't have to try to guess what Ryan is thinking.

At the end of the song, I grab Jase by the hand and lead him out into the hallway. As the door closes, the videographer turns and his blinking red light is on us. Jase and I smile and wave and he pans to the next couple standing in the hallway. The door behind me opens, closes and Ashleigh and Ryan are now facing me.

Ryan doesn't say anything to me but walks to Jase and shoves him hard on the left shoulder. Jase, surprised by the action, stumbles backward a few feet and then regains his composure. Glancing quickly toward the video camera, Jase grabs Ryan by the arm and guides him farther down the hallway and away from everyone else. Ashleigh and I hurry behind them, not wanting it to become a fight.

"That's the second time in a week that you shoved me, Ry," Jase says through clenched teeth. "I thought we talked about this last night and put it behind us. What is your problem?"

"Don't you have any respect, Jase?!" Ryan yells, louder than I think he even expects because he jumps as the sound echoes down the hall.

He immediately lowers his voice.

"I mean, really, my brother is gone for a half hour and you're all over A?"

"Whoa," I start to protest, my hand in the air in front of Ryan.

Before Jase can respond, Ashleigh faces Ryan and grabs the collar of his jacket in both of her hands.

"Honey, think about it. Don't Jase and Ayla make a cute couple? Maybe Tate and A are just friends."

She smiles up at him and pats him on the chest, releasing her grip on his jacket. I'm thankful for Ashleigh in this moment because Ryan seems to gather himself and calm down a bit.

"Bullshit, my brother is head over heels for Ayla. He's told me that many times. And you," he spins toward Jase again and jabs a pointer finger into his lapel, "are trying to ruin it for them."

Jase doesn't want to fight, and I can see in his eyes that he is hurt by Ryan's accusation.

"I would never, Ry. You and Tate are like my brothers. You are my family. I would never disrespect him or you. Don't you know I wouldn't do anything like that?"

Ryan laughs.

"I thought I did. In fact, you were the last person I'd expect it from, but I see the way you two look at each other. I know you well enough to know that you have a thing for her. And I know her well enough to see that she likes you, too. So, what the hell happens to Tate?"

Jase puts his arms up in the air, a peace offering.

"Ry, you're right about one thing. I'm in love with her, but we're not doing anything wrong, and we're certainly not doing anything behind Tate's back."

Ryan looks as though Jase has just slapped him across the face. He turns to me, his voice rising again.

"And you, A? Are you in love with Jase?!"

I look down at my feet, then at Jase, and then finally at Ryan. I nod my head, my voice failing me.

Ryan turns and swipes his arm down a table that is near us in the hallway. Everything on the table, including a metal vase, comes crashing to the floor.

"Babe, don't make a scene," Ashleigh pleads, trying to calm Ryan down, but he pushes her out of his way.

I catch Tate stumbling down the hallway and silently plead for him to turn around and walk the other way. He doesn't and continues his stumble as Ryan turns back to Jase.

"You bastard!" Ryan yells as he lunges at Jase.

"Stop! Please stop!"

Tate's pleading voice stops Ryan dead in his tracks.

Ryan spins around on his heels and he's now facing Tate, his back to me, Jase and Ashleigh.

I notice that we have the attention of some of the other guests from down the hallway. There are a few people even pointing at us. One of the other doors to the ballroom is behind me, and I've heard it open and close a few times, but haven't paid much attention to it.

"Tate, you don't understand. There's something going on here that you need– "

"I'm GAY!" Tate yells loudly, interrupting Ryan.

The door behind me opens and closes again.

Ryan stands in shock, staring at Tate.

"What are you talking about?" Ryan asks him.

I am frozen in my spot, unable to move, unable to utter any semblance of words that may help Tate out. Tate loses his balance, but quickly steadies his feet.

"That's what I needed to talk to you about tomorrow. Jase and A, they aren't doing anything wrong. They've been trying to help me."

Ryan shakes his head and laughs.

"Give me a break, Tate. You. Are. Not. Gay."

Ryan crosses his arms over his chest and shakes his head.

Tate, unaware that he now has the audience of everyone in the hallway, starts out in a low voice which rises quickly.

"I am gay, Ryan. I'm Gay. I'm GAY. I'M GAY!"

Thirty Three

The last time Tate yells the word "gay" it seems to echo inside the ballroom. I spin around and see the red blinking light of the videographer. He's been filming the whole scene and it is playing live inside the ballroom.

I run through the ballroom door and can see Tate and Ryan displayed on both large screens, staring at each other in silence. The horror sinks in as I glance over to our table and see that Mr. Gematti is standing in front of one of the large screens, his face bright red. Everyone around him is staring at either the screen or at him.

I turn back into the hallway and connect wide eyes with Tate, who is now realizing that we aren't alone in the hallway and spots the videographer as he does. His face drains of all color and his knees buckle. Jase runs to him and puts an arm under his shoulder to steady him.

"Sunshine!"

Tate calls for me and I run over to him. I grab him by the arm and walk him in the direction of the front door, trying to get him out of here as quickly as I can. I glance over my shoulder to see Ryan standing in the same spot in disbelief, Ashleigh's arm linked through his.

As we walk through the lobby, people are staring and pointing at Tate. I hear a few people snicker. It lights a fire of hate in my heart, and I push Tate through the lobby even faster. Jase is right behind me, but I turn around and tell him to go back and make sure that Ryan and Scott are okay. Jase looks at me for a few moments, trying to decide whether or not to argue with me. He finally nods and heads back to where Ryan and Ashleigh are still standing.

When we are outside, Tate drops to his knees on the pavement. He lets out a cry that sounds like a wounded animal and crumples to the ground. I crouch on the ground next to him, not caring that I'm in a dress. I put my arm on his back and sit without saying anything because I can't think of anything to say. My heart breaks watching Tate fall apart. I can actually feel it split in two as I sit next to him and listen to his sobs.

After a few minutes, Tate seems to gather himself and looks up at me. His eyes are red and puffy and there are tears still clinging to his eyelashes and cheeks.

"I'm so sorry, Tate-I-Am. I'm so sorry."

That's all I can think of to say because nothing else seems to sound right.

At that moment, two elderly women walk out of the front door. They look at the two of us crouching on the ground in the parking lot and shake their heads.

As they walk away, the one leans toward the other to whisper.

"What is that about, dear?"

"You were in the ladies' room when it happened. Poor boy announced he was queer on the big screen. That's Scott's boy, you know?"

"No, I didn't know that. On the big screen?"

"Yes ma'am. The screens played the whole thing like a show. Scott stood in the same spot turning more and more red. It was a better show than the Playhouse put on."

They both continue their walk to the valet, laughing hysterically.

I look down at Tate wanting to protect him and hope he hasn't heard them, but Tate pushes away from me and stands up. He starts toward the parked Hummer, thinks better of it and takes off toward the street in a full run.

"Tate!" I yell after him, cursing myself for not bringing flats with me like I've done in the past.

Tate doesn't turn back when I yell, but I know where he is headed; the same place he went two years before and a year before that. I peek inside the Hummer, but the driver and keys are gone.

I know Jase will be upset if I go after Tate alone, but I hope he will forgive me. I take off the pumps and leave them in the Hummer, not wanting to ruin the heels on Ashleigh. Instead, I start following after Tate in bare feet. I can almost make him out in the distance, but he hasn't slowed down and he begins to disappear from my view.

I pull the skirt of my dress up in my hands so I can jog after Tate, bare feet and all. It's beginning to get dark now and will be harder to spot Tate. It will be more difficult for cars to spot us on the side of the road, too. With Jase's voice in my head, I get closer to the ditch in the road so I'm not too close to oncoming traffic.

A few cars go by and honk their horns, and it's déjà vu all over again. I speed up my jog and silently wish Jase would show up with his truck. Why didn't I go in to get him, I think to myself as a rock cuts the bottom of my foot. I yell out in pain. I know by now that Tate has slowed down to a walk because the few times we've run together on the beach, his stamina is short-lived. Thankful that I ran almost every day this summer, I pick up my speed and try to ignore the stabbing pains from the rocks underneath my feet.

It's now pitch-black outside, and I keep tripping. Another car, coming toward me, honks their horn as they pass, making me jump at the sound. Maybe I am too close to the road, and I move even farther off the side.

Fifteen minutes later and about a mile away from Jake's house, I can just barely make out Tate in the distance. He's walking slow now, with his head hung low.

"Tate-I-Am. Please stop. Please!" I yell out to him.

He stops at the sound of my voice. I pick up speed and the gap between us is starting to get smaller. He turns around and begins to walk in my direction.

Just then, another car drives by, coming from the direction of the gala. I see the lights slow down and am thankful Jase must have come to find us. I turn around, but it's a black Jeep that I don't recognize. As they drive by me, they shine a flashlight on me. I can see from the light of it that the four passengers are wearing the comedy and tragedy masks from the gala. Something hits the front of my dress and explodes. The force of the blow of the egg feels like getting shot and it stops me in my tracks.

"Fag Hag!"

I am in a daze and almost don't hear the girl's voice from the Jeep as I watch the egg drip down the front of my dress. Tate and I are about 30 feet apart now. I see Tate run at me, but that's the last thing I want him to do. Something about the masks fill me with fear and I want Tate to run as far away as possible.

The Jeep pulls over in front of me, cutting off my view of Tate, and three masked men get out on Tate's side. There's one female in the Jeep, but she makes no move to get out. She remains in her seat, staring creepily through the mask.

I run to Tate, and as I'm coming around the back of the Jeep, I watch as two of them hold Tate by the arms while the third hits him over and over again in the face and body. Something red glimmers from the third one's ear in the streetlight and I realize he is wearing an earring. It's a skull with red eyes.

"Get off of him!" I scream as I jump on the attacker's back, but he throws me to the ground easily.

My head hits the pavement with a thump and my vision gets blurry.

"Hold her down!"

The earring is a red blur. The girl in the mask has gotten out of the Jeep now, and straddles me while I'm on the ground, pinning my arms above my head. She's stronger than I expect, and I struggle to break free as the guys continue to punch Tate over and over.

"Stop struggling, bitch, or it'll be worse for you."

"You fucking faggot," I hear them say over and over to Tate.

I am kicking and fighting with everything I have in me, and I finally manage to knock the girl's grip loose on my arms. I swing wildly and connect with the side of her face. The mask sits crooked on her face now. The second swing connects underneath her chin, snapping her head up. I use all my strength to push her off of me and scramble to Tate's attackers.

I lunge at the one holding Tate's left arm, and he stumbles backward in surprise.

"What the fuck?" but he lets go of Tate's left wrist as he does.

Terror fills my stomach as I watch Tate's arm hang limply at his side. Tate falls to his knees, making soft gurgling noises as blood drips from his eyes, nose, ears and mouth.

"No!"

I scream as the second attacker regains his balance and hits me across the side of my head before grabbing both of my wrists and twisting my arms behind my back. He forces me to my knees, right in front of where Tate is still receiving punches to the body and face.

"Now you can watch, bitch."

When I try to turn my head, he grabs my chin with his free hand and twists my face so I am staring at Tate. The attacker's face is very close to mine and I can feel the spikes of his gelled hair poke my cheek as his hot breath hits my face.

The first masked man has shaggy dirty blonde hair that falls over the forehead of the mask as he struggles to hold the weight of Tate's limp body. The last punch breaks Tate's jaw, and I can hear the crunch of bone as it happens. I think he may be unconscious now, because his body sags, and the one with dirty blonde hair drops him so that his body is lying sideways in front of me.

They both look at me, the comedy masks grinning wide. The one who was holding Tate's arms comes around to where I am thrashing wildly to no avail. He grabs a handful of my hair and drags me away from spiky hair's grasp. He twists my face so that I am staring straight into Tate's swollen eyes. That's when skull earring kicks Tate as hard as he can in the stomach three times and then finally his face. I hear a horrible snapping sound and Tate's body doesn't move.

I'm vaguely aware that I am crying now. I hear the squeal of car tires and all of a sudden, the force twisting and holding my hands behind me releases, forcing me to fall to the ground. The three attackers grab their female companion, jump in the Jeep and speed away.

I can hear someone screaming.

Voices are yelling things that I can't make any sense of. I pick myself up on my arms and crawl through a puddle of Tate's blood to where his body is lying unmoving. I pick up his face in my hands, and his eyes roll into the back of his head. His features are swollen, and his face is almost unrecognizable. His mouth is hanging open at a horrible angle and he's missing some of his teeth. I cradle his head in my arms and sob uncontrollably. There's a gurgling sound coming from his throat and I look up to see that his eyes are rolling around. I pull him closer to me.

"It's okay Tate-I-Am. I'm here. I'm here. We're going to be okay."

And that's the first time I've ever lied to Tate.

My dress continues to sop up Tate's blood, and the swelling in his face is getting worse by the second. His breathing is ragged, and I try to choke back the vomit that keeps creeping up the back of my throat.

Another gurgle noise escapes from Tate's mouth.

"Shhh. Don't talk. It's okay. I'm here. I love you, Tate-I-Am."

I can't believe I can even speak sensible words. I hear a siren in the distance and more voices, but I can't concentrate on what they are saying. Without me realizing it, there's a crowd growing on the side of the road, as more and more guests leave the gala. Someone in the crowd recognizes me and calls Ryan and Jase.

Tate's breathing is slowing, but I refuse to believe I'm losing him.

"Someone, please, help me!" I scream to the crowd.

A few people come forward, squatting next to me, but I won't let Tate out of my arms.

"Oh my God!"

One of the people cries out, and then clamps a hand over his mouth. He turns around and makes the crowd move farther back, giving us room.

One long, shallow breath escapes from Tate and his chest stops rising and falling completely. Everything in his body relaxes and his head lulls to one side in my arms.

Someone in the crowd is screaming again, but then I realize it's me.

Someone tries to help me to my feet, but I am sobbing and screaming and refuse to let go of Tate. His lifeless body is still in my arms when the ambulance arrives. The paramedics hop out the back with a stretcher and the man who moved the crowd back just shakes his head at them. They stop with the stretcher a few feet from me, but don't come any closer.

I feel a shaky hand wrap lightly around my wrist and I look up into the shining eyes of Jase. This just makes me cry harder, sobs that come from deep within me and shake my entire body. Jase has tears streaming down his face, but he won't look directly at Tate, only into my eyes.

"Babe, you need to let him go."

"No!" I scream at the top of my lungs and grasp tighter to Tate.

"No," I shake my head violently, not sure whether I'm trying to convince Jase or those around me.

Somewhere far away, I hear Ryan's voice.

"No, that's not Tate. No!"

I look up and watch Zac push him away from us with the help of Alex and Jackson.

"You don't need to see that, Ry. You don't want to."

Zac's quiet voice paralyzes Ryan and he falls to his knees in sobs. Zac holds him while Alex and Jackson stand there, terrified expressions on their faces.

Jase still hasn't let go of my wrist. I turn my face back to him, tears continuously streaming down my cheeks.

"Why? I don't understand. Why?!"

Jase shakes his head.

"I don't know, baby, I don't know."

He stops as he loses control of his voice and starts to cry. He puts his forehead to my forehead, and I flinch in pain. Jase's hand flies to the side of my face that is starting to swell a bit.

"Did they hurt you, too?" Jase asks, his voice immediately rising in anger.

I shake my head.

"Not like — Not like they did to — I tried to stop them — They wouldn't stop. Jase, they kept punching him and kicking him and saying horrible things. And oh, God, the sounds."

I let go of Tate without thinking about it and cover both of my ears with my hands, the sickening noises replaying in my head at a deafening level.

Jase takes the opportunity to carefully pull me into his arms and away from Tate at the same time. There are police officers rolling out caution tape around the scene. People in the crowd are crying. Someone is taking pictures.

One of the paramedics motions to Jase to walk me over to her and he does, very slowly. I stumble alongside Jase, unsure of how my legs are holding me up. I'm somewhere far away at the moment and in a trance. I'm confused. I hear noises and see motion, but nothing makes sense to me. I blink a few times, trying to clear the fog.

I sit down on the back of the ambulance and the paramedic checks my vitals. She does something with a light in my eyes and makes me follow her fingers. I can barely concentrate and there's a loud ringing in my ears.

I hear her whisper to Jase.

"I think she may have a concussion. Her heart rate is high, but that's understandable. There's some bruising and swelling on the side of her face, but nothing seems to be broken. We should keep an eye on her tonight, but she doesn't seem to have any serious injuries."

Jase stares at the woman and nods his head. He sits down next to me and puts my head on his shoulder. I immediately start to sob, and he pulls me to him so my face is hidden from the crowd and any additional pictures. I cry uncontrollably. I can't even feel grateful for having Jase next to me because I feel completely empty inside.

The only thing that stops me from sobbing into Jase's chest is the booming voice that is unmistakably Mr. Gematti's.

"I want to see my son. NOW!"

The police officer standing with his hands on Scott's chest drops his hands to his sides and steps out of the way. The coroner and his staff have already put Tate's body into a black bag stamped County Coroner on it. They have him on a stretcher and are about to put him into the back of their van when Mr. Gematti's voice interrupts them. The coroner himself shoos the others away. He slowly and carefully pulls back the zipper when Mr. Gematti stops alongside of the stretcher. He stops the zipper after a few inches, displaying only some of Tate's face. Mr. Gematti sucks in a surprised breath and a cry of grief escapes from deep within him.

"No! That is not my son. That is not Tate. This is a mistake. A mistake!"

His whole body begins to shake, and Jesse and Ace are quickly by his side, soon followed by Mikey and Austin. They stand around him in a circle, supporting his weight, and walk him away from the Coroner's stretcher.

The bag is slowly zipped back up and his staff continues with their task of getting Tate in the van. No more words are spoken; only cries and sobs can be heard with an occasional grief-stricken moan.

A police officer walks over to us and stops in front of me.

"Miss, I am so very sorry for your loss. My name is Detective Van Wagner, and when you're ready, we need to ask you a few questions."

I'm not sure I'll ever be ready to talk about anything that just happened, but I don't say so out loud. I don't have it in me to respond, so Jase does for me.

"I think she's been through enough tonight, don't you? Can't she come to the station tomorrow instead?"

"Sir, I respect the fact that she's been through a horrific tragedy tonight, but the sooner we can find out anything we can about the perpetrators, the more chance we have to catch them and put them away."

Jase nods and looks down at me in question.

"Masks," I whisper so low that Detective Van Wagner has to lean in to hear me.

I clear my throat, my voice sounding weird to my own ears.

"There were four of them and they were all wearing masks from the gala."

Another sob escapes me before I can swallow it.

"One girl, three guys."

I think back trying to remember what they were wearing or anything that might stick out in my mind, but all I can see is Tate getting punched and kicked over and over and hear the noises their blows make. I once again cover both ears and shake my head.

"That's a good start."

The Detective walks a few feet away to talk on his cell phone.

"A black Jeep Wrangler," I croak out, my voice still not sounding like my own.

The detective's head snaps up.

"And let's get an APB out on a Black Jeep Wrangler with four possible suspects, one female and three male, possibly in possession of four masks."

Thirty Four

The whirring sounds of the machines around me keep me from sleeping, although I doubt I would have slept at all anyway. I'm at the county hospital one town over, and Mr. Gematti is asleep in the chair next to my bed.

Jase is lying next to me in the bed, his arms wrapped around me and snoring softly in my ear. Ryan is sitting in a chair next to Mr. Gematti, but his head is lying on top of his folded arms in my bed. His hand is wrapped tightly around one of mine.

The hospital didn't think it was necessary to keep me overnight, but Mr. Gematti insisted, and I didn't have the strength to fight it. The rest of the guys are sprawled out across the room in various chairs and cots that the hospital staff had brought in.

Thanks to Mr. Gematti, I had a hospital suite all to myself. I didn't even know there were hospital suites. I know that visiting hours ended at eight, but when the nurses came in to tell the guys they had to leave, Mr. Gematti insisted they stay. No one argued with him.

The Detective asked me a few more questions on the scene, and then came to visit me at the hospital. Tomorrow, I will have to replay the night's events to him. I asked him if we could do that in private. I don't want Ryan or Mr. Gematti to have to listen to what happened. I know that seeing Tate the way they did would stay with them for the rest of their lives. They don't need to hear every detail of how it happened.

I'm already broken in two. There's no longer a whole Ayla, just the part of me that was before Tate died and the part of me that exists now. I feel numb, and painfully sad all at once. My heart shattered into a million pieces as Tate took his last breath in my arms, and I'm not sure it'll ever go back together again. I am now the human version of Humpty Dumpty. I laugh out loud in spite of myself, and cover my mouth quickly. I don't recognize the sound. Jase stirs next to me but doesn't wake up.

I play the events over in my head again, a continuous loop that doesn't stop. I keep thinking if only I had run faster, we might have made it to Jake's before the Jeep drove by. If only I hadn't called out for him, he might have kept going and maybe the Jeep wouldn't have seen him. If only I hadn't let him run away from me in the first place at the gala, this would be a whole different kind of night. If only.

If only.

I put my fist in my mouth and bite down hard, trying to avoid the sobs that are waiting at the back of my throat. No more crying, I try to convince myself. Everyone who has seen me since looks at me with pity in their eyes. I hate pity. My lip trembles, but I bite it until it bleeds. I need to help find the people that did this. I bite harder and can taste blood in my mouth.

All of a sudden a thought strikes me so powerfully that I sit upright in bed.

"Jake!" I yell out into the quiet room.

My outburst wakes everyone up with a jolt and they sit around my bed staring at me wide-eyed.

Ryan tugs on my hand and I look down at him.

"What is it, A?" Ryan croaks, his throat dry from too many tears.

I shake my head.

"No. No. No."

I turn to Jase.

"Somebody has to tell Jake."

Mr. Gematti leans over in his chair and rests his hand on my shoulder gently.

"Who's Jake, A?"

Thirty Five

"So, Tate was, um—"

Mr. Gematti swallows hard.

"—seeing someone?"

I finish telling everyone about Tate and Jake's relationship. I cry through some of it because I can't keep the tears at bay. I pray silently that Tate will forgive me for telling a secret that he should be revealing himself if he were only still here.

Everyone cries with me, even Mr. Gematti. I explain why Tate kept his secret for so long, believing that he would disappoint all of them or let them down.

Ryan holds his father while I talk. As I continue, I watch a wave of emotions run across their faces. Tate only longed for their acceptance and approval, something they could no longer grant him.

The reality of what had happened the night of the last island party reflects in each of the guys' eyes. I watch Zac's face go from sorrow to horror and then guilt. I shake my head at him when he glances up and tears stream down his face.

When Ryan lets go of his father, he walks over to where Jase is now standing next to my bed. Ryan grabs Jase in a long hug, apologizing to him repeatedly as he does. They stand together for a long time, and when I finish speaking, Ryan apologizes to me, too.

"If I had known, A— Jesus, I am so sorry. This is all my fault—"

Ryan's voice trails off as he bends over, rests his arms on the hospital bed, and sobs. His sobs are painful, like a knife slicing me. Mr. Gematti starts to cry softly and puts his head in his hands.

I clear my throat. My voice sounds husky.

"This is not your fault, Ryan. None of this is anyone's fault except those bastards in that black Jeep."

Both of my fists grasp the blanket on either side of me.

"What I wouldn't give—"

"What any of us wouldn't give," Zac interrupts me.

All of the guys nod their heads with the same look of anger in their eyes that I feel.

Mr. Gematti slams a meaty fist onto the bedside table, making me jump at the sound.

"I want those sons of bitches found. They should be tortured the way they did to — my boy — they took my poor boy from me."

His shoulders bob up and down as he cries more silent tears.

Thirty Six

Mr. Gematti and Ryan leave to talk with the funeral home, so I ask Jase to drive me to the police station while they are gone.

At the station, I ask Jase to wait in the truck. He isn't happy about letting me out of his sight, but he agrees anyway. I'm not looking forward to doing this alone, but it'll be easier for me if I don't have to worry about anyone else's reaction to what happened.

Mr. Gematti had called my parents sometime last night, and they are both on their way to Virginia, but I want to get this over with before they get here. I can't bear the thought of my mother having to hear in detail what happened last night, but I know if she and dad were here, they would insist.

Detective Van Wagner stares at me with sad eyes from across his desk.

"I'm so sorry for the delay," Van Wagner and his sad eyes say to me.

"Should only be a few more minutes."

He strums the desk with his fingers, and I wish those pound puppy eyes would stop looking at me. The back of my head is throbbing, and while the ringing in my ears is much softer now, there's a huge egg-shaped lump at the back of my head.

We're waiting on the conference room to open up. A door across the large room opens and someone calls Van Wagner's name.

"That's us," he says to me.

I follow him to the open door and inside are two other men in police uniform and a video camera on a tripod. There's a tape recorder sitting on the conference table next to a glass of water. My eyes are wide as I walk into the room. The other officers introduce themselves, but I forget their names as soon as they say them.

"Isn't there anyone with you, Miss?" the one officer says to me looking worried.

I nod.

"My boyfriend is out in the truck, and Tate's — uh, the victim's — family is at the funeral home."

My voice drops to an almost inaudible volume. I look back up at them and clear my throat.

"I prefer to do this alone. I don't want any of them to hear any more than they have to."

The officers nod at me from across the table and Van Wagner's sad eyes flicker with respect.

"So, here's what we're going to do, Ayla. I would like you to go as far back as you can and tell us everything that you can remember. Any detail that may seem insignificant to you may help us in the investigation. We are going to catch all four of them, with your help. I give you my word on that."

I don't say anything, but nod at him. I can't bear to smile, but his words somehow give me a glimmer of hope.

"We're going to turn on the video camera and the tape recorder, but those are just formalities. We want you to be as comfortable as possible, given the circumstances. And if you need to stop at any point, just let me know, and we'll take a break."

I nod again.

"I think I'm ready."

My hands tremble a little along with my voice, but I tuck them underneath me.

Detective Van Wagner motions to the other two, and one officer turns on the tape recorder while the other turns on the video camera. The blinking red light of the video camera flashes me instantly back to the hallway at the gala. I take a deep breath and start from there.

Thirty Seven

Detective Van Wagner escorts me outside, and the bright sunshine temporarily blinds me. I put my hand up to shield some of the glare as he reaches out a hand.

"We'll be in touch, Ayla, but you did a very good job in there. We've got a good chance at catching these guys, sooner rather than later, because of you. Thank you."

I shake my head at him.

"No, thank you, Detective."

I try to smile at him, but the corners of my mouth have forgotten how. I manage a small wave instead as I walk down the front steps of the police station.

Jase is out of the truck and wrapping me in his arms before I reach the bottom step. He walks me to his truck, his arm across my back, and opens the passenger door to help me in. Once he's in the driver's seat, I push myself over to the middle seat and curl into him. He doesn't ask me about what happened inside, only whispers, "Love you," into the top of my head. We drive to the Gematti's house in silence.

When we pull in, my father's Chevy is in the driveway. My heart jumps, and all of a sudden, I want to cry. Cora walks outside with my mother, and my father is a few steps behind them. My mom is already crying, and when she encircles me in a hug, she sobs out loud. I hold her tight, trying desperately to hold back tears. Jase shakes my father's hand, who looks solemnly at him and puts a hand on his back.

"I don't know how to thank you," is all that my dad says, but I can tell by Jase's face that it means the world.

"No thanking necessary. My only regret is that I wasn't there to protect her – and to protect him."

Jase clears his throat. His eyes glimmer and I silently beg him not to cry because that will be the end of me.

Mom finally lets me go and hugs Jase, kisses him on the cheek and holds him tightly. I pretty much jump into my father's arms, and I'm a little girl again. I'm fighting a losing battle with the tears, and they pour out of my eyes like a dam has been released. My father stands still, holding me as I sob into his shoulder. I wish I were still small enough for him to pick me up.

Finally, I am able to calm down and dad pulls me back so he can look at my face.

"I'm sorry we weren't here last night. We came as soon as Scott called us."

I swipe at my tears as Cora hands me a tissue. I look at her gratefully, and then my heart tugs again because I know how much this must hurt Cora. Her and Tate were close from the time Tate was small. I nod at her in sympathy, and she pulls another tissue from her pocket to dab at her own wet cheeks.

"I'm just happy you and Momma are here, Daddy."

He stands next to me, his hand on my lower back unmoving. I think part of him wishes he could make it all go away for me, everything that happened.

Mom finally releases her death grip on Jase, and Cora walks over and gives him a quick hug. As she lets him go, Mr. Gematti and Ryan pull in behind Jase's truck. I hear a sob come from my mother, and she's crying again, anticipating the pain and sorrow that Scott and Ryan must be experiencing. My mother has always been like that. She senses other people's pain and experiences it with them.

Ryan shakes my father's hand while throwing an arm across my shoulders at the same time. My mother hugs him tightly, but lets go after only a few moments. Scott, who has never met my parents in person, but spoke to them on the phone quite a few times, introduces himself to my mother and father.

"Helluva way to meet you," he says to my father with sad eyes, and dad wraps both hands around Mr. Gematti's handshake.

Dad nods his head and lowers his eyes.

"I'm sorry for your loss. I'm so very sorry."

That's my dad. Short, sweet and to the point. Scott walks to mom next, but before he can say anything, she wraps her arms around him. He lets a few silent tears fall and mom cries openly. When she pulls away, she dries her eyes with a tissue from Cora.

"Tate was a good friend to my Ayla. He was always there for her when she needed him. They had a very special bond."

"Mom—" I say to stop her, slightly embarrassed, but Mr. Gematti nods his head vigorously.

It takes him a minute to find his voice.

"I don't think anyone argues with that. The two of them, they were nseparable whenever she was here. I will forever be grateful to your daughter. She's like a daughter to me, and she will always be a part of this family. By extension, you will, too."

And I'm crying again. I'm a huge puddle of tears on the floor. Dad nstinctively reaches his arms out for me, but Jase grabs me first. I see something licker in dad's eyes quickly, and a very small smile crosses his face for an instant, out then it's gone.

Jase pulls me in tight, rubbing my back until the tears stop. Cora tells us all o come inside. When we do, she has tea and coffee ready with pastries and pie. I welcome the coffee but can't imagine eating anything. Mom tries to protest, but dad shakes his head at her and she gives up quickly.

As we sit, Mr. Gematti and Ryan tell us bits and pieces about their meeting with the funeral home. Ryan quietly explains when the services will be held, and Mr. Gematti talks about getting pictures ready.

Jase's dad stops by and gives me and Jase a quick hug. I introduce him to my parents before he sits down with a mug of steaming coffee next to Scott. One by one, all of the guys arrive, some with both parents, some with just one. The sitting room houses enough chairs for most of us, with some of the guys sitting on the loor and on tables.

We begin to share stories about Tate, something that seems to temporarily give Mr. Gematti some peace. We sit for hours, eating and talking, Cora making ure there is plenty of food and drink.

Mr. Gematti mentions the idea of having boards with photos at the viewing ervices, something the funeral home had suggested. He asks around the room ind the guys say they will bring photos to the house tomorrow. Mr. Gematti also mentions that the photographer from the gala has some photos, but that he isn't ure if those should be included or not. They quickly slide a glance at me and hen decide not to include the photos. My face must read like a book, because t the mention of the gala, horror rises in my belly. I cover my mouth; afraid it will escape and try to shove it back down deep. Mr. Gematti nods his head in agreement.

Next comes the task of asking if anyone would like to speak at the funeral. Mr. Gematti starts to cry again, and there's an uncomfortable silence. Jase's dad puts a hand on Scott's shoulders.

Ryan clears his throat.

"I'd love to speak, but I'm not sure I'll be able to—"

His voice trails off, thick with emotion. Everyone nods around the room in silent agreement.

"I'm not such a great public speaker," Zac says quietly to Alex.

"Me either," he replies, but looks down at his hands sadly.

"I'll do it," I say quietly, and then nod my head as if to convince myself.

"Yes, I would like to speak at the funeral."

Mr. Gematti looks at me.

"Oh, A, do you think you will be able to?"

More tears fall down his face.

Ryan looks at me with tears in his eyes and shakes his head.

"How are you going to speak, A? You were so close. It won't be easy — and I don't want you to have to relive — everything."

I nod my head fast now, trying to convince all of them. My mind is already made up.

"It won't be, but it's something I want to — something I need to do."

Dad clears his throat as I finish, and everyone looks at him.

"When Ayla's grandfather passed away last year, she read a beautiful eulogy at his funeral. I think if Ayla thinks she can do it, then she can do it."

Not one person argues with dad and I look at him with big, brown grateful eyes.

Mr. Gematti gets up from his chair and walks across the room to give me a hug. He doesn't say a word, but his appreciation can be felt in every hot tear that drops down his cheek and onto the shoulder of my shirt.

Thirty Eight

The next few days are a blur. None of us go to work, including Mr. Gematti. Mom and Dad stay in the attic suite that was my room for the past two summers. The rest of us don't have the heart to go back to the summerhouse to sleep, so Mr. Gematti hires someone to pack everything up and deliver our clothes to the appropriate houses.

He also purchases a number of extra pillows and sleeping bags and we camp out in the Gematti's living room for the next few days. I think having all of us in the house is a comfort for Mr. Gematti.

We spend time going through old photos and baby albums. The guys tell me stories about Tate before I met him, and Ryan shares family stories from when they were both little. Sometimes Mr. Gematti or Cora will chime in, but mostly they just sit quietly and listen. I share stories about the times we spent with Jake, mostly funny ones that I know will make everyone laugh. And we do laugh, quite a bit more than I expected. At first, I feel guilty, but it feels good to laugh and it seems to become easier and easier to do so as the days go on.

Detective Van Wagner stops by each day to check in on us and let us know how the investigation is going. Dad talks to him for quite awhile the second day, and Mr. Gematti sits with them when he does. When the detective leaves, Mr. Gematti explains to us that they should have four suspects in custody by the end of the week. I eagerly wait to hear who they are, but Mr. Gematti only shakes his head. When he doesn't speak, I look to my dad for more information.

Dad reaches for my hand and we walk out onto the back patio, facing the water and the dock that made me fall in love with this place from the first moment I saw it.

"You're going to have to go down to the station to see if you can pick them out of a lineup, A. Mr. Gematti asked him if it could wait until after the services, so you could get through that first, but the Detective was insistent and I reminded Scott that you have school to think about next week."

I haven't even thought about starting my senior year of high school. That seems like worlds away. I haven't thought about going home, either. Having mom and dad here made me forget that I'm supposed to be going back to New York in only a few days. My heart wrenches at the thought and I start to cry again, before I even realize I'm doing so.

Dad puts his arms around me.

"I know this is hard, A. I'm so very proud of your strength, but you don't always have to be strong. It's okay to be sad, and it's okay to cry. I'm not leaving your side, so you lean on me when you have to. I'll go with you to the station. We can leave mom here if you think that's best. And as for school next week, let's just take this one day at a time. We'll figure everything out. I'll stay here with you as long as you need."

I look up at my father through tears.

"But what about your job, Dad? And Mom's? And what about the girls?"

It is the first time since they arrived that my mind flies to my sisters.

"Gram is staying at the house, so don't worry about them. I'm sure she's spoiling them both as much as she can. And you let me and Mom worry about work."

Dad kisses my forehead the way Tate used to, which just makes me cry even harder.

"It hurts so much, Daddy. Every time I think about him. Every time I let what happened really sink in, it hurts. I feel like my heart has been ripped out. But I'm not just sad, Dad. I'm so angry. I'm so very, very angry. And not just at the people that did this to him. I'm angry about the whole situation. I'm angry about the reasons behind their actions. I am angry that Tate was right about wanting to hide his feelings, and how naïve I was to believe that people would be more understanding. I wish you could have seen the way people reacted at the gala when everyone accidentally found out. It didn't matter who Tate was or the good things he has done, people made fun of him right away. I hate the way people hate, dad. It makes me hate, too."

Dad wipes a tear from my cheek.

"Hate has a way of inspiring more hate, A. You can be angry, but you have to rise above that anger. You have to be strong and smart and good to counteract the anger and the hate. You have a voice, A, and you've never been afraid to use it. You should find a way to use that voice now."

I look up at him.

"You mean at the funeral? In the eulogy?"

"I don't think a eulogy is a place to be political, but it may be a good time to address who Tate really was, the person that so many didn't get to see because of their hate, or because Tate was afraid of their hate. And perhaps you can talk about why he was afraid, and the hate that caused his death. Hate is a powerful weapon, A, but love is so much stronger. And you inspire love in others. You have since you were a little girl. Perhaps you can find a way to make some good – some love – come out of such hateful actions."

"Oh, Dad–"

A surge of emotions come over me. I curl into his lap like I used to do when I was young. We watch the sun go down together before we walk back inside and join the others.

Thirty Nine

The next morning, my father and I sit in the backseat of the Gematti's car while John drives us to the police station. Ryan and Jase are in the row seats behind us, and Mr. Gematti sits in the passenger seat, talking quietly with John.

Mom stays behind to help Cora get the food ready for later today. This afternoon and evening is the wake, and family and friends would be coming to the Gematti's after the viewing hours end.

I can't wait for today to be over, but I know this is only the beginning of a very long day that lay ahead of us. Dad reaches for my hand when we first get in the car, and he squeezes it every now and then, sensing the nervousness that keeps creeping into my stomach.

Part of me is anxious about seeing who is brought in for this lineup, and part of me is a little scared. I'm more nervous that I won't be able to identify anyone, and this makes me panic in the backseat as we get closer and closer to the police station.

I don't want to let everyone down, but I've played the events from that night over and over in my head and there are still pieces missing and things that don't make sense to me. I try to picture the attackers each time, but as a dream that you can't quite remember, their features and clothing are fuzzy, and their faces are hidden behind the masks that I see every time I close my eyes.

The one thing that I can't seem to forget is their voices. I desperately grasp onto the sounds of their voices that night as tightly as I hold onto all of my memories of Tate, afraid that if I let them go for a moment, they'll be gone forever.

When we arrive at the police station, Detective Van Wagner shakes everyone's hands, but gives me a hug. He explains to Ryan and Mr. Gematti that they aren't allowed into the room with me. This is something else that I requested of the Detective.

When they start to protest, I feel guilty and drop my head, but Detective Van Wagner holds up his hands.

"It's department policy. We can't let any emotions or reactions cloud Ayla's judgment. We need her to focus, and she can't be distracted by you both being in the room."

I grab hold of Dad's hand, and flash the Detective a secret, appreciative smile. The Detective returns one that Ryan and Mr. Gematti miss as he turns to me.

"Your father can go with you, Ayla, if you would like him to."

He nods at Dad, who turns and looks at me. I nod furiously and look over at Jase. Jase, looking relieved that someone would be with me in the room, turns to the distressed looking Gemattis.

"I'm going to wait with Scott and Ry, A. You okay without me?"

Jase looks from me to my father and back at me. I nod again, still unsure of my voice. Van Wagner gets another officer to walk Mr. Gematti, Ryan and Jase to a separate part of the station that I can't see. Dad squeezes my hand tighter as the Detective opens a door and leads us into a small room with a large viewing window. There are two other officers in uniform already inside the room. Detective Van Wagner shows me where to stand and dad stands directly behind me, his right hand still holding mine.

The Detective pushes a button and says something over the intercom. A door opens, and eight young men walk into the room on the other side of the glass.

"Now, Ayla, no one in that room can see you in here. You are perfectly safe, and I don't want you to be afraid at all."

I feel myself stiffen and stand up tighter as a rage boils deep within me.

"I'm not scared, Detective. I'm angry."

I look him dead in the eye, and for the first time all morning, my voice and hand stop trembling. Dad squeezes again, and when I look out the window into the other room, I know immediately that at least one of them was there that night behind a mask. Every hair on my body stands on end as if I can sense it. It's as if a current races over my skin, leaving goose bumps in its wake. I know then that Tate is somehow here with me, and this makes me feel even stronger.

The Detective pushes the button again and asks them all to face to their left. They all do, and I recognize a few of the faces from parties I've been to or around town. When they are all asked to face the front again, something about the second and third person in the lineup sits uneasy with me.

"What is it, A?" Dad asks me, reading my thoughts.

"I don't know," I say cocking my head to one side in thought.

"There's something about two and three, but I can't place it. I recognize them, but I'm not positive it was them that night."

The Detective nods at me and he asks them to face right. As they all turn, something flashes on the guy standing under the number six. I step closer to the glass and squint at the side of his head. It's a skull earring, its red eyes catching the light and giving the illusion that they are glaring at me.

"That's him, Detective," I say, my voice rising. "Number six was the one who kicked Tate — the last time."

My heart is racing as the memory comes flooding back.

"His earring. I remember the skull earring and the red eyes."

Detective Van Wagner looks through a few pages from his notepad and pushes the button again.

"Starting at number one, please say 'Hold her down!'"

Each of the eight take their turns, but it's when number six says it gruffly that I'm immediately taken back to that night. It's like reliving the events all over again, except this time I'm not alone and this time, I'm no longer helpless.

I clench my teeth together and look at the Detective.

"That's him, and two and three, also. I remember two's dark spiky hair from when he held me down and three's blonde hair hung over his mask when he pulled me by my hair."

The Detective pushes the button once more and asks them to repeat different phrases that were said during the attack. He asks two, three and six to step forward and it only reassures me that they were the ones who attacked us.

Behind me, Dad tenses and I can feel his anger as the three step forward.

I nod once more to the Detective.

"There's no doubt in my mind. That's them."

"That's great, Ayla. You're doing great. Those are the three who we arrested this morning. They had four masks from the gala in their possession and a black Jeep wrangler is registered to one of their parents. Your positive identification only strengthens our belief that we have the right gentlemen in custody."

"Those aren't gentlemen, Detective. They're animals."

My Dad's gruff voice makes us both glance in his direction. Dad's hands are balled into fists, and I realize that in my need to have him by my side for strength, I didn't think about how difficult it would be for him to face his daughter's attackers.

"Yes, sir. I completely agree with you" the Detective responds.

He looks back at me as the last of the eight leave the room on the opposite side of the window. He says something else into the intercom and six girls are brought into the room and asked to line up. Two of them, number one and five, I know immediately are too short to be her. Number two looks around nervously, and three and six have their arms crossed in front of them. At first, I worry that none of them are her, but then four looks straight ahead and smiles through the viewing window, like she is staring right at me. Her long blonde hair is pulled back into a ponytail, and there's a bruise on her cheek under her left eye.

"Detective, can you ask them to lift their heads? Number four has a bruise on her cheek and I think she may have one under her chin as well."

Sure enough, as the Detective asks, four slowly lifts her head and the bottom of her chin is covered in a veil of purple and blue.

He asks them each to repeat the words, "Stop struggling, or this will be harder for you."

They all do, and as four finishes the sentence, she smiles again. The anger rises in my throat and I pound my fist on the glass. The noise echoes through the intercom and four's grin widens.

"That's her, Detective. That's definitely her, and I can't wait to look her in the eye in court and say so."

The Detective says something to the officer beside him and in a moment, he is ushering the six young women out of the room on the other side of the glass. Detective Van Wagner faces me and clears his throat.

"We picked number four up with one of the three young men this morning. She resisted arrest and assaulted the arresting officer. She's facing some additional charges because of it."

Dad walks over to me and hugs me, and even though the anger is still bubbling inside me, I tremble from head to toe in his arms. The Detective shakes my father's hand when I finally let him go, and then does the same to me. He asks me to follow one of his officers to where Mr. Gematti, Ryan and Jase are. Dad stays behind to talk with the Detective about the details of the case, and my responsibilities for it.

When the officer opens the door to the conference room where I had been only a few days before, Jase rushes to my side with Mr. Gematti and Ryan only a step behind him. All three of them look at me anxiously.

I pick my head up and it feels like I use every ounce of strength to speak.

"All four of them are in custody, and I was able to identify all of them. We got them, Mr. Gematti. We got them."

My knees feel weak underneath me. Mr. Gematti puts his hand on my shoulder and squeezes. We exchange an unspoken moment with our eyes, and then he breaks down in sobs. He turns to Ryan and hugs him as if he's holding on for dear life, and they both cry in relieved grief.

I don't have to say a word to Jase, because he's already holding me in his arms and rocking me slowly back and forth. I let my head rest on his shoulder, feeling only some of the relief that Mr. Gematti and Ryan are experiencing.

When Detective Van Wagner returns to the room with dad, handshakes are exchanged all the way around, and an appreciative Mr. Gematti hugs the Detective in a tight embrace that embarrasses both of them momentarily.

I'm suddenly exhausted, and I want to go home and sleep. Instead, we have just enough time to change before heading to the funeral home for the wake.

Forty

Mr. Gematti walks in first with his head bent low. The funeral home is the largest one I have ever seen. It has a large open room with pews that remind me of a church. There are two side rooms that are connected to the larger room, but slightly more private. Mr. Gematti walks directly to the room on the right and the staff from the funeral home offers him a glass of water.

Walking into the funeral home is eerie. There is a chill in the room, even though it is the very end of August. I shudder quickly, and Jase who is holding my left hand and Ryan who is holding my right, both look to me as I do. I shake my head to tell them that I am okay and keep walking forward.

My eyes go directly to the closed casket at the front of the room and a wail starts from deep within me. I stop it in my mouth, clamping my jaws tight and covering it with both hands, letting go of Jase and Ryan at the same time.

Ryan's gaze follows mine and his knees buckle. He bends over and rests his hands on the tile floor and begins to sob. Jase quickly kneels next to him and Mr. Gematti is not far behind Jase. The rest of the guys are making their way inside slowly, but at the sound of Ryan sobbing, they come rushing through the door. Behind them are both of my parents, and mom rushes to Ryan's side right away. Zac, Alex and Jackson circle around Ryan, but Ace, Jesse, Austin, and Mikey stand back near the door waiting.

While they are attending to Ryan, my gaze drifts back to the casket. There is a beautiful spray of flowers, white roses mostly, lying on top of it. My eyes fill with tears that I won't allow to spill, and I start a very slow walk up to it. When I am only a few feet away, the silence is deafening, and I look behind me.

Jase has gotten Ryan into a chair and Mr. Gematti is sitting on the other side of him. The guys, too afraid to come in any further, are all gathered at the back of the room. Their attention is on Ryan as my mother walks over to hand him a tissue. He seems to have calmed down, and Mr. Gematti is speaking in a low voice to him. My father is the only one with his attention on me. He catches my eye and gives me a tight smile.

I turn back to the casket. I run my fingers along the dark wood and jump at how cold it feels to the touch. I can't describe the loss that I feel, but it is strong and almost overpowering. Seeing the casket in front of me makes me want to open it up and crawl inside, just to be next to him again. But I know that Tate is no longer here. I know that whatever body is left inside the casket, it's not the Tate who I'm longing to see again. I want desperately to hear his voice just one more time.

I look up and see a heart of sunflowers hanging just above my head. In the middle of the heart is a white ribbon with gold letters that say, "Love, Your Sunshine." It's enough to bring me to my knees and I try to make it look as though I'm praying instead. I rest my forehead on the cool wood and allow a few quiet tears to fall down my cheeks.

I whisper very softly to Tate, who I know is somewhere listening to me.

"I miss you so much that it hurts. And I'm so sorry."

I start to cry a little harder.

"God, Tate-I-Am, I am so sorry. We shouldn't have been out on that road that night. I shouldn't have let you take off like that or let the fight with Ryan get that far. And I'm sorry I told your secret about Jake, but I hope you can forgive me. Ryan went to talk to him, but he wouldn't let me go with him. Can you believe that? Ryan went to Jake's house and had a conversation with him. He misses you so much, Tate, and your dad— your dad is a mess, Tate. He loves you so much. And I'm sure you know this, but he's sorry, too. We all miss you and love you and would give anything to have you back with us. I don't know how to get through something like this without you. How am I supposed to? Who am I going to run away with now? I want to run away right now so badly, but I know you can't come with me anymore and it breaks my heart."

I can feel my shoulders rise up and down as I gasp silently between tears. I hear Tate's voice in my ears, and it makes me cry harder. I feel a hand touch my shoulder softly and I look up to see my father. He hands me a tissue and lets me wipe away tears before he helps me back to my feet.

Looking past him, I see that everyone's eyes are on me now. Jase stands a few feet behind dad, his eyes glistening with tears as he looks at me in front of the casket. Mr. Gematti and Ryan are standing off to the side. I don't think either one of them wants to come any closer just yet, but I can tell by the expressions on their faces that they are experiencing the same emotions I am.

The guys are sitting in the pews a few rows from the front, and their parents have joined them. Mom is sitting next to Zac, who is holding her hand while she cries into a tissue. She uses the sign language hand gesture she taught us as little kids that means, I love you, and I return it. This seems to make her cry a little harder, but she smiles at me through tears.

Dad holds my hand and walks me to a seat next to where Jase is standing. He sits next to me and puts his arm around me as Jase walks to the casket and kneels himself. His right hand brushes the sides of the wood and I know a small part of him is admiring the artwork of it. He stays kneeling for a few moments more, and then he gets up, turns around, and sits on the other side of me. He reaches for my hand and squeezes it quickly. I turn to him as two tears stream down my cheeks. He reaches up to wipe them away and Dad pulls his arm from around my shoulders so that Jase can hug me.

When Jase lets me go, I turn back in my seat so I'm facing front again. I look at the clock on the wall and realize the wake starts in a half hour. People will be arriving shortly and there will be a lot of them, especially because of Mr. Gematti's many employees.

Mr. Gematti and Ryan walk to the casket together.

With their backs facing me, I make a promise out loud.

"No more tears from here on out."

"A, it's okay to cry," Dad starts to say, reassuring me once more.

"No, no more. Not today, anyway."

I wipe the evidence of any crying from my face. And not one more tear falls until I look up from the receiving line and see Jake.

Forty One

As the wake starts, Mr. Gematti and Ryan stand next to the casket, shaking hands and sharing hugs as family and friends give their condolences. Each of us take turns over the next four hours standing next to Ryan, making sure that there are at least two of us standing around him at once.

I make a few trips to the side room to bring him and Mr. Gematti glasses of water or tissues. Cora stands toward the back the entire time but checks with Mr. Gematti every now and then to see if he needs anything. I'm so thankful she's here with us.

I look up at the clock to see that there's only another hour left of the wake. I'm standing next to Ryan, and Jesse is on the other side of me. I have my head down, whispering to Jesse about how tired I am when he grabs for my hand and tugs on my arm. I hear Ryan take a sharp breath in. My eyes connect immediately with Jake's, and even from across the room I can see his legs tremble. He looks at me with tears in his eyes, and then glances around nervously, obviously uncomfortable. I can tell right away that he feels like he doesn't belong.

For a moment, I worry that he might turn around and run outside, so I break away from my spot beside Ryan. Jake is looking behind him as I approach and when he turns around, I wrap him in a quick hug. He immediately begins to cry in my arms, so I hold him tighter.

"I'm so sorry, A. I wanted to come see you, but I couldn't. I just couldn't bring myself to."

Jake's tears won't stop.

"I wanted to come see you, too. I miss him so much, Jake."

The tears that I had been holding in for the past few hours spill over and down my cheeks in two steady streaming rivers. Jake only nods in my arms as his tears puddle on my shirt. A hand on my back makes me lift my head and I look directly into Mr. Gematti's face. I try to introduce him to Jake, but my throat is full of tears now and no sound comes out. Mr. Gematti clears his throat and awkwardly throws a hand out in front of Jake.

"I'm Tate's father, Scott. It's nice to meet you, Jake. I hear that you are a very important person to my son, and I'm sorry that we are only just meeting now and like this."

Mr. Gematti looks down at his outstretched hand and then back at Jake. Jake pauses for only a moment, and then pushes Mr. Gematti's hand out of the way to hug him.

It is an awkward hug at first, but after only a few seconds Mr. Gematti puts his arms around Jake as well and they stand that way for a few moments. Everyone around them is silent, and as I look around I realize that all eyes are on them.

If only Tate was here to see this.

Ryan walks up beside me and taps his father as Mr. Gematti drops his arms to his side once more. Ryan doesn't say anything to Jake but follows his father's embrace with one of his own. One by one, the guys join in and silently hug Jake. In this moment I know that somewhere Tate is smiling with me as he watches it all unfold.

As the last few people trickle out of the funeral home, Mr. Gematti seems to come undone. He falls in front of the casket, and sobs loudly, his hands resting on his knees. Ryan walks slowly to him and helps him to his feet. My father, silent and strong, grabs Mr. Gematti's other arm and helps Ryan walk him out to their car. I tell mom to go back with the Gematti's, asking her to make sure they are okay. I think she's thankful to have a purpose, and she gives me a quick hug before she makes her way outside.

The guys all whisper plans to meet back at the Gematti's house, and they file out of the funeral home after they say final goodbyes in front of the casket. Jake left about fifteen minutes ago, but he promised to stop by the house, too.

After a few moments, the funeral home is almost silent, other than the tic-tic-tic of the clock on the wall. I realize that Jase and I are the only ones left in the room with the casket. Even the staff seems to have disappeared.

Jase kisses the top of my head and tries to walk to the back of the room to give me some time alone, but I grab for his hand instead and won't let go. Sensing that I want him with me without me having to say so, he pulls me to my feet and we both walk to the casket one final time.

"I don't want to leave him," I whisper to Jase, but keep my eyes on the sunflowers above the casket.

Jase puts his hand on my lower back, but only nods. I glance over at the photos that we put together only yesterday, even though it seems like a lifetime ago. My eyes stop on a photo of me and Tate sitting in a canoe together. Tate's dimple is out and he's smiling at me like I'm all he sees in the world. I'm looking at the camera and laughing, my hair blowing in the wind. I wonder to myself if I'll ever be able to be that happy again.

I place my hand on top of the casket, on top of the area where I imagine Tate's chest would be.

You're my heart, Sunshine, Tate's voice floats into my mind.

"You're mine, Tate-I-Am," I whisper back, imagining the shape of a heart breaking into tiny little confetti-like pieces.

With the little bit of strength left in me, I turn around, hand in hand with Jase, and walk out of the funeral home.

Forty Two

When I climb into Jase's truck, we're the only vehicle still in the parking lot. I curl into his shoulder as he shuts the driver side door. We sit in silence for a few moments this way.

"I don't want to go back just yet," I say to Jase and he nods down at me, feeling the same.

"Let's go to the renovation house for a little bit. Take a little break before going back to the Gematti's. I think everyone will understand."

I smile weakly at Jase, and he puts the truck into gear without letting me go even for a moment.

A short while later, I'm on my back in the field of sunflowers behind Jase's renovation house. Jase is lying next to me, and he hasn't let go of my hand. Every few moments, he kisses my fingers.

We don't speak, but I keep thinking about having to leave Jase to go back to New York and part of me senses he is thinking about the same thing. Both of us seem afraid to say it out loud. The loss of Tate is so all-consuming that it takes up all the room in my heart, and I haven't fully let the idea of leaving Jase behind sink in. I know we should talk about it, but I haven't had the heart for the conversation yet.

"What are you thinking about right at this moment?"

I turn to Jase to ask him. He kisses my hand again before he answers.

"About you and how I can't imagine being without you."

He pauses for a moment and looks embarrassed.

"And I feel guilty, too."

I sit up and Jase does the same. I put my hands on either side of his face and pull him close to me.

"What on earth could you possibly feel guilty about?"

"A, I hate what happened to you and Tate. I'm angry about it. I miss Tate. I love him like my own brother and hate what happened to him. As much as I hate those assholes for doing what they did – I am so grateful you are safe. I was actually relieved that night that you were okay and not badly hurt. That was my first thought before anything else, even Tate, and then I felt horrible for feeling that way."

I pull his face even closer and kiss him. He lets me kiss him, but after a moment, he takes over and is the one kissing me. He pulls my whole body into his embrace and continues to kiss me until we're both breathing heavy.

"I'm sorry, A," he says between kisses. "I should have been with you. My biggest regret is that I wasn't with you to protect you and to protect Tate, and that you had to go through all of this alone."

I shake my head at him, but he continues.

"If anything had happened to you, I don't know what I would have done, A. What happened to Tate is horrible – it's disgusting and heart breaking, and yet you've managed to be so strong through all of it. I'm not as strong as you are. If anything had happened to you that night, I wouldn't have survived it, A."

I wrap both arms around Jase, resting my cheek to his cheek.

"I'm just barely surviving this myself, Jase, but if it weren't for you, I wouldn't have. I love you."

Jase rests his hand at the back of my head, holding me tighter to him.

"I don't know if you'll ever know how much I love you."

We sit like this for a few moments before I sit back to look into Jase's eyes.

"I know I have to go back to New York in a week or so, but I don't want to go anywhere without you, Jase. School and my family are in New York, but the rest of my family and my heart are here. How do I leave everyone after all of this? I don't know if I can."

Tears start to form in the corners of my eyes. Jase kisses both of my eyelids.

"We'll make it work, baby. We'll figure out a way to make it work. We can talk on the phone every day and we can visit each other. I promise you that I'll make sure that Ryan and Scott are okay while you're gone."

"What about you, babe? Will you be okay while I'm gone?"

I take Jase's hand and kiss his fingers, mimicking his kisses from earlier.

"No, but I'll figure out a way to be. I'll just have to make many, many trips to New York. Will you be okay?"

I shake my head at him.

"I'm not sure if I'll ever be okay again. The only time that I feel like I might be since everything happened is when I'm with you."

Jase puts a stray strand of hair behind my ear and lets his thumb linger at the side of my face.

"We'll just take it one day at a time, A."

It strikes me that Dad said the same thing to me. I feel a strange sense of comfort that I haven't felt since I lost Tate, and I lean into Jase's touch.

Forty Three

I didn't sleep at all last night, knowing that today is going to be the hardest day of my life. There were people all over the Gematti's house when Jase and I returned last night, and the last visitor didn't leave until after midnight. Almost everyone had passed out or went to bed right after that, but Jase and I stayed awake out on the dock. I watched the sunrise while wrapped in his arms, reading and re-reading the eulogy that I wrote for this morning.

Now that we're pulling up in front of the church, butterflies fill my stomach and part of me wants to stay in the car. As we file in the church for the funeral mass, I sit up front with Ryan and Mr. Gematti.

The extended Gematti family fills into the front pews, and my parents are right behind us. The rest of the guys act as pallbearers and walk the casket down the main aisle of the church. I can't look, so I stare straight ahead at the large crucifix on the wall behind the altar. I fix my gaze there and refuse to look anywhere else in an attempt to keep my emotions in check. If I am going to make it through this eulogy, I have to keep my attention focused on something else. Being in church has always comforted me, and I try to find that peace of mind while fixing my gaze on the cross in front of me.

Once the casket with Tate inside rests at the front of the church, the guys fill the rest of the front pew where we are sitting. Each of them has their head down as they sit. Jase sits next to me and grabs for my hand as soon as he does.

The mass begins, but I keep my eyes fixed in front of me. I thought the mass would drag on, but it goes by too quickly. Before long, it is time for me to get up and read the eulogy. I'm shaking from head to toe. Jase squeezes my hand one more time before letting me go. I stand up on shaky knees, the folded pages in my hand trembling, too.

I walk up to the podium at the left of the front of the church and put the trembling pieces of paper down in front of me. For the first time since I sat down,

I look up and around the church. I had no idea how many people were here until this moment. Every pew of the church is filled, with people spilling out into the aisles. The entire back of the church is crowded with people standing shoulder to shoulder. The doors at the back of the church are open and I can see there are more people standing outside.

A slow panic begins to rise, but I push it back down. I take a deep breath and glance over at Mr. Gematti and Ryan. They both have their heads down. I look at Jase and he winks at me. One by one, I make eye contact with each of the guys and then finally my parents before I begin to speak.

"For those of you that don't know me, my name is Ayla, but to Tate, I have always been Sunshine. And to me, Tate has always been Tate-I-Am because that's how he introduced himself to me the very first time we met."

I hear a few muffled laughs and I look up, momentarily distracted. Ryan is looking up at me now and smiles, so I continue.

"I have only known Tate for two years now, but he is – was – my closest friend. We told each other frequently that we were soul mates, meant to be in each other's lives. Most people that knew the both of us assumed we were in a romantic relationship, but our relationship was much more than that. Tate wasn't my boyfriend, but he was my best friend. He knew me better than anyone and knew how I was feeling just by reading my face or my voice. We were connected from the moment we met, and I told him constantly that he was my heart. He knew all of my secrets and I know all of his. I helped him keep a couple of secrets, too. Secrets that we kept even from his own family and our closest friends."

I look to Mr. Gematti now and he smiles up at me reassuringly. I can sense Dad's gaze and when I glance at him, he nods his head at me to continue.

"Tate's biggest secret was that he was gay. There were many reasons why Tate kept this secret, even from me at first. Reasons that run the gamut of being ashamed of how he felt, to worrying what people would think, to thinking that his feelings would disappoint his family. I would argue with him all the time, trying to convince him that people would love him regardless and that he shouldn't be afraid to be himself. Tate would tell me that I didn't fully understand. It wasn't until his death that I realized that he was right. I was naïve to the hate that exists in this world. I didn't understand that people do judge others without getting to know them first, and that something as simple as who you love, can define who you are to someone else. I'm speaking today because I want everyone to know who Tate really was. I want each of you to walk away feeling like you knew Tate, even if you didn't. You see, being gay wasn't who Tate was, that was just one thing about him. A good friend of mine once said that you miss out on some really great people in your life if you judge them before getting to know them. I want all of you to know how special Tate was, so that each of you don't miss out on knowing one of the good ones.

Tate had a kind soul, and he had a way of making you feel special when you were around him. He looked out for others, and whenever Tate and I were somewhere together, he always kept an eye out for me to make sure I was okay. Sometimes I would look at him from across a room and he would know what I was thinking without me ever having to say a word. He was intuitive and deeply caring, and he never stopped wanting to help people. As much pain as he dealt with internally because of his own struggles, he never let that stop him from taking care of anyone else.

Tate was the kind of person that you felt like you knew for years after only meeting him for a few minutes. His smile was a comfort, and he smiled often. His dimples – just like his older brother Ryan's – had a way of making you smile, too, regardless of how you were feeling. Tate's laugh was contagious and inspired many long nights of laughter with all of our friends."

I glance up and see all of the guys in the front row smiling in memory. A few of them are nodding in agreement.

"Most importantly, Tate loved, and he loved unconditionally. He loved everyone around him and created special bonds with the people in his life.

Tate loved his friends and spending time with all of us. Tate and I are the youngest of our group of friends, and it's no secret that he would get upset when we were too young to go out with everyone else. He shared with me that some of his favorite memories were of the nights we spent all together on the island, or at our summerhouse or at his father's house. All of you – Jase, Jesse, Ace, Zac, Jackson, Alex, Austin, and Mikey – you meant the world to him and I want you to know that even though he kept his secret from most of you, it wasn't for lack of love or respect. He looked to all of you as older brothers, and each of you were special to him.

And, of course, Tate loved his family. Ryan was someone that Tate always looked up to. He wanted to be just like you, Ry. He always admired your drive, your ability to make friends everywhere you go, and how you never let him forget how important he was to you. You have always been his protector, taking the lead and doing things first as an older brother. And he shared with me that he always felt safe with you around.

Mr. Gematti, you were Tate's hero. Tate looked up to you and admired you for raising him and Ryan as a single dad. Tate may have been afraid to tell you his secret, but only because your opinion of him was so important and he never wanted to let you down in any way.

Tate also had a special relationship with Cora. For those of you that don't know Cora's famous cooking, you're missing out, but Tate had a special place in his heart for Cora. He confided in her and told me once that she was like a mother to him."

I look out in the crowd to find Cora. She is rocking slowly back and forth with tears in her eyes and her grandson's arms are wrapped around her.

I take a deep breath and continue.

"Tate also loved Jake."

The church is so silent you can hear a pin drop, but I continue anyway.

"Jake was Tate's best friend, too. He helped him understand things about himself that I never could. Jake helped Tate realize the things he wanted in life and what it felt like to be in love. Jake, I think you know by now that Tate loved you, but if there's any question in your heart, let me assure you, he did. He may not always have known how to show it or express it, but he did. Tate struggled with his feelings, but only because of the way he thought the world would view them. Regardless of Tate's struggles, he always found his way back to Jake."

I take a big breath, turning to the last page I have written.

"The main theme woven through Tate's life is love. That's the best way I can describe Tate and the life that he lived. He loved. He loved universally, unconditionally, and without pause. He loved to help people. He loved to make people laugh. He loved to spread love. That's why his death is so difficult for me to accept. Not just because he was my soul mate. Not just because this world lost a beautiful person when he passed. But because Tate was stolen from us and his life of love in an act of hate. My father said to me the other night that hate has a tendency to inspire more hate. He said that the hate that took Tate from us could only be battled with love, and while hate is a strong weapon, love is stronger."

A single, silent tear falls down my face. Everyone in the church seems to be crying now, but I don't notice.

"I was there, right alongside him, when Tate left this world. I watched what was done to him and I couldn't do anything to stop it. I feel helpless and angry and lost without him, but I'm trying to overcome all of that by spreading love. I ask you to do the same in Tate's honor.

His entire life was about loving those around him, and we can continue that legacy even though he is gone. I want you all to leave today knowing that the world is a little less beautiful without Tate in it, but that we all can inspire more beauty in this world with love and understanding. Even though Tate is no longer with us, he'll never truly leave those who continue to love him. And for those that didn't know him, I hope you leave today with a better understanding of Tate and the love he inspires. Hopefully his story inspires it in you, so that you can inspire it in others, too."

I turn to face the casket at the front of the church, no longer looking at my paper. My lip trembles a bit, but I try to steady my voice.

"Tate-I-Am, my heart, my soul mate, I don't know how to say goodbye to you. I sat up all last night trying to think of what to say, to express the feelings I have knowing that I face the rest of this life without you in it. I keep coming back to what you said to me as I was leaving for New York my first summer here, the first summer I met you. You told me, 'Hey, this isn't a goodbye, silly. It's just a see you later.' and I'd like to think that is still true now. Somehow it brings me a little peace to know that someday, I will see you again. I miss you, Tate. I love you, Tate. And I'll be seeing you."

I look up and realize that there is not a dry eye in the place. Something about watching how everyone reacts to what I have said brings me a little peace. I take notice of people sharing hugs and tissues, making sure those around them are okay. Somehow, I know that Tate's story has left an impression on all of them, and I hope that the love he shared in his life continues to be shared amongst all of them and beyond.

I walk slowly back to my seat in between Jase and Ryan. When I sit down, they put arms around my shoulders and Mr. Gematti grabs my hand. My mother hugs me from behind and Dad squeezes my shoulder. I know he is proud of me without having to turn around.

Shortly after, we are standing at the cemetery in front of the Gematti family plot. After a short reading from the priest, everyone takes turns saying goodbye before returning to their vehicles.

I feel numb through all of this. People move around me in a blur and the only thing I am aware of is Jase holding my hand. I go through the motions, but nothing seems to set in until we are back inside our cars. As we pull away, I watch with a heavy heart as Tate's casket slowly lowers into the ground.

Forty Four

Saying goodbye to everyone at the Gematti's house is difficult for me. I always feel like I leave a part of me behind when I leave Virginia at the end of the summer, but this year, the feeling is so much worse.

I stand in the Gematti's driveway as Mom and Dad say goodbye to everyone, not willing my feet to move from the spot they are planted beside Dad's truck.

Cora walks to me first, wrapping me in a hug that almost hides me completely.

Before she lets go, she kisses my cheek and whispers in my ear.

"Don't worry about Jake. I'll make sure to stop by once a week with some goodies."

I smile in appreciation at Cora, thankful for her kind heart. Jake stopped by earlier so I could say goodbye to him, and the guys had all promised me that they'd look out for him, too. I kiss Cora's cheek and whisper a quick thank you.

The boys have all lined up in front of me, but none of us seem to want to say goodbye. Austin is usually the quietest, but he's the first to speak.

"I don't know what we're going to do without you, A. You may have to come back sooner than next Summer."

Austin hugs me tightly and I nod into his chest in agreement. When he lets me go, I continue down the line and say very long, tearful goodbyes to the rest of them. Jesse and Ace hug me at the same time, with Mikey following right behind them. Jackson kisses my cheek, and Alex can't even manage a sarcastic comment. His voice catches as he says goodbye to me. Zac's hug lifts me off the ground, which just makes me think of Tate, and I cry into his shoulder.

Mr. Gematti puts his hand around the back of my head and pulls me into a long embrace. He thanks me again, even though he already has multiple times in the past few days. He shares with me that he is going to buy a house close to us in New York so that the guys can all visit whenever they want. I make sure to tell him that he and Cora have to come, too. He nods and finally lets me go.

I look at Ryan, who hasn't cried since the funeral, but his face is full of tears now. He kisses and hugs me, and I can feel his tears on the side of my face. I cry for a few moments with him, and when he lets me go, everyone else is crying, too.

Finally, it's time to say goodbye to Jase. I have been avoiding it, but he is the last person left. I wish he could hop in the car with us and come back to New York. Instead I jump in his arms and he rocks me back and forth.

"I have to let you go now, babe, because if I don't, I won't ever let you go," he whispers to me.

"I'll see you in a few weeks. I love you."

Jase already has plans to come visit New York, my parents insisting that he stay with us.

"Love you, too," I whisper into his neck.

I let him put me back on the ground. I take a step back, tell them all I love them, and blow kisses into the wind. My feet feel like cement, and I don't want to get into the car. Finally, Dad pries me away and helps me inside.

They all stand in the driveway, waving with arms slung over each other's shoulders. Cora is hugging Mr. Gematti, and I watch Ryan turn to Jase to give him a hug.

Dad pulls out onto the road, leaving them all behind us, but I still have one more goodbye left.

Forty Five

"You have to promise me that you'll stay with me, because I can't imagine going back home without you."

I sit waiting for a response that I know will never come. I'm sitting with my legs crossed in the grass. The black stone in front of me is etched with Tate's name, his date of birth, and the date of the night I will never forget.

I cry silently, not wanting Mom or Dad to get upset or get out of the car. The large, wet tears form small puddles of mud beneath me.

"Tate-I-Am, how am I going to get in that car and drive back to New York? I just don't know what to do without you. Maybe I should just run away."

I pause for a moment.

"Hey, I know," I say smiling in spite of the tears. "Let's run away together tonight. We'll find some island, just you and me."

I stop speaking, because this is where Tate would usually chime in. I brush myself off and kiss the top of the black stone. I stand for a moment, not wanting to let go, before I walk to Dad's Chevy and open the back door.

I climb into the backseat slowly. Mom is crying again and blows her nose in a tissue. Dad doesn't say anything but looks at me in the rearview mirror. His look is enough to make me want to cry again, so I break the gaze and stare out the window instead. He starts the car and begins the long drive back home.

I sit in the backseat of the truck, my face pressed against the glass of the back window. I watch Tate's stone get smaller and smaller, and then I watch as the cemetery gets smaller and smaller behind us.

"This isn't goodbye, silly. It's just a see you later."

Tate's voice echoes in my ears as I stare out the window, leaving Virginia behind me.

Acknowledgments

I would like to thank some of the people who made this book possible and helped me along the way on this journey.

First, and foremost, I have to thank my mother, Roberta, and my sister, Krista, for reading, re-reading, reading more and finally editing this with me. You both have been a large part of this three year project, and I can't thank you enough for your constant love and support. I could not have done this without you.

To my sister, Kacie, who read the entire draft in one night on the small screen of her cell phone. Thank you for helping me develop the characters and their dialogue, and for always believing in me no matter what.

To my cousin, Meg, who not only offered insight into the interaction between characters, but who also provided me with the beautiful picture for the front cover. Your advice and constructive criticism is much appreciated, and helped me redevelop the first few chapters to make them better than I thought possible.

To my always supportive aunts, Teresa and Deb, thank you for taking the time to read my drafts. Anything always seems possible with the two of you behind me.

And a special thank you hug goes out to Dad, Erin, Aunt Margaret, Jel, Tammy, and Kelli for being a sounding board for my ideas and characters, reading drafts, and offering advice and direction.

Thank you all from the bottom of my heart.
Thank you. Thank you. *Thank you.*

Summers After

Coming in 2021

Read how Ayla and Jase are doing now in this two chapter preview included on the next few pages.

1 - Ayla

I glance down at my feet and realize my flip flops are filthy and wet. I must have walked through a puddle and not realized it, lost in a daze that seems to plague me lately. I shiver despite it being the dead of summer.

I continue on my journey, something that has become a bit of a routine for me. I glance down at my arms, covered in goosebumps that seem to appear every time I am close. It's been dark for a few hours now and the moon is high and bright in the sky above me. I reach for the gate and pull it open with a bit of a struggle, the heavy weight in my hands making them shake with effort. It closes behind me with a loud crash, echoing through the darkness. A calm spreads over me as I approach him and I soak it in like a drug. It's the feeling I've been chasing for the past two years—the feeling I can never seem to hold onto anywhere else. He's had that effect on me since the moment I met him. As I walk up the last part of the hill, I close my eyes and breathe deeply, the scent of fresh dirt and just-cut grass hanging heavy in the air. A smile slowly finds its way across my face and I silently wish I could run up to him and jump in his arms. My heart aches at the thought.

When I'm close enough, I take my usual place on the ground facing him. I sit with my legs crossed in the wet grass, not caring that I'm wearing a dress. I instinctively reach out and place my hand on the dark stone in front of me, running my fingers across the smooth surface and tracing the letters of his name.

It's hard to believe it's been almost two years since you left me.

It feels like yesterday and a lifetime ago at the same time. So much has happened since, and I quickly push away the thought of how messed up things are now. Because that line of thought brings me to a dangerous place, where the memory of that night taunts me, threatening to replay on a torturous loop that doesn't end without the aid of something that helps me to forget.

I reach into the pockets of my dress and pull out the cans of beer I grabbed on the way here. I open both quickly, the soft pop making my mouth water. I sit one in front of the stone and then tilt mine to my mouth, allowing the now slightly warm beer to fall down my throat without tasting it. I finish more than half of it with the first few gulps. I smile and clink my can to his, a toast to him I'm not sure he's aware of. I close my eyes and try to imagine his laugh, but I can't seem to get it right in my mind. I open my eyes again and envision him sitting across from me, laughing at me for being so ridiculous, and I laugh out loud in spite of the ache that sits heavy in my chest.

"That's the first time I've laughed all night," I say to Tate, hoping that wherever he is he can hear me.

I proceed to tell him about the day, my latest fight with Jase this morning, and the prank I played on Alex before we all went out tonight.

Most people I know are out partying along the beach, drinking at a local bar or dancing in one of the clubs downtown. I attempt to do those things, too. I try to pretend that I am okay and everything is normal, but it never lasts long. Despite my best efforts to pretend that my whole world didn't change in a matter of minutes that night two years ago—to pretend my insides aren't constantly churning with loss and anger and heartache—it isn't long before all of that bubbles to the surface and I have to leave quickly before I completely lose it in front of everyone, or worse, in front of Ryan or Jase. The both of them seem to always be waiting for me to break down, dancing around me cautiously as if one wrong move may cause me to completely shatter. It drives me insane, even if they are mostly right. And so, regardless of where I am or who I am with when I do feel like I may shatter, I typically leave without so much as a word. I disappear, wishing I could actually disappear for a while, and my feet almost always bring me here even if I hadn't intended on it. I know that it drives Jase crazy that I leave him wherever we are without an explanation, more so because he worries like crazy about me now. And while I should find that sweet, it makes me angry instead and I can't fully explain why. I also know how weird the guys think it is that I'm here, even if they won't say it out loud. I guess the truth is that most nineteen-year-olds don't typically hang out in a cemetery at midnight, but then again, most nineteen-year-olds haven't had to watch their best friend die in their arms.

2 - Jase

"She's gone again," I say out loud to no one in particular.

I shake my head in Ryan's direction, but he won't meet my eyes. I swallow what's left of my drink and scan the room again. Ryan motions to the bartender for another round and when I put my hand up to stop him, he shakes his head at me. His eyes flicker with sadness and pain for only a moment before both disappear into the smile he tries to always carry now. Even that seems pained though, a far stretch from the laid back, carefree grin he used to always have.

"We both know where she is—where she always ends up. Have a few more drinks with me and then we'll head home. You know she'll be back at the house before you know it."

I also know there is no point in arguing with Ryan, because for all intents and purposes, he is right. I know she is either already at the cemetery or on her way there. And yes, she almost always finds her way back to me, to all of us, eventually. She won't say it out loud, but when her eyes meet mine I always know exactly where she's been.

I try to be understanding, but I still worry about her all the time. Every moment she's not with me, I fear the worst. I could have lost her, too, that night two years ago, and the mere thought of that is enough to bring me to my knees. I'm not sure I'll ever know what she went through that night or all of the details of what happened before we arrived. I want to, only to help her carry some of it, but she insists on carrying it alone. She is constantly trying to prove something, although I have no idea to whom. We all lost Tate. He was like a younger brother to each of us, and Ryan's actual little brother. The pain in his eyes is present every time he talks about Tate, but at least he talks about him. At least we can have conversations when he's having a tough time with it so I can try to help, even if it's only to listen.

I can't do that with Ayla. She shuts down completely, like she's flipped a switch to turn off that entire night and everything she feels about it except anger. She seems to be angry all of the time now. And that's okay. If that's what she needs to do to keep moving forward, I understand, but I also know that avoiding things usually only makes them worse. I don't want things to be any worse for her. I hate that she had to go through what she did alone. I hate that I wasn't there for her that night, for both of them. I should have been. And that's my burden to carry. It's yet another regret to add to my pile.

I think about how I found her that night—wrapped around Tate so tight that you couldn't tell where she ended and he began. They were both covered in so much blood that a surge of panic locked my feet in place. I felt the world sway beneath me while something inside my chest exploded as I watched her rock him back and forth. She sounded like a wounded animal, so full of pain and so achingly sad that I knew he was gone before I moved any closer. The world stopped around us and I couldn't hear anything but her pain. I spoke to her softly at first, but I'm not sure that she heard me right away. She was lost somewhere, a distant look in her eyes that I see return often now. She looked like she was lost somewhere far away and it scared the hell out of me. I closed the distance between us and pulled her into my arms gently, trying to see if she was hurt. Her eyes focused once again, and she folded into me like she wanted me to hold her and never let her go. If it were up to me, I would have done just that. There are days now that I have trouble looking Ryan in the eye because of the guilt I carry for feeling relief in that moment—relief that Ayla seemed to be mostly okay once she was in my arms. But she's not really okay, even when she pretends to be.

Who would be?

That distant look in her eye returns often. I've become used to it now. I think she spends most of her time somewhere else. Her body is here, but her mind is lost in another place and time. She holds everything in. She's built a wall around everything that happened that night and won't let anyone inside—not even me. She used to tell me that me and Tate were the two people she was never afraid to tell anything to, but now there are days that I worry she won't ever let me in again. It's not like this all of the time. There are moments where she catches my eye and she smiles that smile that will forever make me stop in my tracks and the world is right again. I've never stopped being thankful that she chose me, and continues to choose me. But I know that smile hides what she's really feeling and I can't seem to get her to understand that it's okay to let me see what's underneath.

Don't get me wrong. We all try to pretend that everything is okay even when we all know it's not. Some days it's easier to pretend that we can all move on and somehow be okay or that things are like they used to be. We know they never will be.

Ryan shoves another drink toward me, so I take it without argument this time. Ace approaches us both, asking if we know where Jesse is tonight. We both shrug and shake our heads, and Ace sits down on the stool next to me, defeated.

"I give up. I can't keep track of him anymore. He stopped telling me anything."

Ace hangs his head a bit and I motion to the bartender for him. I can relate. He's going through something similar with his younger brother Jesse, who seems lost since everything that happened to Tate. Jesse and Ayla bond now, both trying to escape things instead of dealing with them. They have their own private club that's heading down a dangerous path, but that's something else that Ayla doesn't want to hear about from me, regardless of the personal experience I have with it.

I wash away the jealous anger with another sip of whiskey as I think about the fight we had earlier today and how she went running to Jesse immediately after because she knew it would make me angrier.

Sure, I understand wanting to escape things. I understand wanting to have a drink or two and relax with friends to help unwind. I just wish she wouldn't drink as much as she does. I watched my mom do the same thing and it brings back many memories from growing up. I try not to let those memories bleed into how I react to Ayla's drinking, but I can't keep it from seeping into the edge of every argument we have about it. She doesn't want to hear it. And now she disappears all of the time without ever saying anything to me first. It's like I'm not even here. Sometimes I think she forgets that I am. I can feel her slowly slipping away from me. Before Tate died, we never fought—ever. Things are different now. She's different now. Everything I say seems to make her angry and we're constantly frustrated with one another. She used to be the only person I could talk to about anything, and now we have trouble communicating about everything.

"Earth to Jase. Hello in there?"

I pick up my head and realize that Jessica, Ayla's friend who works for Ryan's dad, has been trying to talk to me. I hadn't noticed her walk up beside me and I hadn't heard her say anything. Apparently, Ayla isn't the only one lost in thought lately.

"Sorry."

I smile weakly at her as she places her hand on my arm.

"Where's A?"

A is how most people in town refer to Ayla, a loving nickname our friends had given her that spread beyond us quickly. I shrug at Jessica and shake my head slowly.

"Cemetery, I'm guessing, but she didn't mention it before she left."

She never does, I think to myself as I motion to Ryan that I'm ready to leave.

About the Author

Kara DeMaio loves to connect with people through writing and is inspired by everyday interactions between people and the role that relationships take in shaping who we are.

She is a firm believer that listening, understanding, and love can breed acceptance and inspire peace. She strives to write books that raise awareness, encourage hope, and help open our eyes to the silent struggles we may not otherwise recognize.

Kara grew up in the Hudson Valley, and splits her time between Highland, New York and Naples, Florida. She is currently working on Summers After, the sequel to Summers Away, and recently released her debut poetry collection, *To You Love Me*.

To read more, please visit LifeTranscribed.com.

CPSIA information can be obtained
at www.ICGtesting.com
Printed in the USA
LVHW032123051220
673449LV00005B/827

9 781735 845524